To the Only Thug I'll Ever Love

K.L. Hall

Dedication

To lovers everywhere.

Author Acknowledgments

To God be the Glory,
The book is finished. After *YEARS*…the book is finished!

Synopsis

As the daughter of a fallen police officer and former marine, Golani "Gotti" Evans has her head on straight and her life planned to the T. Education. Career. Then love, *maybe*. With only months left until she graduates with a master's degree in criminal justice, she meets *him*. Two strangers. One uninhibited night of pleasure. *Zero regrets*.

He was just supposed to be a *distraction*.

A *diversion* from the pain.

An *interruption* to her every day routine.

Yet her lungs can't find air and her feet can't find the ground when he's around.

Dashiell "Dash" Graham is six feet of perfection and the epitome of a thug. Every woman wants him and every man wants to either be him or kill him. Just nine months out of jail for serving time for his past endeavors, he makes sure he handles his business in the shadows. His outlook on both life and love changes when he meets Gotti. The only thing that can threaten their future together is his past. He knows she'll want nothing more to do with him when she discovers the skeletons in his closet.

She's not ready for love. Neither is he. They are from two separate sides of the law. Yet, the explosive chemistry between them is undeniable. Their outlook on love begins to change as they embark on a love story as complex as it is passionate. When Gotti finds out the truth about his past, will she leave her broken heart behind or give Dash the opportunity to fix what he shattered?

Epigraph

"Tell them I was the warmest place you knew,
and that you turned me cold."

-Rupi Kaur

Prologue

January 1, 2012

Golani "Gotti" Evans

"Five! Four! Three! Two! One! Happy New Year!" my mother cheered as we welcomed in the new year.

"It's my birthday! It's my birthday! It's my birthday!" I cheered and then jumped in the air.

"Yes! Happy sixteenth birthday, baby girl!" she said as she pulled me into a warm bear hug. "You're turning into such a beautiful young woman. I can barely believe it every time I look at you."

She walked over and started lighting the candles on my cake, then brought it over to me.

"Where is Dad at? I thought he was supposed to be here by now."

She sighed. "One of the newer officers on duty called out sick, so he got called in to take his place on patrol."

"Are you sure he's not out cruising around the city in my brand-new car, wink, wink."

My mother rolled her eyes. "I'm positive."

"Ugh," I groaned. "That's annoying. I'm his only daughter. He should be here celebrating with us!"

"It's okay. He'll probably be here soon. Go ahead and blow out your candles before they melt, or worse, you set the house on fire. Then this will really be a birthday to remember, huh?"

She chuckled, and I rolled my eyes at her. "Okay, fine."

"Wait! I'm gonna record this for your father," she said while running over to grab her phone off the living room couch.

"Ready yet?" I asked.

"Yup, I'm recording now. Okay, here we go. Happy birthday to you! Happy birthday to you! Happy birthday, dear Gotti! Happy birthday to you!" my mother sung.

I closed my eyes, made a wish, and then blew out all sixteen candles. My mom slapped her thigh as she cheered in the background, and then put her phone down on the kitchen countertop. "How do you feel now that you're almost an adult?"

I shrugged. "No different."

"Good, because you'll always be a little girl to your father and I."

"I'm about to call him," I said.

"Be my guest."

I grabbed my phone and scrolled through my favorites and clicked my father's name. Instead of putting the phone up to my ear, I pressed the speaker button and listened to the phone ring over and over again before finally going to his voicemail. I hung up and went to our text messages thread.

Daddy [8:42 p.m.]: Hey, baby girl. I better be the first one to tell you happy birthday since I'm saying it so early. So, here it goes...HAPPY SIXTEENTH BIRTHDAY, GOTTI! You have made me so proud. Keep chasing your dreams, baby girl. I love you, Dad.

Me [8:47 p.m.]: Thanks, Daddy! I love you too! Come home before I cut my cake! You know once Mom and I get into it there may not be any left!

Daddy [8:50 p.m.]:That's a 10-4 baby girl. I'll do my best to be there before it's officially your birthday.

"He didn't answer," I announced to my mother, who was about to answer her own ringing phone.

"Maybe this is him," she said before pressing accept. "Hello? This is she. Yes. What? What! What happened? Where is he now? Okay, okay—I'll be right there!"

"What's wrong? Who was that on the phone?" I asked

frantically.

She stood frozen in her step for a few seconds before sprinting into action. She ran toward her purse and then to the door without even grabbing her coat to shield her exposed arms from the frigid New York winter air.

"Mom!" I stressed as soon as her hand touched the brass door knob.

She turned her neck in my direction and kept the rest of her body facing the door. "It's your father, Gotti."

My eyes bulged wide as I ran over to her. "What happened? Is he okay?"

She slowly shook her head as tears sprang out of her eyes and raced down her cheeks. "No," she whispered.

"Mom...," my voice cracked. "Tell me what happened, p— please."

"Gotti...he's dead."

Chapter One

January 1, 2020

Gotti

"Five! Four! Three! Two! One! Happy New Year!" Bellamy screamed along with the rest of the twenty-somethings in the crowded club I was standing in.

Liquor bottles and beer cans clinked together in celebration, while I stood with my heart and my mind somewhere else. The start of a new year and my birthday turned into nothing but a constant reminder that it had been eight long years since my father was killed in the line of duty. Eight years and it didn't seem like my eyes had fully dried yet. I could still hear the screaming of my mother as if I was right back in the morgue, watching my mother fall across my father's dead body after identifying him.

Bellamy hip bumped me and jolted me back into the moment. "Happy birthday, bitch!"

She flashed all thirty-two teeth at me and then started twerking to the beat. I curved the left side of my mouth into a smirk, but the truth was, I didn't feel like smiling. I didn't even know what I was doing in the club on my twenty-fourth birthday in the first place. It wasn't my scene, but my best friend, Bellamy, insisted I needed to try something other than moping around in my flannel onesie and binge watching all the seasons of *Being Mary Jane* I'd missed before the show was cancelled.

"I think I'm ready to go home," I announced.

She took one look at me and rolled her russet brown eyes. "Leave? Are you serious?"

"I told you I would stay until the ball dropped. It dropped. I'm ready to be out."

"How about you take a shot with me and see if that changes your mind?"

"I'm sure it won't," I assured her.

"Never know unless we try, c'mon," she said, before locking arms with me and dragging me to the bar.

After we pushed our way up to the front to make eyes with the closest bartender, she waved her hand in the air as if she was hailing down a taxi. "Excuse me, can we get two shots of gold tequila? Top shelf."

"That'll be thirty dollars," the bartender told her.

"Thirty dollars?" I asked, scrunching up my forehead. It might've looked like liquid gold, but it sure didn't taste like it.

"It's okay, put it on his tab," she said, pointing a few people down to a man who looked to be in his mid-to-late forties.

"Do you know him?" I mumbled to her.

"Nope, but so what." She shrugged, followed by a giggle.

Bellamy handed me a full shot glass filled with liquid regret and held her glass in the air. "To no regrets!"

I closed my mouth around the lime and sucked on it before throwing back the shot of tequila. "No regrets!"

"Jesus! That shit was strong as fuck!" she said, coughing and smacking her chest.

I screwed up my face as if I'd just finished sucking on a tart lemon. "See, this is why I don't drink!"

"Don't drink? Bitch, you don't do anything!"

I rolled my eyes. "There you go again! How many times are we going to have this conversation, Bellamy? I'm good!"

"Tell that to your pussy! Oh, but I bet it can't hear you through all the cobwebs!" she joked.

"You're so fucking annoying."

"Truth hurts doesn't it?"

"Whatever!"

"I'm just saying, girl. It's the first day of a new year! It's also your fucking birthday! I know this day is hard for you for a thousand reasons, but if you ask me, you need to do something to get your mind off it."

"You mean do someone, right?" I asked, raising my thick arched eyebrows.

"Preferably, damn! All you do is school shit and work as a damn professor's assistant. How boring is that?"

"I'm perfectly fine with my boring ass life, thank you very much," I told her.

She sucked her teeth. "Why be fine when you can be great?"

"What are you talking about?"

"I'm telling you, all you need is a nigga to break your back real quick, and I promise you'll have a brand-new outlook on this thing called life."

"Because that's what you'd do to remember the day your father died? Fuck a stranger?"

"Calm down, Gotti. It's not like that and you know it. Admit it, you're wound as tight as a damn yo-yo straight out the pack. You need to let your hair down and let loose for once. Stop looking at the day you were born as just the day your father passed away and look at it as a chance at a new beginning for you. You have to put the happy back into your birthday, girl, or you'll be sad forever," she told me.

I rolled my eyes while looking in the opposite direction of her and remaining silent. I couldn't remember the last time I'd taken advice from anyone. There was no way I was going to admit to her that there was truth in what she was spewing. Both she and my mother had been telling me the same thing for years. It seemed like everyone had moved on from my father's death but me. Maybe they were both right. Maybe, I did need to try something new.

I shrugged. "So...what do you think I should do?"

"Hold up, is this you telling me that I'm right for once?" she asked.

"Some things are better left unsaid," I mumbled.

"Fine, I'll take that! Okay, okay, so, hmmm...let's find you someone in here to take home."

"Wait, in here? Tonight?" I asked, immediately getting nervous.

"Yes. There's no time like the present."

I sighed. "Before anything happens, I need another shot. Two of 'em!"

"Coming right up!"

While Bellamy stepped back up to the bar, I scanned the club. I'd spent every birthday for the past eight years in pain. I'd just turned twenty-four, and I was at the point where I would much rather fuck instead of feel.

"What about him?" Bellamy asked me after downing her first shot.

I followed her deep-set eyes across the club. "Who? The nigga with the grill?"

She giggled. "Yeah."

"Pssh. Girl, bye," I told her, tossing down my first shot.

"Okay, okay, fine. What about….him," she said, pointing to a white boy.

I shrugged. "He's cute and all, but I like my meat well done, if you know what I'm saying," I told her.

She sucked her teeth. "Girl, you are IMPOSSIBLE to please. You point out what you like then, how about that?"

We both downed our second shot as my eyes scanned the packed club full of drunk and sweaty party goers. I'd almost given up hope and was about the chuck the place up to a dud when I saw *him*.

"Damn," I mumbled.

Bellamy's eyes followed mine and by her speechlessness, I knew she'd seen who I did. He was six feet of solid, dark chocolate perfection. There were two large princess cut diamonds that shined in his ears underneath the busy strobe lights. His haircut and facial hair were edged up to the T. He stood in his private section with a bottle of champagne glued to his hand and a bunch of hooligans around him, popping bottles and drenching everyone around them with champagne showers.

"Oh, hell yes," Bellamy mumbled, "definitely him. He look like money."

"What do I do?" I asked as my heart fluttered. I could feel my round face turning from honey brown to deep blush.

"Walk over to him and try not to trip, stutter, or drool."

"Really? All that?"

"Shit, as good as his ass look, you better hope you don't go over there and forget how to speak," she told me.

I drew in a deep breath and nodded. As soon as I took my first step, my legs felt like Jell-O, and I couldn't find my balance. I swiftly turned back around to Bellamy while shaking my head. "I can't. I fucking can't. He's too fine. Look at me! He's already got me off my game, and he's all the way across the fucking club!"

She steadied my balance by placing her hands on my shoulders. "C'mon, bitch! Get your head in the game, okay? This is exactly what you need to do to pull yourself out of that funk, okay? Trust me! He definitely looks like he can get the job done and then some."

I took another quick breath and nodded. "Okay. Here I go."

Before my brain had the opportunity to talk my legs out of moving forward, I began pushing through the sea of people to make my way over to the finest man I'd ever seen in my life. Just as I approached his section, I looked up, and he was gone. I looked left and then right, searching for my black unicorn and got nothing.

"Fuck," I mumbled.

Feeling defeated and a bit relieved, I turned around to head back over to Bellamy.

"Lookin' for someone in particular?" I heard a man's deep voice say in my ear.

I quickly jerked my neck around, ready to cuss a bum nigga out when I froze. It was *him*. He was even finer up close.

"Huh?" I asked him.

"I asked you were you lookin' for someone in particular."

"Actually, yes. You."

"Me? You know me?" he asked.

I shook my head. "No."

"Fuck you doin' lookin' for me then?"

I drew in a deep breath and held it a few seconds longer than normal while taking in the sight of a man standing in front of me. There were skeleton fingers tattooed around his throat as if he was being strangled by the Grim Reaper every day of his life. He looked almost as dangerous as he looked divine. I shook my head. "You know what, never mind. It's stupid."

"Nah, I don't like secrets. Tell me."

I shook my head repeatedly. "No, trust me, it's dumb. I'm sorry."

He reached out and grabbed my arm to stop me from leaving his presence. "Nah, that look on your face is sayin' somethin' different."

"I—um, it's my birthday, and my best friend dragged me out the house to make me have a good time. To be honest, I was really ready to leave and then I saw you...so, she pretty much dared me to come talk to you."

"Well, now you can tell your friend you succeeded."

I nodded quickly. "Yup. Um, it was nice meeting you," I said, looking down at his hand still holding onto my arm.

He slowly slid his fingertips down the front of my arm and made each hair follicle stand on end. "Likewise."

I felt my entire face go warm as I turned to walk back over to Bellamy, who was staring at me with her mouth wide open. "Bitttcccccchhhhhh."

"What?"

"What? What the fuck you mean what, Gotti? What the fuck was that?"

"We talked, that's all."

"About what?"

"Nothing really, just an exchange of words. I don't even remember what I said," I admitted, tracing my hand down the arm he'd grabbed.

"Didn't look like nothin' to me," she said, nudging my

side.

Before I could respond, the sea of people parted as two bottle girls with sparkling bottles of Moët in their hands made their way over to us.

"Follow me," one said to me.

Bellamy and I looked at each other and followed them back over to his section. The girls poured both Bellamy and I glasses of champagne as I locked eyes with him.

"Happy birthday," he mouthed from a few feet away.

I managed to smile and raise my glass to him even though there were butterflies trampling through my abdomen. "Thank you," I mouthed back.

Bellamy nudged my side again. "See, told you that wasn't nothin! Look where we standing at, bitch!"

*****

AS THE NIGHT went on, I found myself stealing looks at him every chance I got. The more I looked, the more intoxicated I got by him than the fusion of tequila and champagne in my system. I'd never encountered a man that I couldn't seem to form complete sentences around. I was drawn to his creamy, dark chocolate skin and could only image that it felt as soft as it looked. I'd secretly nicknamed him *The Black Adonis* in my head. Just as I was going in to steal my thousandth peek at him, I caught him making his way over to me. I tried to remain as cool and laid back as possible on the outside although I was flipping my shit inside my head.

"You enjoyin' your birthday yet?" he asked me.

"This has made it much better, thank you."

"You're welcome."

His eyes burned with passion as he looked at me, and I felt my hands get clammy. My arms remained tense at my sides as I balled my left fist.

"You got any New Year's resolutions?" I asked him over the music.

"Nah, you?"

"Yeah, I think I do."

"What is it?" he asked me.

"To let loose and not be so wound up all the time."

"What your little ass so stressed for?"

"A lot. School, finding a job after I graduate in a few months..."

He stroked his beard. "What you in school for?"

"Criminal justice. I'm about to graduate with my master's," I said proudly.

"Word? Congrats."

"Thank you."

"I think that deserves a toast," he said, pouring some of his champagne into my half-empty glass. I found myself staring at the bubbles in my champagne flute with a smile on my face.

"What's on your mind?" he asked in my ear.

He slowly pulled his lips away, allowing his juicy bottom lip to graze my earlobe. My heart skipped a beat, and I tightened my thighs.

"Absolutely nothing."

"Gotta be something. Let me guess, you thinkin' 'bout the nigga you got waitin' on you at home, right?"

I shook my head. "No, definitely not that."

"As pretty as you are, I know you got a nigga. Just let me know who ass I gotta beat upfront. As much as I hate secrets, I hate surprises even more."

I smiled at him and shook my head. "That won't be necessary. I'm one hundred percent single, I promise."

"You wouldn't lie to me would you?" he asked.

"No reason to."

"Good."

"I'm just tired of running in circles with niggas, you know?" I stated honestly.

"Uh oh"

"What?" I asked.

"Why you fuckin' with me while your heart broke?"

16

I giggled. "Who said I was fuckin' with you? I'm just making a new friend."

"Oh, so we just friends?"

"Yeah. For now." I smiled.

Just looking at him smile lifted my mood to heights I hadn't felt in a long time. It was the first time in years that I felt fully alive. It was almost as if I was floating above both of our bodies standing there, letting the floor vibrate underneath our feet. He had me cheesin' like the Cheshire cat from limited conversation. I stole another seconds worth of glances, trying to capture as many of his Herculean features as I could. From his chiseled jaw to his hulking stature, I was hooked on the stranger with the Godiva skin. And those hands. *Goddamn.* He couldn't be real. He looked *that* damn good. When the DJ started blasting throwback twerk jams through the speakers, the entire section went wild. I glanced over at Bellamy, who wasted no time letting her ass bounce back against the closest nigga to her.

Without saying a word, he stepped behind me, and I started swaying my hips to the beat. The way he clenched my waist felt like a prison of pleasure. I was embarrassed to admit how mesmerized I was as he gently caressed my ass on the dance floor. It was probably more than wrong, but it all felt devilishly right. My pussy throbbed to the beat. I wanted him. I *craved* him. The universe owed me a night of toe-curling, lip biting, sheet-gripping pleasure, and I wanted him to deliver it to me.

"What are you doing after this?" I asked, looking back at him. His chestnut-colored eyes twinkled underneath the strobe lights.

"Shit, whatever you want," he said.

I turned to look at him, and he didn't bother to take his hands from around my waist. I was hoping the look on my face would say everything that my lips were afraid to. My lips needed to say *kiss me,* and my eyes needed to say *right now.* He was the man who I had set my sights on for the night. I was inflamed with passion and the urge to know him intimately, if only for the next few hours.

"I want you to fuck me tonight," I whispered in his ear.

He took a step back and looked me up and down while biting his bottom lip. "You got a name, sweetheart?"

I shook my head. "No. You?"

"Nah."

"Good. No strings."

He smirked. "No strings, huh?"

"Nope."

A part of me felt like I was acting out only because my misery needed the company. I couldn't believe how I was acting or the things that were spilling out of my mouth. A man like him was far from my type. He was refined, but I could tell he still had some hood in him. I preferred someone with his head in the books rather than his hand in the streets. The only place all those differences would disappear? The bedroom. I already knew he didn't like secrets or surprises. I didn't want to know anything else about him. The more I knew, the more everything I was thinking about doing with and to him would be too real for me to handle the next morning. It was the first time I'd been unguarded with a man in my entire life. I was ready to give every piece of myself to a stranger and feel no remorse about the shit.

"You ready to get out of here?" he whispered in my ear.

I swallowed hard and then looked up at him. "Y—yeah. Let's go."

I slipped my hand in his and caught eyes with Bellamy. She winked at me and motioned for me to text her my location. I walked out of the club with him drunk with happiness. As soon as the cold winter air hit my bare arms and legs, I began to slowly sober up.

"Where are we going?" I asked him.

"I got a room for the night we can go to," he told me. "Right now, I'm just trying to get us to the car. It's brick out here."

I nodded and focused on walking faster. As soon as we got into a blacked-out Mercedes, he turned the heat on full blast and rubbed his hands together while blowing warmth into them. It didn't take long for me to feel warm air blowing across my face and against the back of my thighs from the heated leather seats. Seconds after we pulled out of his neatly parallel parked spot, I made sure to drop my location to Bellamy's phone just in case the night turned from sugar to shit real quick.

*****

WE PULLED UP to the hotel within ten minutes, and he had valet park his car. My heels brushed against the plush carpeted lobby as we made our way over to the elevators. As soon as we stepped inside, he pressed the number fifteen while I relaxed my back against the wall and watched the doors close. When the elevator began gliding up floors, he stepped up to me and pressed his chest against mine.

"You sure you wanna do this?" he hissed in my ear.

The closer we got to the fifteenth floor, the quicker my heart started to race. All I could do was nod. He wrapped his rough hands around my throat and pulled my lips only a breath away from his.

"Come here then," he said before gently pressing his lips against mine.

My entire body froze up like a popsicle when he kissed me, yet I couldn't get enough. His tongue snaked its way past my lips as his hands glided up and down my spine. His breath was a mixture of mint and cognac while mine tasted like fresh tequila shots and bubbly champagne.

DING

As soon as the elevator doors began to part ways, he broke the kiss. "We're here," he said, brushing his lips against mine.

Before my brain was able to formulate a response, he scooped me into his strong arms and carried me to the room where I could only hope my deepest desires would be filled. Within seconds, he'd plunged our bodies onto the bed. I was going to let him take control with no restraint. He tightened his grip around my hips as he toyed with the hem of my dress and then slid his cold hands in between the warmth of my thighs.

He placed wispy kisses down my neck, shoulders, and chest before sliding my dress up to my stomach and sliding off my panties. Butterflies surged through my body as the flood started between my legs. *It was go time.* With my eyes fixated in the back of my head, I let my fingertips creep down the back of his head before tugging on his shirt. I watched as he sat up and pulled his shirt over his head, letting his solid gold chain swing freely against his hard chest. Just staring at Olympian abs let me know that I was head over heels in trouble. He flipped me over on my stomach and unzipped my dress before peeling the straps over my shoulders and kissing down my spine.

"Mmm," I moaned at the feeling of his facial hair tickling the small of my back.

He slid his hand up the back of my neck before grabbing a fistful of my hair and latching his lips to my neck. "You like that shit?" he asked before running his thumb over my lips.

"Mmm, yeah."

The Black Adonis gently turned me back over onto my back and kissed my erect nipples before sucking on each of them. I sliced my teeth into my bottom lip as to not let another moan burst past my lips. Then, he began kissing down my stomach and gently rubbing on my dampened pussy lips. Before I had the chance to draw in my next breath, I felt his full, juicy lips gliding against my wetness.

"Ooooh shit. Mmm, that feels amazing. Yeah, right there," I coached as my hands reached out to grip the sheets.

He continued to suck on my pearl as I bucked my hips forward, grinding against his beard until I came.

"Fuckkkkkkkk!"

It was a spine tingling.

Toe curling.

Eyes rolling back in my head, climax.

He gently blew his breath against my sensitive clit while drinking my juice like water straight out of the faucet. With my legs spread from east to west, he dipped into his pocket to pull out a condom and then dipped his chocolate inside my sex.

"Mmm, shit," he groaned.

My back arched with more pleasure than pain, although it had been an unspeakable amount of time since I'd entertained the mere thought of a penis. My fingernails clung to the strong muscles of his back as he began circling his hips while pushing deeper inside my whirlpool of warmth. Just as I became accustomed to the rhythm of his stroke, he untwined my legs from around his waist and placed them over his shoulders, hitting my G-spot with every blow. There were so many squeals and moans coming out of my mouth, I knew any straggling hall walkers in the hotel knew I was getting my back broken somethin' proper.

"Turn that ass over," he demanded.

After he recoiled his dick from inside me, I was able to see his package in its full glory. I had no idea how all of him fit inside of me, but every inch felt like heaven, and I couldn't wait to feel it some more. The Black Adonis bent me over the side of the bed and began fucking me doggy style. He pushed deep inside me, making sure I knew what it felt like to have every inch of him inside of me.

"Shiiiiiiiittttttt! You're gonna make me cum!" I squealed.

"Throw that ass back at a nigga."

I pushed back against his wood, while inching closer and closer to my climax. I was ashamed to say I'd fallen in love with the sound of my ass slapping against his strong thighs. The pounding was hard and steady.

"Damn, this shit feels so good!" I screamed as he continued fucking me with no mercy until my voice went hoarse.

I felt my juices slowly trickling down my inner thigh as he pulled out and replaced his girth with the warmth of his long tongue, coiling his lips around my clit. My body shook helplessly under his grasp. I could barely control my motor skills. The Black Adonis slurped me like a popsicle on the hottest day of summer, and I couldn't wait to return the favor. Once I began to get the feeling back in my legs, I turned to face him.

"Take the condom off," I told him.

Puzzled, he stared at me in silence before obliging. As soon as the sticky wet rubber hit the ground, I took as much of him in my mouth as possible without choking to my death.

"Mmm shit, yeah, get that dick nice and wet," he instructed, while gripping the sides of my face to inch himself deeper inside my mouth.

I managed to sneak a peek up at his face, and he looked to be in as much bliss as I'd been only minutes prior. His stance was wide and firm, and the dark chocolate skin wrapped around his muscles flexed so hard, I could see veins cracking through. I was quickly brought back to reality when he slid out of my mouth and brushed the tip of his dick against the outside of my lips.

"Stick that fuckin' tongue out."

I obliged, looking like a dog with her head stuck out of the window on a long car ride. In that moment, he probably could've gotten me to do anything he asked. He tapped his dick against the length of my tongue before I curled my lips around his thickness once more, tasting his pre-cum. With one hand at the base of his dick and the other caressing his balls, I sucked until I was sure his soul had left his body.

"Mmm, fuckkkkkkkk!" he growled, extracting his cream into my mouth. He leaned against the bed for stability as I lapped his warm milk up until the very last drop.

I didn't know what had overcome me. It could've been the liquor or just the good pipe he'd laid down. No matter the case, he'd managed to fuck me so good that it was the first time I could remember what it felt like to feel no pain. If only for one night, he'd unleased the freak I kept bottled up inside. The beauty in it all was that when the sun came up, I'd never have to see him again.

Chapter Two

Two weeks later.

Dashiell "Dash" Graham

"Virgil got a Patek on my wrist going nuts. Niggas caught me slipping once, okay, so what?" Drake spit through the speakers of my blacked-out Mercedes as I pulled up to my building. I had every intention to swing right into my parking spot when I saw a large U-Haul truck haphazardly parked half in my space with the other half sticking out in the street.

"What the fuck," I mumbled, ready to go off on the mothafucka that was slowing me up from getting inside my parking spot and getting in the crib.

My hazard lights blinked as I swung open the driver's side door and stepped out with the engine still running. I walked up to the back of the truck and saw two girls standing there, arguing over who was going to pick up a box.

"Yo, you gotta move your shit," I said, announcing my presence.

They both stopped their bickering to look at me and all three of us froze.

"You..." she said.

"You," I repeated.

It'd been a couple weeks since my encounter with *the shorty from New Year's* as I called her. I was accustomed to women throwing themselves at me, but there was something about her that was different, innocent even. The last place I ever expected to see her was standing outside of my building.

"Oh shit," her friend mumbled. "Is that...that's not...

damn, bitch."

"I'm sorry, we're almost done. We just got a few more boxes left to move into the building, and I'll move," Shorty told me.

"Or you could help us...it'll make the process go *much* faster," her friend chimed in.

"Bellamy, I'm sure he's busy. He looks like he just wants to get to wherever he's going," she said without redirecting her gaze toward me.

"I'm just sayin', if he want his parking spot as bad as he says he does, then maybe he should put those muscles to work and help us out."

Shorty rolled her cat-like eyes. "Please excuse my friend. She has this condition where she says the first thing that comes to mind."

"It's called honesty," she retorted.

"You good. I'll help," I told them.

"Really?" Shorty asked.

"Yeah, on one condition."

"What's that?"

"You never block my space again."

"Your space as in...you live here?"

"Yeah, I do," I said, waving my key fob in her face.

If Shorty had been a cartoon character, she would've melted into a puddle and slid right off the back of that truck. She was shook.

"Wait, are you serious?"

I nodded. "I don't give a fuck enough to lie to you."

"What a coincidence! My girl is your newest neighbor," her friend announced.

My eyes widened for a split second and then went back to normal. "Word?"

"Yup..."

"Well, it sounds like you two have it all covered, and I can go ahead and get out of here. Call me later, Gotti. Smooches!" her friend blurted out before hopping off the back of the truck and scurrying down the street to her own ride.

"Good help is so hard to find these days," she said, rolling her eyes once more.

"It sure is. Consider this your housewarming gift. Pass me the box," I told her.

*****

"Thank you..." she said as I placed the last box inside her empty two-bedroom apartment.

"You welcome." She looked around the space filled with cardboard moving boxes and plastic bins before reverting her gaze back in my direction. "You got somethin' you wanna say?"

"It's just that I didn't expect to run into you again—"

"So soon, right?" I asked, cutting her sentence off at the knees.

"No, ever," she said brashly. I could see Shorty turning red inside and out. "I—I'm sorry. I just, I've never done anything like that before, and I just figured if I never saw you again then I wouldn't have to worry about being embarrassed about it."

"Then, you really gon' hate what I'm about to tell you, sweetheart."

"What's that?"

"I lay my head about six floors up from you."

"Wow...yeah, this is...mortifyingly awkward."

"I mean, I'm good, but how you wanna play it? You wanna act like you don't see me and I don't see you, or what?"

She nervously shook her head, looking more like a child than the grown ass woman she was. "Nah, we don't have to do all that."

"Cool, well I'm about to go move my car."

"Um, yeah...sure that's cool."

"Unless..."

"Unless what?" she asked.

"Unless there was something else you had to say to me."

"Oh, no. I was just going to offer you a bottle of water or

something for your trouble."

I chuckled. "It's like thirty degrees outside, Shorty. The last thing I need right now is a bottle of ice-cold water, but good looks though."

"I have hot chocolate in here…somewhere," she offered.

"Nah, I'm good. Maybe next time."

She tilted her head to the side. "Next time? I mean, sure, yeah. Next time is cool," she said while bobbing her head.

"Bet," I said before turning away and exiting down the hallway back to the elevators.

Gotti

I flopped my tired body against the couch after he left. Although I'd moved the truck, I knew I needed to return it so that I wouldn't get charged an extra day for no reason. But before I could do anything, I needed to take a second to get my bearings. There was just something about being in that man's presence that made me want to surrender everything, even my common sense. It angered me how I could barely form an intelligent sentence around him when I was months away from graduating with a dual master's degree in criminal justice and political science. He must've thought I was just another dumb broad or something.

After a few more minutes of self-loathing and sulking, I picked up my phone to call Bellamy.

"Why am I hearing from you not even an hour after seeing you?" she answered.

I scoffed. "Um, because we're done moving the boxes that your ass left us with!"

"Girl, that was the Christian thing to do. Who am I to get in the way of your opportunity to get your back broken for the second time by *The Black Adonis*." She giggled. "Ain't that what you call him?"

I rolled my eyes while secretly cursing myself for telling her the nickname I'd given him in the first place. I should've kept my indiscretions to my damn self, but Bellamy had a way of pulling even my deepest, darkest secrets out of me.

"Whatever. I didn't call to talk about him. I called to see if you can meet me at the U-Haul place so I can return this truck today."

"Bitch, please. You know damn well you wanna talk about that nigga. I don't even have to see you to know his face is plastered all over the walls of that brain of yours and your pussy too!" She snickered.

"Ugh!" I groaned. "Bellamy, like what the fuck am I supposed to do? He was just supposed to be a distraction. A one-night diversion from the pain. Not my fuckin' neighbor!"

"Take a chill pill, Gotti and just see where the shit goes," she advised.

"I can't do that. He's not even my type and you know that."

"Girl, fuck a type! Did you see how fuckin' good he looked? Plus, a vibe is a vibe. Just go with it! At the end of the day, y'all both grown, so what's the big deal? It was one night of hot, sexy, uninhibited sex! You're single, bitch! You're supposed to do single shit. The only one feelin' bad about the shit is you, and I don't know why because we both know if given the chance to hop on that chocolate pole again, you'd do it in a heartbeat."

I absolutely hated it when she was right. "Whatever."

"Riddle me this, then bitch. Do you wanna see him again?"

I sighed. "I don't know, maybe before, but now that he lives here, no. That's awkward, right? I mean, what if I see him with another female when I'm leaving the building or coming in? How am I supposed to act?"

"How do you wanna act?"

"Ugh, you're no help!"

"I'm the most helpful bitch you know! But because you're my girl, and I love you, I'm going to leave you with a word. You ready?"

"Yeah, I'm ready..."

She cleared her throat. "In the true words of my girl, Cardi B, grow up, bitch and suck a dick!"

We both burst out into a roar of laughter. "Just shut up and meet me at the U-Haul place. I'm about to leave now!"

Chapter Three

Bellamy Daniels

I'd been in love with music all my life, or at least as long as I could remember. As soon as I heard Lauryn Hill's *The Sweetest Thing,* I knew becoming a singer was what I wanted to do with my life.

Boy, don't stand too close to me or I might just fall in love.
Love the way my body fits in your arms like a glove.
I never thought I'd fall so hard for someone I just met.
Other girls want you too, but baby, I'm as real as it gets.

I wanna get to know you, boy in every kind of way.
Every time I talk to you, you know just what to say.
You must be an angel 'cause you treat me oh so good.
Have me feeling ways that I never thought I would.

I finished writing the lyrics to my newest song inside my notebook and closed it as soon as my cell phone vibrated. Usually when I was in my zone, I sent all of my calls straight to voicemail, but I decided to answer it anyway.

"What you want?" I asked, smacking my lips.

"Where you at, hoe? Mama is gettin' ready to put Sunday dinner on the table," my older sister, Tatiyana, told me.

"Tell her I'm on my way now. I'm just leaving work."

"Okay, well, hurry up. There's someone I want you to meet."

"Who?" I quizzed.

"You'll see whenever you get here. Bye!"

I rolled my eyes as I started the engine to my car and

pulled out of the Sephora parking lot. I'd been working as a makeup consultant there for over a year and a half, not once getting the opportunity to put my associate's degree in music to good use. Nevertheless, I was a makeup consultant by day and a bartender at night to keep a roof over my head. There was no way I could go back to living under the same roof as my mama. No matter how much I loved her, I'd grown out of not having any privacy and having to answer to where I was going and when I planned to be back, even in my almost mid-twenties.

I swung my cherry red Nissan Altima into my mother's driveway, parking next to a snow-white Bentley truck I'd never laid eyes on before. "Whose ride is this?" I mumbled to myself before reapplying my lipstick in the visor mirror and stepping out of the car.

My heels clicked against the ice-paved driveway as I headed up to the front door and knocked. I rubbed my hands together before sliding them in my coat pockets for warmth.

"It's about time you got here," Tatiyana snapped as soon as she opened the door for me.

"Whatever," I said, swiping past her and taking off my coat. "Who fancy ass car is that in the driveway?"

"It's mine," I heard a male voice say from behind me.

I quickly snapped my neck around to put a face to a voice. My eyes met that of a man I'd never seen before, and God was he gorgeous. He stood towering over my frame even with three-inch heels on, landing him somewhere over six feet tall. His pore-less caramel skin looked sweet enough to eat, not to mention his wavy jet-black hair, supple lips, and freshly groomed facial hair. Perhaps, his most intriguing feature was his smoky gray bedroom eyes; with those alone I knew he could charm the skin off a snake.

"And you are?" I asked.

"Bells, this is Jaron, my boyfriend," Tatiyana interjected, swiping her shoulder-length bob behind her ear.

"Oh, so this is the surprise guest you wanted me to meet," I said, extending my hand to him.

His large hand swallowed mine whole as he shook it while giving me a glimpse of his set of cocaine white teeth. "It's nice to meet you."

"Likewise," I told him.

Before I had the opportunity to grill him, I heard my mother's voice in the background. "Dinner is ready!"

The three of us shuffled into the dining room and took our seats around the table that seated six. As much as I couldn't stand living with my mother, I could still appreciate her love for tradition. Ever since our father passed away, she made it her business to keep up the tradition of family dinners one Sunday a month with both Tati and me. Only this time, Tati had invited a boyfriend that I was sure neither I nor my mother knew about.

As soon as each of our plates were filled with helpings of fried chicken, collard greens, mac and cheese and mashed potatoes, I kicked off the conversation. "So, Tati...how long have you and..."

"Jaron," he answered.

"How long have you and Jaron been dating? Must not have been long since this is the first time I'm hearing about him."

"Me too," my mother chimed in.

We both let out a cackle, and then I directed my attention back to my sister to answer the question.

"Actually, we've been together for about six and a half months now."

My eyes widened. "Really? And yet somehow you managed to keep him under wraps this entire time?"

She rolled her narrow eyes at me while arching her brows. "Everything I do ain't your business, Bells. Besides, he spends a lot of his time out on business."

I tossed up my imaginary white flag. "Touché. Jaron, I hope you know you've got a feisty one on your hands," I warned him.

"Oh, I'm quite aware."

"So, what is it that you do, Jaron?" My mother asked, taking over the conversation.

"Oh, I'm a music producer."

"As in, in a studio?" I asked for clarity.

"Yeah, Jaron has a studio downtown," Tati answered for him.

"Own? Wow, that's pretty cool. Tati got herself a nigga with a big boy job," I teased.

"Watch your mouth at my table, Bellamy!"

"My bad, Mama! My bad!"

"Actually, I've been telling him about your songs and how good they are," Tati told me.

"Oh, really?"

He nodded. "Yeah, she said you were dope."

I smiled. "Tati always did tell the truth."

"Nah, but for real, if you're as dope as she's hyped you up to be, then you should bring your songs. I'll play you some of my beats, and we'll see what we can cook up," he told me.

"For real? You'd do that?"

"He'd do anything for me," Tati beamed.

I watched her reach out for his hand while showing all thirty-two of her braces-straightened teeth. I knew first-hand how many toxic relationships Tati had been in over the years. I'd sat and listened to her cry over nigga after nigga on a million different occasions. She had a way of falling fast and hard for men and always ended up getting her heart broken in the process. It was good to see a genuine smile on her face and it didn't hurt that it was all due to the fine ass nigga on her arm.

"Yeah, bring it by and let me hear somethin' soon."

"And whatever it is, you better make it good! Don't embarrass me!"

I sucked my teeth. "We all know I'm the only one in this family with any true talent anyway."

"Bellamy!" My mother scolded me.

"So tell me, how'd the two of you meet? I mean, you've been together this long and neither of us ever heard of you. I'm just curious about all the secrecy."

"We met on Instagram," Tati said.

"I would've come around sooner, but I travel a lot, doing business with different artists, so I'm rarely ever here."

"Must be hard to keep your relationship strong like that," Mama mumbled, while pushing her food across her plate.

Tati smiled, raising her elevated cheekbones even higher. "Mama, Jaron and I are good. In fact, we're more than good."

"And what exactly does that mean? I better not see no babies comin' around here without a ring on your finger!"

"No, I'm not pregnant, but Jaron and I have decided to move in together. My lease is almost up and being that he's hardly ever home, it just doesn't make sense for us to keep paying separate bills because when he's in town, we spend every waking moment at one another's places."

"Don't you think it's a little too soon for y'all to be shackin' up?" I asked, egging on Mama's suspicions.

"My sentiments exactly."

"With all due respect, we're grown, and we're in love."

"So, you gon' do what you wanna do. We get it," I told her.

*****

After dinner, Tati and I both helped Mama with the dishes while Jaron sat in the living room watching TV.

"You been workin' on any new songs?" Tati asked me.

"You know me, I'm always workin' on new music."

"Then, why don't you go in there and talk to Jaron? I mean, I like music just as much as the next girl, but I don't connect with it like y'all do."

"I don't know what to say," I admitted.

"Don't think, just go. He's harmless, I promise."

I shook away the butterflies that were producing in my stomach and told myself that Jaron could be the key to my big break. The last thing I wanted to do was mess it up by letting the moment pass me by. Who knew if or when I'd get another one? I walked into the living room and stood a couple feet away from him.

"Hey, you got a sec?"

"What's up?" he asked.

"I just wanted to talk, you know, and pick your brain about this music shit."

"No problem. I can play some beats for you that I have on my phone. You want me to play 'em in here or outside?"

"The acoustics in the car would probably be better, right?"

"Definitely."

"Cool, I'll grab my coat."

"So, how long you been into music?" he asked as he unlocked the doors to his luxury truck.

I shrugged. "For as far back as I can remember. What about you?"

"Shit, me too. It's just somethin' about it that speaks to my fuckin' soul, you know? Pardon my language."

"I'm not my mama, Jaron. You ain't gotta censor yourself around me."

"So, you gon' let me hear you sing somethin' or you too shy?" he asked.

I immediately felt those butterflies fluttering in the pit of my gut once more. "I—uh, yeah sure. Play me somethin', and I'll see what I can come up with on the spot."

"Bet," he said, scrolling through his phone. After finally selecting a beat, he let the melodic tune set the vibe as he turned the volume up. "Go 'head."

I closed my eyes and slowly nodded my head to the melody.

"Boy, don't stand too close to me or I might just fall in love.
Love the way my body fits in your arms like a glove.
I never thought I'd fall so hard for someone I just met.
Other girls want you too, but baby, I'm as real as it gets.

I wanna get to know you, boy in every kind of way.
Every time I talk to you, you know just what to say.
You must be an angel 'cause you treat me oh so good.
Have me feeling ways that I never thought I would," I sang.

"Yo, that shit was fire! Tati wasn't lyin' you are talented as fuck! You just came up with that shit on the fly like that?"

"Yeah, earlier today when I got off work."

"No lie, that shit was dope."

"Thank you!" I beamed.

"Lemme see your phone real quick."

"For what?" I asked.

"I'ma call my cell from your phone, then I'll text you the address to the studio and you just let me know when you tryna fall through."

"It's just that simple?"

"Pretty much. Come through. I always got bottles on deck when I'm in town. Anything you need."

"Well, I appreciate it, more than you know."

"It's nothin'. I'll do anything for Tati, so if that means helping out her sister, then so be it."

Jaron Mitchell

A couple days passed before I got a text from Bellamy asking to fall through to the studio. I had business to handle that kept me tied to the city, so I didn't mind the company. If I had to put it into words, her voice was a blend of the delicateness of Jhene Aiko and the modern sultriness of SZA. I couldn't wait to hear her sing again.

Bellamy [9:45 p.m.]: I'm pullin' up now.
Me [9:47 p.m.]: Bet. I'm in suite 301.

About ten minutes passed before I heard a faint knock on the door and then looked up to see Bellamy standing on three-inch heels in the doorway. "What up?" I greeted her.

"Hey," she said, walking in and taking off her coat.

I watched her coat hit the couch and couldn't help but notice how good her plump, heart-shaped ass looked in the jeans she was wearing. Her hourglass figure and full lips definitely had the dog in me interested in more than her music, but the man in me knew better.

"I can't lie, I was surprised to hear from you."

"Why is that?" she asked.

I shrugged. "I meet a lot of people who claim they 'bout this music shit but then when they get the invite, they flake."

"Well, you don't have to worry about that with me," she assured me.

"Then, why you look so nervous?"

"Because I am. It's not like I get this type of opportunity every day," she admitted.

"Shit, this place should have you feelin' like a kid in a fuckin' candy store. Unless..."

"Unless what?"

"Unless you not as serious about your music as I thought you were."

She sucked her teeth while fluttering her lash extensions. "Boy, bye. I'm dead ass serious, aight?"

"Bet, then show me what you got. Pass me the book," I said, pointing to the small notebook she had clutched between her fingers. She took a few steps closer to me and handed it off. I quickly flipped through her journal of song lyrics, noting one familiar theme. "What nigga hurt you?"

She frowned. "Excuse me?"

"I mean, the lyricism is there, but at the same time, it's all about the same shit."

"What do you mean?"

"Love and a nigga breakin' your heart."

She shrugged. "I write from experience."

"You need to try writing when you're happy or when you're feelin' sexy and turned on. Write then and get some variety in your collection!"

"Are you serious?"

"Hell yeah, I'm serious. Trust me, after we're done here tonight, I want you to go home, put on some slow jams, take off all your clothes and just before you get in the shower, I want you to take a good look at yourself in the mirror. Stare at yourself and let the music move your fingertips all over your body. Do that, and I promise you'll write a sexy ass hit by the end of the night," I advised.

"So, let me get this straight. You're telling me that masturbation will get me to write a bomb ass song?"

"It'll get the juices flowin' in more ways than one." I chuckled.

She playfully rolled her eyes. "You know what, you're dangerous with how smooth you talk."

"What that mean?" I quizzed.

"Nigga, you know exactly what that means. Everything that drips off your lips is smooth and sweet like honey. My sister better watch her back. I bet you got groupies on groupies on your dick, huh?"

I shook my head while pulling my dreads back into a low ponytail. "You got me all wrong."

"Mmhm, yeah, okay."

"I'm tellin' you right now, whatever you heard about me, that's just street gossip."

"Who said I heard anything about you?"

"I'm just lettin' you know off top."

"Fine, so you read my stuff, so let me hear what you got since you claimed to have all these beats and shit."

"As soon as you told me you were comin' through, my wheels started turning. I got the perfect song for you. I been workin' on this shit for a minute, just waiting for the right voice to come along, and I think I found that in you. There's just one tiny issue," I told her.

"What is it?"

"It's a duet."

"A duet? With who?"

"Me."

Her russet brown eyes widened. "Hold up. You?"

"Yeah, me."

"You mean to tell me that not only do you own this studio,

produce music, but you sing, too?"

"Yeah, man. You wanna hear the song or not?"

"Hell yeah, I do."

"Now this is some top-secret shit, aight. Don't a mothafucka alive know I got the pipes of an angel and shit."

She belted out a quick laugh. "An angel, huh? I'll be the judge of that. Play the song."

"You think a nigga playin', I be bussin' it down in the shower like that nigga, Drake."

She chuckled. "I think I would pay big money to hear you sing in the shower."

"I bet you would," I joked.

"Whatever! I'm anxious! Hurry up and play the song!"

[Female verse] Boy, I think you're scared/to love me like you want to.
You don't know what you want/so your boys gotta tell you.
So you side with them/then get mad at me
All I'm askin' is where you wanna be?
I love you with all honesty/but the things you do are so confusin'
You say you love me too/but boy I think you usin'

[Male verse] Girl, I think you're scared/to love me like you want to.
You don't know what you want/so your girls gotta tell you.
So you side with them/then get mad and say you leavin'
All because you caught a nigga creepin'
I love you with all honesty/but you think everything is a game
I swear this shit is crazy/thought about givin' you my last name.

"How you feelin' about that shit so far? You think it's somethin' you can fuck with?" I asked her.

"Hell yeah, that shit was fire. Send me the lyrics and let's try it out."

"Bet," I said while twisting open the cap of a brand-new

bottle of Hennessy and grabbing a glass. "You drink Henny?"

"Yeah, I do."

I poured two glasses for us and then escorted her over to the booth. We stood beside each other with our phones in one hand and drinks in the other. After about three runs, and two glasses of Henny later, I took the headphones off. She showed off her skills, switching octaves with ease, and making melodic riffs as her voice blended with the acoustics of the song.

"Yo, you killed that shit."

"Nah, *we* killed that shit."

"We make a good team," I told her as we stepped out of the booth.

"We definitely do."

"I got a question for you," I said, wrapping my hand around the neck of the bottle and taking it straight to the head.

"What?"

"What is your creative process like when you write?"

She shrugged. "Um, I don't know. I keep my notebook on me at all times so whenever I get a thought, I stop to write it down. You remember what I sang for you the first time we met?"

I nodded while sparking the tip of a blunt I'd rolled before she arrived. "Yeah."

"I'd just written that while sitting in the parking lot outside my job before I came to the house for dinner."

"Just off the top of the dome like that? No instrumentals for inspiration or nothin'?"

"If I'm home, I'll bust out my guitar from time to time, but if I'm out and about, it's just whatever comes to my mind or heart."

"Guitar, huh? See, I knew under all that glamour you had a bohemian vibe." I chuckled.

"What about you, Mr. Big shot music producer? You play any instruments?"

"Piano."

"I always wanted to learn how to do that. How long have you been playing?"

"Believe it or not, I grew up in the church. Me and my brother. He played the hell out of some drums, and I played the shit outta the keys."

"Wow, your own little family band."

I bobbed my head up and down. "Yeah, something like that."

"Your family must've been proud."

"Everything was cool until he got killed and then shit just seemed to spiral out of control for me. I broke away from the church and my family."

I could instantly see the sadness in her eyes. "I know that must've been hard."

I took a long pull from my blunt and nodded. "It was, but I learned to put my pain in the music . That's how I cope."

She didn't need to know my brother was actually still very much alive; he was just dead to me. I still did business with him, but we stopped seeing each other as true family long ago.

"Well, for what it's worth, you're talented as hell."

"Takes talent to know talent."

A rosy-pink glow glimmered across her warm caramel cheeks. "Thank you."

"I'ma take my time with you and your music to get it just right. You definitely have the potential to be a big star, Bellamy. I don't say that to just anybody."

She rolled her eyes. "Stop gassing me. You're not going to get anymore cool points with my sister or me for that matter."

"I'm dead ass. Stick with me, and I really think we can make somethin' big happen. I got connects all over."

"Singing is my dream, Jaron. Like, you don't understand how bad I want this. You think I wanna be a makeup consultant and bartender for the rest of my life? If you're as serious as you say you are, then I'm going to trust you. I'm putting my future in your hands."

"I won't let you down, Bellamy. I got you," I assured her.

Chapter Four

Dash

Over the years, I'd made a name for myself on the streets, so much that niggas knew to be cool whenever they were in my presence, or it was gon' be a problem. Niggas said I was so ruthless that my heart had to be as black as coal. I was nowhere near as hot headed and wild as I was when I was coming up. After recently coming off a bid, I made it my business to take the hands-off approach and stack my money lowkey, moving forward. I was never going back to jail for nothing or no one. Shit, I was happy that in the nine months I'd been out, I was able to take the bread I'd stashed and flip it to make a half a million. I was slowly making my way back on top as if I'd never left.

I pulled up to the hole in the wall pool hall to meet my boy, Devil. Before I could even step out of the warmth from my vents, I saw him coming outside bundled up with an oversized red jacket with a fur hood, Timbs, and a skully covering his wavy jet black hair.

"What's good, my G?" he asked, sticking his hand through the window to dap me up.

"Shit, you called, and I pulled up. What's up?"

"I need you to ride out with me."

"Where we goin'?"

"Does it matter?"

"Nigga, you know it do. You already know what type of time I'm on now," I reminded him.

He rolled his gunmetal gray eyes. "Don't tell me you gone soft on me."

"You know me better than that. My attitude ain't change,

just my mindset, nigga."

He smirked as he shoved his hand in his pocket to grab his keys. "Let's ride then."

I shut off the engine and stepped out of my car just to hop in the passenger seat of his snow-white Jaguar. "This shit clean as a bitch," I said, complimenting him on the red leather interior.

"Good looks. Just paid cash for this pretty ass bitch two days ago."

Devil pulled the car out of the lot, and we headed to the interstate. Not too long after getting on the road, his phone rang. "Hello? Bet. Good. Just make sure it's wrapped and vacuum sealed."

I chuckled at the fact that his call had ended almost as quickly as it had started. I'd known Devil for over half of my life, and he'd never been one for talking on the phone too long. He was my day one. Wasn't shit thicker than our blood. We fell into the game as young niggas, making money, which also meant making enemies for ourselves. Our motto had always been "high risk, high reward." It was nothing new, just the mentality of a New York nigga. When the situation came my way that landed me in jail, I stood ten toes down, and he held me down on the outside.

After eight long years of being incarcerated or being sent off to "school" as he called it, he knew more than anybody that I was ready for my homecoming and to reclaim my spot at the top of the food chain alongside him.

"You gon' tell me where we goin' or who we pullin' up on?" I asked him.

Instead of responding right away, he reached into the center console and grabbed a pre-rolled blunt and a red lighter. Red had always been his favorite color, and he had no problem letting niggas know it. Any outfit he wore had some attribute of red in it, whether it was the ruby red diamonds in his ears or the expensive ass Rolex on his wrist with the red dial. There was no questioning as to why niggas from New York all the way to Miami knew his light-skinned ass as Devil.

As soon as his blunt was lit and he'd inhaled at least twice, he passed it to me. "Niggas man, you try and show 'em the way and they go and try to play with your money like you a sucka."

He didn't need to say more than that. I already knew what was up and what I might be forced to do if shit went left. "You got the heat?"

"Always. Pop the glove box."

I followed his words and popped open the glove compartment to see the Glock staring back at me, and then shut it. Devil knew that ever since getting out, I sat back and made all of my moves in silence, but he was ready to be loud and in color with whoever had fucked with him and his money. As his right hand, I had no choice but to be right there with him. The two of us pulled up to a vacated parking lot where there was only one other car parked there. Devil parked six spaces away before killing the engine.

"You ready?" he asked.

I nodded, while grabbing the Glock out of his glove compartment. Seeing that put a smile on Devil's face. "Let's get at these niggas," I told him.

My rust colored Timbs hit the icy black pavement as I stepped out and tucked the gun in the back of my jeans. I looked across the way and saw three niggas leaning against an older model BMW. Two were Hispanic and one looked to be a half-breed between the black we were and the brown mothafuckas he was with. Without an ounce of fear in his heart, Devil stepped up to them with me by his side.

"You got my money?" he asked the mixed one.

"Nigga, how many times I gotta tell you? I don't owe you shit. None of us do! We gave you your cut and that was that."

"Now, my black ass may not have finished high school, but a nigga knows his math very fuckin' well. Your cut was short five thousand fuckin' dollars. How you think I wasn't gon' catch that? I gave your bitch asses the last forth-eight hours to get me my shit and now what it sound like, Dash?" Devil asked, turning his attention to me.

"Sound like they ain't got it," I replied.

"Sounds like y'all ain't got it," Devil said, while shaking his head. "Now what the fuck do we do from here?"

I chuckled on the inside at the way Devil interacted with them. He rested his hand on his chin to really look as if he was debating on his next move when both of us knew what was about to come next. His mannerisms were comical, but there was no pleasure in his face. If any of them had an ounce of sense, they would've known never to fuck with him the way they did. If it was one thing Devil ain't fuck with, it was his money and his family. I kept my eyes on all three of the strangers standing in front of me, taking note when the Ricky Ricardo lookin' nigga to my left widened his stance.

"I put you young mothafuckas on and this is how you repay me, by stealing from me? Taking food off my plate? Taking food out of my kids' mouths?"

"Relájate, esto no debería ser nada para ti," one replied.

The fact that he didn't have the balls to say what was on his chest in English, pissed me off. He was speaking Spanish at us like we knew what the fuck he was talkin' about, knowing damn well he understood the entire conversation before that moment. I didn't know about Devil, but I felt disrespected enough for the both of us. "Speak English, mothafucka!"

"Dile a tu madre que hable inglés," he muttered, followed by a chuckle.

Although I didn't know what the fuck he was saying, I could hear the intensity in his tone. He was taunting me, snickering as if he knew he'd gotten the best of me. "You better stop while you're ahead, before I slide your head clean off your neck, nigga," I warned.

"Comer un d—"

Instead of letting him finish or wasting my energy with another response, I drew back and connected my fist with his mouth. Three of his teeth instantly went ice skating across the pavement. He stumbled back into the rear of the car while holding his aching face. My impulsiveness had taken his ass by surprise. From then on, it was all out war.

The other two stepped up to us without being invited, sending four pairs of cold, rough hands our way. Devil took on one, sending a gush of pain into his ribcage, while I thrusted my cold, balled-up fist into the chest of the other. He gasped for air as his arms lost tension, and his legs began to buckle underneath him. The two of us were breaking bones with every blow. Although they'd swung on us first, their agile movements were just too slow.

"Where. The fuck. Is my money," Devil asked, drilling his fist into his victim's face with every word he spoke.

"I'll get it to you. I—I swear on my motha, I will!" he said, trying to start negotiations in order to stop the ass whoopin' he was getting in the dead of the New York winter.

Devil and I both knew it wasn't about the money to him at that point. He'd seen a few thousand come and go within the matter of minutes. It was the principle of it all. He had to prove a point, and he was using me to help him do it. Just as I'd sent one sliding across the ground, the one I hit first came leaping at me like a panther, trying to wrestle me down to the ground. We tussled, beginning a choreographed dance of ruin until both of our bodies thudded against the ground. I quickly rolled over, balling up my fist and repeatedly crashed it into his cheekbone like a broken record. His loose neck flew up and back against the ground like a yo-yo until his head and face were soaked in the aftertaste of blood.

"That's enough, Dash. I got these mothafuckas from here," Devil said, resting his hand on my shoulder.

I immediately snapped out of my daze and looked down at him. One of his eyes was swollen shut and there were welts and gashes on his face with blood leaking out of them. I stood to my feet and looked around at the three of them all laying on the cold pavement with their wounds oozing.

"Bitch ass mothafuckas," I mumbled, while eyeing my fist stained with blood.

Devil popped the trunk, pulled out a jug of gasoline, and

started dousing it all over the ground around them in a circle. When he was done, he reached into his pocket and pulled out the blunt we hadn't finished on the ride over and lit it again.

"This will teach you not to fuck with me or my money again, mothafuckas! This fuckin' city is mine," he said, flicking the blunt into the circle, watching it ignite almost instantly.

We pulled off and left them bleeding out and burning on the pavement almost as if it was nothing. If there was one thing I knew, it was that anything went in the streets. All that mattered in the end was who came out on top.

Gotti

My eyes were as heavy as lead by the time I'd gotten off work. I barely remembered holding up my key fob to get into the building. As soon as I walked through the door and popped around the corner to the elevators, my fatigue was instantly interchanged with nervous energy when my eyes landed on Dash's.

"H—hey," I said.

"What up?"

"Just getting in from work."

"Long day?"

"Definitely. I have a shit load of student emails to read and respond to before midnight, plus I'm still working on my thesis paper so I can graduate in a couple months."

"You a teacher or somethin'?"

"Teacher's assistant. I work alongside one of my poli-sci professors."

"That pays for all this?" he asked, stepping onto the elevator when the doors opened.

I chuckled. "No, my uh...let's just say I have my ways."

He nodded. "That means daddy's credit card is paying for

it."

I winced at the mere mention of my father. "Something like that. And what is it that you do?"

"I'm in business for myself."

"So like an entrepreneur?"

He nodded once more. "Yeah, something like that."

"Looks like you had a hard day yourself," I said, glancing down at his swollen knuckles with caked up blood on them.

He looked down at his right hand. "Nah, I'll be aight."

"You sure? I'm certain I have a Band-Aid or some gauze or somethin' in my medicine cabinet."

He chortled. "If you want me to beat it up again, all you had to do was ask."

I could feel my face turning beet red. "No, that's n—not what I meant at all."

"I'm joking. I'll take it."

I let out a sigh of relief after stepping off the elevator onto my floor. He followed me down the hallway and waited for me to unlock the door. As soon as I flipped on the lights, I immediately regretted inviting company over as I looked around at all the unpacked moving boxes and plastic tubs. "Excuse the mess. I've been working on my thesis paper and the shit is taking over my life, so I haven't had time to fully unpack."

"You eating Oodles and Noodles like you locked up or you a freshman in college or somethin'."

A smile stretched across my face. "Ha-ha, very funny. I just don't have the time until the weekends and then it's like I'm so tired, all I want to do is lay around and be on some bummy shit."

"Maybe I'll treat you to a real meal one day since you insist on being my nurse and shit."

"That would be nice...but uh, make yourself at home while I try to go find my first-aid kit. I'll be right back."

As soon as I stepped into my bathroom, I rested my hands on the edge of the porcelain sink and drew in three, long deep breaths. My entire aura was off when I was around him. He made me nervous, excited, and all out horny at the same damn time.

I'd never experienced no shit like that, and it scared the living hell out of me.

"Get it the fuck together, Gotti," I whispered to myself before opening the medicine cabinet and pulling out what I needed.

"Found it," I announced, while making my way back down the narrow hallway a couple minutes later.

Dash was sitting on the couch, scrolling through his phone as if he didn't have a care in the world. "Bet."

"Come in the kitchen so I can do this over the sink. I don't want you bleeding all over my couch," I said, half-serious, half-joking. He followed me into the kitchen while I flipped on the lights and put the first-aid kit down on the counter. "Okay, let me see it."

He extended his hand to me, and I winced in pain as if I could feel what he felt just from looking at his wound. "It's not that bad," he assured me.

I frowned. "Sure don't look that way."

"Trust me, I've had worse."

"So, you just go around beating up your hands for fun?" He smirked without letting a word fall from his juicy lips. "What is it? What's so funny?" I asked.

"Ain't nothin' funny."

"I saw the smirk on your face."

"And?"

"And, that tells me there's somethin' you wanna say, but you're not."

"Chill, lil' mama. It ain't nothin', just keep bandaging a nigga up."

I rolled my eyes and placed my focus back on cleaning his wounds. "Fine, whatever."

"You from the city?" he asked me.

"Yeah, you?"

He nodded. "Born and raised."

"That's odd."

"What?"

"Why we never ran into each other before."

"New York is a bigger city than you think."

I shrugged. "Yeah, I guess."

"So, you said you in school and shit?"

"Yeah, why?"

He chuckled while tilting his head toward my half-opened bookbag laying across the dining room table.

I smirked. "I'm wrapping up my last semester in my master's program. All I have left to do is finish my thesis paper, and then it's on to the next big thing; trying to find a big girl job."

"Oh yeah? You don't got nothin' already lined up?"

"As soon as I get done with this paper, I'm jumping head first into beefing up my resume and lining up interviews. It's just right now…this paper is taking over my life. I've been writing it over the past two semesters."

"Damn, fuck you writing, a novel?"

I giggled. "I wish. I'm sort of what you call an overachiever, so I'm actually getting my masters in both criminal justice and political science. Double the major, means double the work. On top of that, I already told you I'm working as a teacher's assistant for my professor. So that means grading papers, answering emails, all that."

He boomed with laughter. "As busy as you are and you still found the time to stitch a nigga up. I'ma stop callin' you lil' mama and start callin' your ass Wonder Woman."

I chuckled. "Thanks…I think."

"Once you finish, hit me up, and we'll celebrate."

"Well, you already know where to find me," I said, oddly nodding my head toward my front door.

"You right."

"I'm all done…with your hand," I said, rushing my eyes up toward his.

He examined his bandaged hand and nodded. "Good looks."

"Um, if that was your way of saying thank you, then you're welcome."

Instead of acknowledging my comment with a response, he walked over to the dining room table and picked up one of my textbooks. "You read this whole thing?"

I shrugged. "Most of it."

He examined the title. *Exploring Criminal Justice,* huh? What made you wanna get into that field?"

"My father..."

"He a cop or somethin'?"

"Was. He was um...killed on my sixteenth birthday."

"Damn, yo. I'm sorry to hear that."

"Nah, it's okay. I spent the first few years warring for my sanity, but now I'm finally at a place where I can talk about it without—"

"Fallin' apart?" he asked, finishing my sentence.

I flashed my eyes up at him and nodded. "Yeah...exactly."

The two of us kept our eyes locked on each other, and I swore I could feel him seeing straight through to my soul.

"So, that night I met you...that was your birthday?"

"Yeah, it was."

"That explains why you looked so uptight."

I lowered my head so he wouldn't see the embarrassment across my face. "Shut up. I wasn't uptight, I was...okay, you got me. I was uptight as hell."

A smile tugged at his lips. "You don't have to tell me what I already know."

"What's up with that?"

"What's up with what?" he asked.

"You...are you just that good at reading people or what?"

"I am. It's a gift."

My eyes traveled down his entire frame, milking in everything about his presence. His ability to read people damn sure wasn't his only gift. God had blessed him ten times over.

"You got somethin' you wanna say?" he asked, snapping me back into the moment.

"No. Why do you ask?"

"I know that look."

"And what look is that?" I asked, folding my arms across my chest.

He smirked. "Like I told you earlier, if you wanna bounce on this dick again, all you gotta do is just say so."

It was the middle of winter, yet my body was on fire as if I was standing two feet away from the sun. I dared to part my lips to offer a response, afraid of what would come out. Dash stepped closer to me. "Is that what you want?" he asked.

His tall frame hovered over me. I saw the danger behind his smile, but I still went forward; fell *deeper*. I couldn't fuckin' help myself if I wanted to. "Yes..."

Silence hung over us as he pushed my back against the kitchen island. He effortlessly hooked his index finger underneath my chin and pulled my lips onto his. I coiled my lips around his long tongue as he held my body close like a prison. My legs slightly parted, allowing him to stand in between them as he nibbled on my ear and the right side of my neck.

Tremors rose in the wake of his guiltless kisses. Just his touch alone was tampering with my sanity. "Mmm."

"Mmm, don't tell me I found your spot," he whispered in my ear.

"You definitely did," I admitted.

"You know what that means then, right?"

"No, what's that?"

"Shit is over for you."

Dash gripped my ass and lifted my body off the ground to sit me on the edge of the countertop, carelessly knocking the gauze, band-aids, peroxide, and other first-aid products to the ground. I couldn't have cared less. I wanted to know what he had in store for me. My body was practically begging for it. He lifted my shirt up over my bra and proceeded to unhook the lace contraption that was holding my 32C breasts hostage. As soon as the clasp was unhinged, he swept both my shirt and bra off of me in one quick motion. Before I even had the chance to react, I felt the warmth of his mouth mixed with the stickiness of his tongue latching around my nipples.

My head flew back in pleasure. He'd found yet another one of my hidden turn on spots. So far, he was two for two. I pushed his head back before running my hands down the front of his shirt; lifting it just enough to see the perfect V-cut of his abs and a peek of his Ralph Lauren boxers. My top teeth sunk into my bottom lip as I reached inside his jeans and began circling his growing length with my hand.

"You know what you want, huh?"

I nodded. "Mmhm."

"Show a nigga how much you want it then."

I took that as a challenge and hopped off the countertop. The second I landed on my feet, I dropped down to my knees. Dash unbuttoned his jeans and let them fall around his thighs. I reached out to pull them and his boxers down the rest of the way, exposing the chocolate wonder that I knew was going to have my toes curling and eyes rolling back in my head in no time. Without hesitation, I let my tongue trace from the base of his dick all the way to the curve before pulling the tip into my mouth.

"Mmm," he groaned. "Suck that shit like you mean it."

I sucked harder, determined to show him that I had skills. Dash ran his fingers through my hair as I continued to work each muscle in my mouth. After making sure his dick was rock hard, he pulled me back up to my feet and started planting a trail of kisses down to my stomach before gripping the edge of my pants with his teeth.

"Take them off."

I quickly unbuttoned my jeans and shimmied them down my hips until I could step out of them. Dash grabbed hold of my panties and ripped them with one swift pull before sitting me back on the counter. He kissed down the front of my exposed chest, stopping to gently grind his teeth across my erect nipples. He continued to place butterfly-soft kisses against the most sensitive parts of my skin. His actions were deliberate. Sinister, almost. With each kiss he was stripping away my restraint, morals, and anything else that was holding me back from giving every inch of me to him.

He spread my legs and dropped to his knees. My clit pulsated against his lips as he planted his face at the junction of my thighs. The moment his tongue touched my flesh, my body thrusted forward in agonizing pleasure. Within minutes, he'd managed to map every peak and valley my body without once using his hands.

"Mmm, shit. Right there! Shit, I'm about to cum!" I squealed as I ran my fingers through the rippling waves of his fresh haircut.

"I want you to paint a nigga face with that shit," he growled.

I scooted closer to the edge of the countertop, bucking my hips forward, determined to dive head first into the sea of pleasure that I knew I was only a few tongue strokes away from. "That's it....right there. Right. Fuckin' there," I cried.

Dash carried me over to the dining room table and laid my back flat against it. His forearms locked underneath the crease of my knees as his hands tightly gripped my thighs, leaving red marks across my lightly melanated skin. The moment his width settled into my depths, he began ravaging my body from the inside out.

My nails dug into his back and shoulder muscles.
My bare legs anchored around his waist.
My lips molded into the shape of an O as feverish moans escaped from the depths of me.
I was his for the punishing.

"Yessss! Just like that!" I screamed, threading my ankles around his waist.

It was safe to say I'd met my match with Dash. Every stroke was calculated as if his dick knew how deep to go and what angle to hit to make my body quiver each and every time. Dash slid the palms of his hands underneath my ass and scooped me into the air while sliding my body up and down his pole.

I hooked my arms around his neck while my boneless limbs dangled over his shoulders, bending at his will. While keeping himself firmly rooted inside me, he carried me over to the couch. I straddled him, rocking back and forth to the sensual rhythm our bodies were making.

"Yeah, show me how you ride dick," he said, pinning his hands behind his head.

Hearing the challenge in his tone, I tossed my head back and bucked forward as if my life depended on it. If he wanted to see how I rode dick, I was going to make sure he never forgot. Dash cradled my ass in his hands like a newborn baby as he slid down so that he could push deeper inside me.

"Mmm, shiiiiiiiitttttt!" I screamed, looking down at the flexing muscles of his eight pack.

He was urging me to my peak while I fed him each of my nipples to suckle on. He continued to drill inside me as I rode him until his dick was drenched in my cream. He flipped me onto my back and slid out of me. I watched him admiring the sticky glaze I'd left behind before pressing his dick to my lips.

"Taste it. I want you to know how good you taste."

I exposed my tongue to the sweetness that was mine before locking my lips around the tip of his dick and slurping it clean. My eyes flashed up towards his, and I caught a grin on his face. *This nigga is as nasty as they come,* I thought to myself.

"Turn around," he said, grabbing the base of his dick.

He grabbed a handful of my hair as he pushed inside me again, fucking me like an animal.

"Mmm, shit! Deeper! You're gonna make me fuckin' cum!"

"You ain't never been fucked like this before, have you?"

I shook my head, on the edge of exploding. "Don't stop!"

He went back shot after back shot, baptizing his dick in my wetness. He was fucking me so good, I just knew I was seconds away from passing the fuck out. He licked the tips of his fingers before reaching around and massaging my clit. I tossed my head back against his firm chest with my mouth wide open.

"Ooooh shiiiiiiiitttttt!"

Dash lifted my right leg up on the arm of the couch while he locked both of my arms behind my back and pushed deeper inside of me, leading me to yet another soul shattering climax.

I rested my head back against the throw pillow on the opposite end of the couch while trying to catch my fleeting breath. Dash stood to his feet and began to redress. I admired the sheen of sweat on his chest from our once intertwined bodies. After sliding his shirt back over his head, he looked down at me.

"What?" he asked.

"Nothin'..."

"There you go with that shit. If you got somethin' you wanna say to me, the floor is yours."

"What's your real name?"

"What?"

"I know Dash isn't your real name."

"What makes you say that?"

"Because...that's not a common name for someone to have," I said, while tossing my shirt back over my head and sliding my panties back on.

"I'm not a common ass nigga."

I rolled my eyes. "You have a comeback for everything, don't you?"

He shrugged. "Maybe, but I don't give out my government name to people, let alone strangers."

"I think we're a little more than strangers at this point, don't you?" I asked, trying my best not to sound offended, although I was.

He shrugged his shoulders for the second time in a row, and I could feel myself getting agitated. I was a big girl, and I knew sex was sometimes just that, but it wasn't the fact that he just had some good dick. I vibed with him, or at least I thought I did. His vibrations had instantly gone from insanely intimate to ice cold.

"Don't take me for a hoe because of...you know...what we're doing."

"I would never do you like that. I can easily spot the

difference between you and them," he assured me.

"Oh yeah, how so?"

"For one, you don't smile. Which means, you don't want to be approached. That's the exact opposite of what a hoe would do. These bit—I mean, females see diamonds or a nice watch and start showing all thirty-two teeth just to get noticed."

I chuckled at the fact that I never thought I'd meet someone who was just as blunt as I was. "So, you're funny and smart...good to know."

Silence washed over the room before he rattled his keys in his pocket and pulled out his phone. He began making his way to the door and then stopped to turn and look at me. "Dashiell."

"Huh?"

"My real name is Dashiell."

"Last name?"

"Why you need to know that? You tryna look me up in ya secret database or somethin'?"

"No, I just like to know who I'm dealing with."

He smirked. "Oh, so you dealin' with a nigga now?"

I sucked my teeth. "You know what I mean."

"Nah, it's cool. My last name is Graham."

I displayed an uncontrollable smile. "Well, it's nice to officially meet you, Dashiell Graham."

"Gotti your real name or it's short for somethin'?" he quizzed.

"My name is Golani."

"You got a last name, Golani? If you need to know who you dealin' with, then I guess I should know the same, huh?"

"Golani Evans."

He nodded. "Yo, you dangerous."

I frowned. "How so?"

"You done got good wood and my government out of me in the same night. Let me raise up out of here before you ask me to hand over my social."

I chuckled. "Yeah, it's getting late, and I still have actual work to do."

"I'm happy I could provide the distraction you seem like you needed."

"You're right…it was *much* needed."

He cracked a grin. "I'll catch you later, G."

"Goodnight," I said, while closing the door behind him.

Chapter Five

Tatiyana Daniels

"I swear to God you ain't shit, Jaron!" I yelled, flinging his phone at him while he laid in our bed, sleeping as peacefully as a milk wasted newborn baby.

It astounded me how someone could sleep like the entire world was completely at peace all the while knowing he was doing the woman he claimed to love dirty.

"Yo, what the fuck!" he roared, jumping up out of his slumber.

"You heard what the fuck I said, nigga! Who the fuck is this bitch sending you naked ass pictures in your DMs, huh?"

"I don't know what the fuck you even talkin' about," he grumbled while rubbing the sleep out of his eyes.

"Like hell you don't! You must think I'm some sort of fool! Is this what your so-called *clients* do to get studio time, huh? Pop a lil' pussy and you'll let they ass in the booth!?"

"Yo, Tati, chill the fuck out with all that shit! I told you I don't know what the fuck you're talkin' about. Bitches slide in my DMs every fuckin' day, aight? That don't mean I'm fuckin' them hoes or givin' they asses no free fuckin' studio time. You know me and you should already know a nigga don't do shit for fuckin' free."

"Exactly! And that's exactly why I said you're getting paid some other way if you ain't gettin' paid in dollars!" I roared.

"You know what, fuck it! I don't need this shit!" he said, grabbing his phone and darting off to the bathroom.

Before I could get to the door quick enough, he'd already slammed it and locked it behind him. I balled up my fist and started banging as hard as I could. "So, that's how you gon' do me, nigga? Huh? You gon' tuck your tail and run because you know I'm right? You ain't even got the balls enough to own up to your shit and fuckin' apologize!"

"Apologize for what? I ain't done shit to be sorry for!" he yelled through the door. "All you wanna do is argue. I'm not with that shit. Your ass be way too controlling for no reason! The entire time we been together, I've never given you a reason not to trust me!"

Seconds later, I heard the shower turn on, which only further fueled my rage. Although his statement was valid, I didn't give a fuck. I'd been through this shit before with exes from my past. I ignored the red flags and the never-ending list of broken promises and stayed true only to get hurt in the end. I wasn't about to do that shit with Jaron, no matter how much I loved him. How was I to know what he was doing whenever he was traveling for work? Before we moved in together, I'd always been able to give him the benefit of the doubt, but the shit hit differently when he was in my face, and I had access to his phone.

By the time he stepped out of the bathroom all squeaky clean and carefree, I was sitting on the edge of the bed with my head cradled in the palms of my hands. Jaron walked over and knelt down in front of me.

"Look, I'm sorry, aight?"

"Oh, now you sorry?" I sobbed.

"I promise you, I ain't done shit with that bitch. I don't even know the hoe you talkin' about."

"So, I'm just supposed to believe some random bitch is sending you naked pics for no reason?"

"That's exactly what you're supposed to do, especially when what I'm telling you is the truth, Tati. Just tell me what you want me to do to fix this, and I got you."

I looked up at him with red-rimmed eyes. "I just need to know that you're really in this with me, Jaron. I took a leap on you...on this whole relationship by moving in with you so soon, bringing you around my family. I—I just can't afford to be out here lookin' stupid on account of a nigga again," I admitted.

"You know I'm in this shit with you, baby. I'm ten toes down."

"Then, why the fuck does it feel like I'm the only one fighting for this to work?"

"You're not, Tati. You my girl and everybody who matters knows that shit," he assured me.

"And as your girl, it's my job to keep your ass out of trouble and away from these hoes. You know what I've been through in my past, Jaron. I'm sorry if I overreacted but seeing that shit just triggered the fuck out of me."

"It would never be my intention to hurt you, but look," he said, pulling out his phone. "I'm blocking that bitch right now. You don't ever have to worry about her again."

As much as I wanted to smile and give him and E for effort, I couldn't. I was too busy winding down the rabbit hole of my negative thoughts. It was no secret that I loved him, but I didn't know if I loved him enough to stay if something like that ever came up again.

Jaron sighed. "The look on your face tells me you still ain't happy with a nigga. What do you wanna do? Go to couple's therapy to work this shit out? Nah, you know what—come to the studio with me and see for yourself that I ain't up to shit."

I shrugged before folding my arms across my chest. "Maybe I will!"

He'd never openly invited me to a session with another artist before. I'd only been to the studio when he was working on one of his own projects. But trust and believe, now that the invite was on the table, I was going to be stuck to his ass like Gorilla Glue.

"Can I at least get a smile?" he asked, giving me a puppy dog look with his eyes.

I forced a counterfeit smile, and he kissed my lips.

"Let Daddy kiss the pain away," he said, placing a trail of kisses from my bare shoulders all the way up to my neck and cheeks.

Deep down, I knew that dick was and never would be an official apology, but I was going to accept it if that meant he'd stay around a little while longer.

*****

"Aight, I'll see you later," he said, bending down to kiss me on my forehead as my naked body laid enveloped in our bedsheets.

I frowned. "Where do you think you're going?"

He sighed. "To the studio, Tati."

I sucked my teeth, silently wishing that his entire studio would burn straight to the ground one day. "Every time you're with me you always gotta run off to the damn studio."

"I'm going to meet up with your sister because YOU asked me to. Do you want me to cancel on her?"

I sighed. "No, I don't want her career caught up in the crosshairs of whatever it is we've got going on right now."

"Exactly, so I'll see you later, aight?"

"I'm not playin', the next time, I'm coming with you!"

"By all means, do so. You have an open invitation."

Bellamy

I was standing outside of the building where Jaron's studio was when a white Bentley truck pulled up curbside and let the window down. As soon as I saw his face, I flashed him a grin. "Oh, you fancy, huh?" I asked.

He chuckled while shaking his head. "I know I'm that nigga, but I don't gotta go around gloatin' about the shit."

"Whatever." I cheesed.

"You ain't cold? How long you been out here?"

"Nah, I'm okay—I haven't been out here long," I lied.

He didn't know that I'd been trying to get into the building off and on for the past twenty minutes, but no one would come in with the code or leave. My ass was freezing, and I had the red pointed Rudolph nose to prove it. As soon as he hopped out of his ride and came around to let me inside the building, my phone started buzzing in my pocket. I quickly pulled it out and saw Tati's name across my screen with a picture of us that was taken six months prior.

"Shit," I mumbled.

"Everything good?" he asked.

"Yeah, you go ahead without me. I'll be up in a sec."

He nodded. "Bet."

"Hello?" I answered, putting the phone to my ear. All I heard in return were sobs and sniffs. "Tati—you okay?"

"Are you with him?"

"With who?" I asked.

"Jaron."

"Yeah, I'm here."

She sighed. "Ugh, I should've known...I'm just ugh, what the fuck is wrong with me?"

My forehead crumpled. "What the hell are you talkin' about? What's wrong?"

"We got into an argument before he left, and he said that he was going to meet you at the studio, and I just wanted to make sure he wasn't lying to me."

"Lying to you? Why would he lie about being at the studio with me?"

"He didn't—he wouldn't. I—I don't know. I freaked the fuck out on him because I went through his phone and saw some bitch sending her pussy through the mail in the form of his Instagram DMs."

"And you asked him about it?"

"More like..."

"Flew the fuck off the handles like you usually do?" I asked, finishing her sentence.

She sighed. "Yup."

"Tati, you've really got to get a hold on your anger issues."

"I know, Bells. I don't want to run him off just because my suspicions are always on ten. You know what I've been through."

I nodded while simultaneously rolling my eyes. Any time it came down to Tati defending herself, she always tossed out the *you know what I've been through* victim card first. We'd all be hurt before. It seemed to me that she needed to toughen the hell up.

"What do you think?" she asked.

"About what?" I frowned.

"Do you think he's cheating on me?"

"How would I know that? I've literally only been around him a handful of times. It's not like I've seen him in the studio with a bunch of bitches salivating over him like he's God's gift to women or anything like that."

She groaned. "I just don't know why I can't shake this fuckin' feeling!"

"Look, Tati—I'm your sister, and I love you, so I'm going to give this shit to you straight with no chaser, aight? ALL MEN CHEAT. It's literally embedded in their fuckin' DNA. The only thing you need to ask yourself is do you love him, and I know you love him, don't you?"

"Of course, I do."

"Okay, so either you're going to put up with the shit or you gon' leave. Whatever you decide, just make sure you keep your mouth and your feelings in check before you let your past run off your future," I said, pressing the up button on the hallway elevator.

I knew I was being selfish and not fully taking her feelings into account. A part of me did feel bad for her, but I knew there was truth in my words. I just couldn't afford to have Tati's clinginess ruin my chance at finally getting somewhere with my music.

She sighed. "You're right."

"I know I am, but look, I gotta go, aight? I'll call and check on you tomorrow," I told her just as the elevator door opened.

The second I stepped into Jaron's studio suite, he had

a blunt up to his lips and a glass of Henny in his hands. "Everything aight?"

"You tell me," I said, tossing my purse down on the black leather couch before sliding off my coat. "Tati just called me."

He sighed. "So, now she got you thinkin' I'm a dog, too, huh?"

"Not even."

His eyebrows raised. "That's surprising. I thought most females stuck like glue to their girls by adopting however they felt."

"I'm not most girls," I assured him.

He nodded. "I can see that. But look, I'ma say this to you once, and I ain't gon' speak on it no more for the rest of the night because we ain't come here to talk about my personal shit, but whatever your sister said I did, I didn't. Hoes be in my DMs all the time trying their best for a come up. They don't give a fuck who they gotta suck, fuck, or swallow to get it."

I rolled my eyes. "Typical. They are the ones out here making it ten times harder for those of us with actual talent who are trying to make it the right way with no shortcuts."

"Ain't no comparing you to them. Your talent is valid. That's always gon' outshine whatever music phase shit they be on."

I smiled. "Well, thank you."

"But look, I got a fresh bottle of Henny and three new beats I want you to hear before we start workin' on the song I played for you last time you were here."

I nodded. "Cool, pour me up." As soon as I took my first sip, I spoke up again. "I thought about what you said the last time I was here."

"And what was that?"

"About my lyrics...and how I needed to make some of my music, you know...more sexy."

"Oh, yeah? So, you took my advice, huh?"

I nodded. "Yeah, and I got somethin' I want you to hear."

"Word?"

"Yeah, play me somethin' smooth."
"I'm all ears. Take it to the booth."

*****

"Mmm, yeah. Yeah."

...

"Skin sweeter than sugar, smoother than butter.
Goin' out my head, boy, you make my heart flutter.
The way that my body craves you must be a crime.
Got my body on fire like it's summertime."

Jaron shook his head in disapproval while pushing his dreads out of his face. "Yo, cut. Stop."

I opened my eyes and looked at Jaron, who had a smug look written across his face. "What? What's wrong?"

"You're singing a sexy song about the way a nigga makin' you feel, and yet I don't hear the passion or the vulnerability in your voice, Bellamy. It's beautiful, but it's flat."

I sighed. "Okay, I'm sorry. Let me try it again. Run it back for me one time."

"You know what, take your shirt off."

I frowned. "Excuse me?"

He sighed. "Trust me. Music is about emotion and passion. It's about the singer being and feeling as vulnerable and naked as the words you're singing. What better way to feel exposed then to take off your clothes?"

"You seriously want me to take off my shirt?"

"That's what I said. You not scared are you?"

"N—no. It just seems weird, that's all."

"Trust me, I've been doing this shit for a long time, and I ain't on no perverted ass shit. I just know what works to get people in the right mindset to get the results we both wanna hear."

I tugged at the hem of my shirt. "Okay..."

"Aight, now let's do the damn thing. You're wasting valuable studio time."

"I thought this was your studio," I said, while pulling my shirt over my head and exposing my black lace bra.

"It is, but I do have a girl to get back to, you know, Tati, the one who don't trust a nigga." He chuckled.

"Yeah, yeah. Fine. There, my shirt is off. Now what?"

He watched me drop my shirt to the floor and then started the song over. I placed my hands over my headphones and let the beat sway my body from side to side.

"Mmm, yeah. Yeah."

...

"Skin sweeter than sugar, smoother than butter.
Goin' out my head, boy, you make my heart flutter.
The way that my body craves you must be a crime.
Got my body on fire like it's summertime"

"Is it crazy that I fantasize about you next to me?
Kissin', touchin' and teasin' my body.
You ask me how I want it and I tell you real slow.
Temptation got me wonderin' how far I'm willing to go."

"Honey drip, my honey dip,
Taste of Henny on your lips."

"Boy you make me crazy, got me climbin' up the wall.
Ready for you whenever you call.
In love with the way your body speaks to mine.
Chills running up and down my spine"

"Mmm, yeah. Yeah."

...

"Weed smoke in the air, beat playin' slow.
Imagining you touchin' places only you can go.
A bad habit you are, got me screamin' your name.
Nothin' in this world could extinguish this flame.
Dreams of your smile and your hands around my hips.
Feels just right, oh boy, you make my..."

"Honey drip, my honey dip,
Taste of Henny on your lips."

Jaron stopped the song and stepped into the booth. He stared at me in silence for a few seconds and then started clapping.

"Did you like it?" I asked.

"Like it? I loved that shit, girl. See, I told you! What the fuck did I tell you!"

"I know, I know! Damn!"

"How do you feel?"

I drew in a deep breath and lifted my eyebrows. "I—I feel amazing. I feel open and like I can take on anything right now. Thank you! Thank you so much!" I said, jumping off the seat and into his arms for a hug.

Jaron enveloped my slim waist inside his arms, pressing my body against his hard chest. I had no idea how he felt, but I hadn't felt connected to a man like that in a long time. I gently pulled away from his hard body and flashed my eyes up at him. His deep-set eyes were the perfect blend of ash and smoke. *Dear God, I wanna have his babies.* I thought to myself.

"You're welcome," he said, still holding my waist.

There was a bright, neon sign blaring above his head that said *Run, bitch* but I didn't. I couldn't. In the blink of an eye, he'd turned into everything I ever wanted and everything I didn't need wrapped into one with a bright red bow on top. The only problem standing in my way of taking things to the next level was Tati.

"Um, I should uh let you get home to whatever plans you have with my—Tatiyana."

"Yeah...you're right."

"When do you think we could pick up and finish the rest of the song?" I asked, swiping my shirt off the floor and putting it back on.

"Uh, shit. I'd have to check my schedule and get back to

you. That shit is fire, though. I'll hit you up when I got the time and we can work somethin' out."

Chapter Six

Dash

As much as I was against getting involved in any way with any female, let alone one who lived in my building, I still found myself unable to get Gotti off my mind. The sexual chemistry we had was ill. Aside from the fact that she was pursuing a career in criminal justice, and she was the daughter of a cop, I admired her hustle. Baby girl was smart, beautiful, and had some of the best pussy I'd ever had. To me, she was a hood nigga's trifecta. I would've been a fool not to pursue her. Simply put, she was a vibe that I'd never felt before.

As soon as my knuckle parted from her front door, I could hear songs by the likes of TLC, Destiny's Child, and Mariah Carey—all staples of the 90s and early 2000s R&B era—blasting through the speakers inside. I knew better than to show up unannounced. Personally, I hated being approached when I wasn't ready, nor willing to see people. So if she answered the door and turned me away, I wouldn't even be mad. I waited twelve more seconds before I heard the lock turn. Gotti flung the door open wearing a sports bra, some gray leggings, and had all of her hair on top of her head in a messy ass bun with no makeup on.

"Oh, shit! Dashiell, what are you doing here?" she asked, her round face flushing a bright shade of pink.

I grimaced and then quickly turned my face back to neutral. Gotti was the first girl I'd ever let call me by my government name without checking her ass. "I was about to go grab a bite to eat and was gon' see if you wanted to come, but then I realized I ain't have your number."

"Oh, right. I guess we never did do the official exchange, huh?"

"Nah, we didn't. So you busy, I see you got your throwback jams on and shit, I'm not tryna kill your vibe."

"No, you're not. I, um—I could eat. Just give me like... forty-five minutes to shower and get myself together. Sound good?"

"You look together to me."

She licked her lush, glossy lips before smiling. "I mean, more presentable for the public eye."

"Why you give a fuck what the public think about you? If I think you look good, then that's all that should matter."

"Forty-five minutes, Dashiell," she responded.

I chuckled. "Put my number in your phone so you can text me when you're ready," I said, ready to rattle my number off to her.

She walked over to grab her phone and brought it back to me. "Here, put it in yourself."

I typed in my number and saved it under "Dash" before handing it back to her. "Cool, so I'll see you a little later."

An hour later, Gotti strapped herself into the vacant seat beside me wearing a pair of faded denim skinny jeans, an oversized sweatshirt, scarf, and a pair of UGG boots that reached her calf. She'd taken her hair down from the bun and wore it parted to where some of it cascaded over her left eye.

"You finally ready?" I asked, putting the car in drive. She swatted her neck in my direction, ready to pop shit and then paused. "What?"

"Nothing...it's just...you have...never mind."
"Say it."
"You have really pretty teeth."
My grin returned. "Thanks, yo."

"Where are we going to eat?" she quizzed as I signaled to get on the interstate.

"It's a surprise."

"If we're going to any place fancier than Chick-Fil-A, I'm going to be mad at you."

"And why is that?"

"Because I would've dressed better."

"You look perfect, Gotti."

I saw her cheesing from the corner of my eye. "Thanks... you don't look so bad yourself. How's that hand of yours?"

I quickly took my eyes off the road to glance down at the hand she'd bandaged up. "It's good. You a good lil' nurse and shit."

"So, you gon' tell me the real story about what happened to your hand?"

"I hadn't planned on it."

"Why not?"

"The sharing and *show and tell* shit just ain't my thing."

She didn't need to know that side of me. I knew she was smart enough to know I had ties the streets and that was as far as I was willing to take it.

"I can tell you're probably more trouble than you're worth."

I shrugged nonchalantly. "You're probably right about that, or at least you would've been if you would've met me in my younger days. A nigga is almost thirty-two years old. I'm wiser now and don't care for the hype."

"Yet we met in the club, and I saw you in your section with your people giving champagne showers to anyone who dared to get too close."

"That was different. It was the New Year. Niggas ain't allowed to celebrate now?"

"No, I'm not sayin' that. I'm just sayin' that your previous statement is a little contradictory in my opinion, that's all."

"You got a nigga feelin' like he's on trial or somethin'. Gotta watch what I say around you."

"No, you don't," she said, and then the car fell silent.

Instead of sparking up a new conversation, I reached over

and turned my speakers up just before the flow of traffic went from a slow creep to a complete stop inside the tunnel. After a few minutes of letting the music speak for us, Gotti reached over and turned the volume damn near all the way down to zero.

"It's too quiet in here," she told me.

"You just turned the music down and now you wanna complain that it's too quiet in here?" I chuckled.

"No, I mean—I think we should talk."

"Talk about what?"

"Let's play a game."

My forehead lined. "I'm a grown ass man. I don't play games."

She rolled her eyes. "Whatever. You ain't got shit else to do until traffic starts moving, right?"

"Fine, what's this game you wanna play?"

"Okay, so I'm going to say something like "best breakfast food," and then we have to blurt out the first answer that comes to mind within like one second."

"What the fuck kind of game is that?"

"One that will help us get to know each other better. Trust me, it'll be fun."

"Fine, you start," I told her, while grabbing my blunt and lighter out of the center console. If I was going to be forced to play a game *and* sit in traffic, I was at least going to make sure I felt good doing it.

"On three, okay?"

I nodded. "Aight."

"One, two…three. Best *Friday* movie?"

I sucked my teeth. "Easy. Next Friday." I chuckled after realizing we'd said it in unison.

"Okay, your turn."

I shrugged while ashing my blunt out of the window. "Shit, um…Best cereal of all time? I don't know."

"Cinnamon Toast Crunch," she blurted out.

"Nigga, what?" I disagreed. "It's all about the mothafuckin' Crunch Berries."

She shook her head. "Um, ew. I mean to each his own or whatever, but no. Nothing is topping fuckin' Cinnamon Toast Crunch."

I chuckled. "You're entitled to your whack ass opinion, G."

"Whatever. Okay, this one is gon' make you think."

"Bet, I'm ready."

"It's gon' be hard," she warned.

"Say the shit."

"The King of R&B of *this* generation?"

I paused for a second. "Damn."

"See, told you it would be hard."

"Who you got?"

"I don't know! It's like I'm at a toss-up."

"Between who?" I asked.

"Okay, before you judge, hear me out. So, of course, there's Chris Brown. But then there's Khalid, Bryson Tiller...they've been putting out fire since they dropped."

"Yeah, but even still, they still ain't touchin' that nigga Breezy," I assured her.

She shrugged. "Yeah, I guess you're right. Chris is the king, hands down."

I let out a quick laugh. "I'm glad we were finally able to agree on somethin' else. You lost some points with that Cinnamon Toast Crunch shit."

"Whatever. You lucky I ain't put Jacquees on my list."

I laughed. "I would've had to put your ass out if you did that."

"Now you know you wrong for that," she said, clutching her stomach as she laughed.

*****

"Do you have to eat like that?" She wore a hint of a frown across her face while sitting across from me at the dinner table.

"Like what?"

"Like a savage," she said, turning her nose up at me.

"How you want me to eat it?" I asked, followed by a sly smirk. As much as she tried to hide it, I could tell my words had made that pussy tingle.

"You know what I meant."

"You know you mad bossy, right?"

"So I've been told, but that's just the way I was raised. I've always been outspoken," she said.

"Only child, huh?"

"How'd you know?"

"I can just tell."

"What about you? You got siblings?"

"A brother."

"You two close?"

"We were at one point," I told her.

"What happened?"

"He was killed."

"I'm so sorry to hear that."

"Everybody gotta go someday, right?"

"I guess so. I guess I just don't process death the way you do."

"And how is that?"

"You're so nonchalant about it."

"When you've seen as much death as I have, then it becomes the new normal. Niggas weren't put here to live forever, G. That's just how I look at it."

"You're the only person who calls me 'G'," she said, changing the subject.

"Good. You're the only person I let call me by my government name. I prefer Dash. That's been my name since I was a young nigga. No nigga alive calls me Dashiell."

"What's wrong with the name Dashiell? I like it, plus it has such a beautiful meaning behind it," she stated.

I chuckled. "You looked up the meaning of my name or somethin'?"

"Maybe."

"And what did you learn, *Miss Bookworm*?"

"Well for one, Dashiell means bravehearted and heaven or sky. I feel like you can learn a lot about a person just from the meaning of their name."

"And what does my name tell you about me?"

"That you seem to be the type of person who knows what he wants and goes after it, and maybe just a little high maintenance too," she joked.

I eyed her closely. She was almost too smart for her own damn good, and funny too. I liked that shit. "And what about you? What does Gotti mean?"

"Well, *Golani* means beautiful," she corrected me.

"So, I should just start callin' you beautiful now?"

She flashed a disarming smile at me. "No, I like it when you call me G."

"Yo, what are you doing with someone like me? I mean, you don't really give off the vibe that you'd go for a nigga like me off jump."

"And what type of nigga do I look like I go for?" she quizzed.

"Some while collar, preppy, smart nigga type."

"Wow, judge much?" she asked, rolling her eyes.

I chuckled. "Chill, G. I'm just sayin'. If I'm wrong, then tell me I'm wrong. I can take it."

"You are so wrong. I mean, yeah, you're not the typical guy I'd see myself dating or taking home to meet my mama, but I also wouldn't bring someone around who had a stick up their ass either."

"So, why you here with me?" I asked again.

She lazily shrugged her shoulders. "I like you."

"It's that simple, huh?"

"To me it is."

"Mmhm."

"Is there a reason I shouldn't like you, Dashiell?"

"There are probably a million reasons, but I already know that ain't gon' stop you."

She giggled. "You're probably right."

"Just know that a nigga like me don't let a lot of people in, but you…you get admission."

"And why is that?"

"Shit, I'm still trying to figure that out myself. I guess that means a nigga feelin' you too."

"It's funny because you don't really strike me as the relationship type of guy," she told me.

"That's because I'm not."

"See, that's something else we have in common."

"Comin' from a female, that's some new shit."

"What do you mean?"

"I mean, most women wanna be wifed up, claimed and shit. They damn near press a nigga to make shit official, but you seem good solo."

"It's not that I never want to be in a relationship or that I never want to get married, I just have other shit on my plate that needs to get handled first like school and my career. Once I have all that, then I can focus on possibly entertaining the idea of a serious relationship."

"So, what I'm hearing is that you're good with what it is we're doin' right now."

She affirmed. "As unorthodox as it may sound to you, yeah, I am. And if and when I'm ready for more, then you'll be the first to know…"

I acknowledged her statement with a simple head nod. G was a whole different breed of female that my ass just wasn't used to. She knew what she wanted and didn't want. She had her head on so straight, she had mine spinnin'.

"You finished eatin'?" I asked her.

"Yeah, I'm just gonna get them to box the rest of this up so I can eat it later."

"No wonder why you so small. Your ass eat like a lil' bird."

She rolled her eyes. "Just because you made that statement, I'm gon' order dessert to go, too!"

"The world is yours, G. Order whatever you want."

"Oh, and next time you decide you wanna take me out, let me know where we're going first. I know you may not care what

I look like, but I know I can do better than this," she said, looking down at her casual outfit as we sat in the middle of a five-star restaurant.

I smirked. "Whatever you say, G."

*****

AFTER SHE ORDERED dessert and the waitress boxed up her leftovers, I dropped two one-hundred-dollar bills on the table, and we headed back to the car. While driving on the interstate, my phone vibrated, and I picked it up to answer Devil's call, ensuring she wouldn't hear his voice through the speakers via Bluetooth.

"Sup?"

"Where you at? I need you to come through."

I glanced over at Gotti whose attention had been captivated by the city lights whizzing by. "You gon' have to give me at least an hour," I told him.

"Aight, bet. Come through in an hour. I got somethin' I need to discuss with you."

"I got you," I told him and then ended the call.

"You got somewhere you need to be?" she asked.

"Not right this second."

"But there is somewhere else you need to be eventually, right?"

"Yeah."

She let out an exasperated sigh. "Okay."

"What I tell you about that shit? If you got somethin' you need to get off your chest, then do it."

"Maybe it's not for me to understand the inner workings of the streets, but I don't think anything or anybody should be worth your freedom or your life, but that's just my opinion."

"And you're entitled to it."

"Well, what do you think?" she asked.

"I'll never tell you what I think, only what I know. And what I know is you've got your head so far up your ass that you're convinced every phone call I take has to do with multimillion dollar drug deals and murders. I know that making it in the streets is a rite of passage. I also know your lil' ass is way too judgmental for your own good. What I do is lucrative, and I'm wise enough now to keep my fuckin' hands clean. Plus you said it yourself, I help a lot of people."

"What about the people you hurt?"

As much as I wanted to break it down for her that hurtin' niggas was just as much a part of the game as helpin' niggas, I didn't feel like wasting my breath or my time. She already had her mind made up and there wasn't shit I was going to say that would convince her to see it otherwise. Instead, I shot her a glance that told her she was barking up the wrong tree.

"Next subject."

"No, I want to finish this."

I averted my attention from the road ahead of me to the car behind me that I'd noticed had been tailing me. "It is finished, G. You already told me your pops was a cop, so I wouldn't expect for you to have the same mentality or outlook as I do on shit. Our circles ain't the same."

"Yeah, I guess we're just going to have to agree to disagree."

"I'm just trying to save you from your ignorance, that's all."

She frowned. "Excuse me?"

"Yo, shut up, G," I said, diverting my attention back to my rearview mirror.

"Excuse me? Don't tell me to shut up!"

"I'm serious. Shut the fuck up and be cool."

"Cool? Cool about what?"

As soon as the words fell off her lips, the car I'd noticed that had been tailing us for the past five minutes finally turned on the flashing red and blue lights.

"Cool about this," I said, making my way over to the shoulder to pull over.

"What the fuck is going on, Dashiell? Why are we being

stopped? If there's somethin' illegal in this car then you need to let me know right now!" she demanded.

I knew better than to put G in harm's way, but her mouth was pissing me off. There was nothing inside my whip that would even give the inkling of foul play, but I knew all too well that wouldn't stop the cops from trying their luck anyway.

"Just be calm and do what the fuck I say, aight? Reach into the glove box and grab my registration and my insurance card," I instructed her while reaching over and pulling my wallet out of my pocket.

As soon as the car came to a complete stop, I grabbed my license, cracked the window, and visibly rested both hands on the steering wheel.

"License and registration, please," the officer said when he walked up to my side of the car.

"Excuse me, officer. Why are we being pulled over?" G interjected.

"You were swerving."

She sucked her teeth. "Bullshit," she mumbled.

"Excuse me?"

"Chill, G," I told her while handing him my paperwork.

He eyed us both for a couple of seconds and then looked down at what I'd handed him. "I'll be right back."

As soon as he walked away, I cut my eyes at her. "Didn't I tell your ass to be calm? Ain't no need for all that extra shit. The quicker he run my shit, the quicker I can get you home."

"Please step out of the car, sir," the officer said as he returned to my window a couple minutes later.

"For what?" I asked.

"Sir, I said please step out of the car."

"Excuse me, officer. What did he do?" Gotti interjected again.

"Ma'am, please be quiet."

"It's cool, Gotti. Just chill," I said, slowly opening the door so that I could step out of the car.

Before I knew it, two more cars pulled up and the officer

placed my hands behind my head and cuffed me before patting me down for any weapons.

Emasculated.
Embarrassed.
Enraged.

That was what it was like to be a Black man in America, and G was getting her very first up close and personal look. With my body facing the car, I could see her moving around and before I knew it, the passenger side door flung open, and she stepped out.

"Excuse me, but I want to know why we are being harassed like this, and I want to know now!" she demanded with her cell phone in hand, recording everything.

"Ma'am, step back and let me see your I.D.," another officer told her.

Red and blue lights danced off her honey brown skin as she frowned. "My I.D.? What did I do? I'm not breaking any laws!"

"Ma'am, give me your identification, or I will be forced to place you under arrest."

"Yo, Gotti! Chill!" I barked from across the car.

"You shut up!" the officer yelled at me, pushing his foot into the back of my leg to push me forward over the hood of my freshly waxed car.

I could see the budding fear in G's eyes, and she complied by pulling out her I.D. and flashing it at him. "Here!"

He took her I.D. and went back to his squad car. A few moments later, he came back. "Let them go, McNealy. They're good."

"What?"

"I said, they're good. She's blue," he said, handing her I.D. back to her.

The original officer quickly uncuffed me and handed me back my license and paperwork. "We apologize for the inconvenience. You two have a good night."

She scoffed. "The inconvenience? Are you kidding me?"

Gotti slammed her body back in the passenger seat with a serious chip on her shoulder as if she'd been the one arrested with the side of her face pressed against the hood of a car that cost more than both of those mothafucka's salaries put together. I restarted the engine and proceeded to pull off in complete silence. That wasn't my first run in with the cops, and I knew it damn sure wouldn't be my last. Nothing they asses did ever surprised me. What did surprise me was the fact that they let us go as soon as they saw her I.D.

"Yo, you good?" I asked, glancing over at her.

"No, I'm not. That was all so uncalled for," she huffed. "I'm so glad I recorded that shit!"

"You sure this is the type of system you wanna work for?"

"They're not all bad."

"You should know, huh?"

"What's that supposed to mean?"

"You gon' sit here and act like I ain't hear that mothafucka call you blue like you was one of them?"

"What do you want me to say? I'm not going to apologize for the career choice my father made or the career path I'm choosing to go down, okay? My father was a great, no—an exceptional cop. Nothing you say will ever make me think otherwise. What happened back there…it just wasn't fair. It wasn't right, but not all cops are like those assholes."

"The shit is more than just unfair, G. It's illegal, but lucky you, you got the get out of jail free card."

She shook her head. "Whatever."

"Yeah, it is whatever. That shit back there is exactly why I don't fuck with cops. You sittin' over there shook because you were forced to see them in the negative light that I've always seen them in, and it's hard for you to wrap your pretty little head around that shit."

"I don't want to talk about this shit anymore."

"Why? Because it makes you uncomfortable? That's how

they make us feel every fuckin' day where I'm from. They are dream killers. They break up families and they ruin lives, but I guess you don't see that because you one of those people who believe blue lives matter over black lives, huh?"

"Let me tell you something, *Dash*. I'm a Black woman first, okay? Nothing will *ever* matter more to me than Black lives, but what about the Black lives who choose to be blue? Where's the line drawn then, huh? And how dare you sit here and put all cops in one basket? Yeah, there are a few bad apples in the bunch, but that doesn't mean you throw them all away!"

"Not in my book. Seeing them take my father away in handcuffs at seven years old and watching them gun down my brother when I was twenty-one, put the type of hate in my heart that can't be erased."

She paused her tirade for a few seconds to let my words sink in, then she sighed. "I—I didn't know your brother was killed by an officer."

"Unarmed, too, but hey, they ain't all bad, right?" I asked, throwing her statement back at her.

Silence dangled over us for the remainder of the car ride as we both sat trapped in the belly of our own thoughts. The next time she spoke up again was when I pulled up to the front of our apartment building.

"Um...thank you for tonight," she said, unhooking her seatbelt.

"You welcome," I said, momentarily putting the car in park.

"Maybe we can do it again sometime. I think I'm free next weekend."

"We'll see." I shrugged.

She frowned. "We'll see?"

"You know what, I'm not even gon' hold you. I been through too much shit to open myself up to a fed, and I think it's best we just leave shit where it is."

"What does that mean?"

"You're a smart girl, G. I know you know what that means."

"Dashiell..."

"Take care of yourself."

"So, that's it? All because we had a difference of opinion?"

"It's bigger than that. After how you acted, it's clear you not ready for a nigga like me to be in your space and open your eyes to some shit you never seen before. I'm not gon' change how I live my life all because of what you perceive me to be. I don't bend for no damn body."

She sighed. "Look, I'm sorry about the cop stuff. It just threw me off guard. I knew you weren't speeding or swerving, so my next train of thought went straight to drugs or an illegal firearm in the car. I just wasn't trying to be blindsided."

"And you weren't, were you?"

"No, I wasn't. And again, I didn't know the backstory on your brother's death. I just wanted you to see where I was coming from. I wasn't raised to hate cops."

"And I was, so that's just something we'll never see eye-to-eye on."

"Dashiell, really?"

"I got somewhere I gotta be, G. Have a good night."

She huffed as she stepped out of the car and slammed my door so hard, it rattled the windows. I didn't even wait to see if she made it in the building before speeding down the street. She was a drug that I didn't want to put down, but I knew because of our lifestyles, I was going to have to break the habit sooner than later.

Chapter Seven

Bellamy

I was sitting at home with a glass of sweet red wine in one hand and a pen in the other as I listened to one of Jaron's new beats over and over again. He was more talented than he knew, and I couldn't wait to write some bomb ass lyrics and showcase even more of my skills to him the next time we were in the studio together. Our last session left me feeling like I was sitting on top of the world. It was crazy how he'd easily been able to bring the confidence out of me yet brought out each and every one of my sister's insecurities.

My thoughts were jarred when my phone vibrated against the couch. I peered at the screen and saw it was a New York number I didn't recognize. It was well after eleven o'clock at night, so I knew there was no way a telemarketer would be calling me. Nevertheless, I decided to ignore it and sent it straight to voicemail. I didn't have time for whoever was trying to play on my phone on some late-night shit. I closed my eyes and quickly got back into my zone when my phone vibrated for the second time. My eyes popped open, and I stared at the phone with an annoyed look plastered across my face.

"Who is this?" I answered with not a hint of compassion in my voice.

"Bellamy, it's me—Jaron."

I pulled the phone away from my ear and looked at the random number he'd called me on. "Whose phone you got?"

"This my other phone. You busy?"

"I was just sittin' here listenin' to one of your beats and trying to write, but you keep callin' and messin' up my vibe." I chuckled.

"Can I come through?"

My eyes widened, and I could feel my heartrate escalating by the second. "Um, tonight? Do you know what time it is?"

"I know it's late, but some shit just went down, and I just… please. I wouldn't ask if it wasn't important."

I sat up straight, sensing the seriousness in his voice. "Uh, yeah, sure. I'll text you my address right now."

Twenty minutes later, there was a knock on my door. My mouth almost hit the floor when I opened it to see Jaron standing there with a black eye and gashes across his face.

"Oh my God, what happened to you?" I asked, placing my hand over my mouth.

"I guess, I should've warned you before I came."

"What the hell happened?"

"I got robbed. Niggas took everything I had on me."

"Oh shit."

"I was leaving the studio about to meet up with someone and as soon as I got to my truck, a car pulled up and four niggas hopped out and started dumpin' on my ass. They took my chain, my money, my phone, everything."

"Oh my God! Did you know who any of them were?"

"Nah, all I was doing was swinging for my life. That's about the only thing I made it out with."

"Well thank God you're okay. I mean, you're not okay, but —you know what I mean," I stammered.

"I'll be aight," he assured me.

"Let me get you some ice for your eye. It looks pretty bad, does it hurt as bad as it looks like it does?"

He chuckled while walking over to the couch. "Yeah, it do."

As soon as I popped into the kitchen, I heard my phone vibrating yet again. "Who is it?" I asked him.

"Shit."

"What? What's wrong?"

"It's Tati."

"What's wrong with her calling? Is there something going on between you two that I should know about?"

"If she asks, just tell her you haven't seen me, aight?"

"So, you want me to lie to my sister...why?"

"Please, I'm begging you, Bellamy. That's the last thing I need right now on top of everything else that happened tonight."

I handed him a frozen bag of broccoli florets and picked up my phone to press accept. "Hey, Tati."

"Hey, is Jaron around?"

"Jaron? No, why?"

"Have you heard from him?"

"Uh, nah. We were supposed to meet at the studio but he ghosted me," I lied.

"Ugh! I've been trying to track him, but his phone must be off."

"Track him? Tati, he's a grown ass man not a teenager."

She sighed. "If you hear from him will you just let me know? We had another argument and now I'm starting to get worried."

"Um, yeah, sure."

"Thanks."

"No problem," I said, ending the call. "Now, do you mind tellin' me what all that was about? Why don't you want her to know where you are? And why didn't you go home after what happened to you? Why come here?"

"I don't want to talk about it."

"I can see it in your eyes something besides what just happened to you is bothering you. Your whole vibe is off. So, if you gon' curl up on my couch holding my frozen bag of broccoli florets on your face, then you need to be real with me."

"It's nothin' I wanna get into tonight. I'm doin' us both a favor, trust me."

"Do you love my sister, Jaron?"

"I care for her and at one point, there was love in my heart for her, but I know for a fact that I'm not in love with her..."

I frowned. "Why not?"

"You know your sister better than I ever will, but she switched up on me quick after moving into my spot. I've never been the type of nigga to have to check in with where I'm going and what time I'd be back. I like the fluidity of being my own man. Rules and me just don't get along," he admitted.

Although it stung to hear, I could respect his thought process. Tati had a way of turning more into a mother hen than a big sister or a parole officer instead of a companion in his case.

"Look, I know she's an acquired taste, but if you want out, you need to tell her now."

"I can't. I know what she's been through, and I don't wanna be labeled as just another nigga who broke her heart."

"That's noble and shit, but why stay in something that you're not happy in or at least feel like you can't be yourself in? I mean, look where you are. You're sitting here with me when you could've easily went home to her, talked some shit out, and had your own bag of frozen vegetables sittin' on your face."

He shook his head. "Not like this. Tonight was fuckin' crazy enough as it is. I don't need any more drama comin' from her."

"You're gonna have to talk to her sooner or later. If you think she's not going to question why you didn't come home plus why you have a busted-up face and black eye, then you're sadly mistaken."

"I guess I'll cross that bridge when I get to it."

"And let me guess…you won't be crossin' it tonight?"

"Hadn't planned on it. I got more pressin' shit on my mind."

"Do you wanna talk about it?"

"Nah, not really."

"Whatever it is you gotta handle, you can tell me."

"What makes you think I gotta handle somethin'?" he quizzed.

"I can look at you and tell you're tied up in some street shit. Niggas just don't run around robbin' music producers for nothin'. Plus, with the type of car you drive and all the traveling you said you did, I know there's more than just music involved in all of that. Are you in some sort of trouble?"

"I don't know yet."

"Are you, Jaron?"

"It's best that you not know."

"Is there anything I can do to help?"

"What do you mean?"

"I mean, is there something I can do to help you? Maybe, I can help if you just tell me what's going on..."

"You really mean that shit?"

"Of course, I do."

"Then, I might need you to hold something for me."

"What is it? "He shot me a look as if to say, *You askin' too many questions, Bellamy.* "For how long?" I rephrased.

"I don't know yet."

"I've never done this bef—"

"Aye, say less," he said, cutting me off. "It was stupid of me to bring this shit up to you in the first place. Forget I mentioned any of it."

"No, Jaron. I wanna help you, I do. I just—you're gonna have to give me more than this..."

He let out a deep breath and turned to fully face me. "I've been running drugs through my studio for a nigga named Devil. I got robbed tonight just before I was supposed to go make a drop to him. I owe...a good amount of money."

"How much money are we talkin'?" I asked.

"Fifty stacks."

My eyes almost bulged out of their sockets. "You owe someone fifty thousand dollars, Jaron? How are you gonna pay this man back?"

He shrugged. "I don't know yet. I just need to buy myself some more time until I can figure it all out. Right now, I got a little product left and some money stashed away for a rainy day."

"And where do I fit in to all of this?" I asked.

"Now that I've been marked, niggas are gonna probably

try to hit my spot next. I gotta move what I got outta there to some place safe."

"And you think the safest place is here?"

He sighed. "For right now until I can think of something else. The shit might sound crazy, but right now it feels like you're the only one in my corner."

"So, I'm just going to go out on a limb and say...Tati doesn't know shit about this, does she?"

"I can't turn to your sister about this shit and you can't tell her. Promise me you won't tell her, Bellamy."

I sighed. I knew what girl code meant, and I also knew that blood was thicker than water, but I couldn't help myself. If there was a reason he didn't want Tati to know, it had to have been a good one. Besides, I wanted to trust the good in him. He was showing me the side of him that no one else got to see. Jaron was real. He was vulnerable. He was flawed. I would feel bad if I didn't help him in his time of need given what he'd done for me with my music. He believed in me, and I needed to show him that same respect.

"I won't. It'll be our secret," I assured him.

"Do you trust me, Bellamy?"

I nodded. "Yeah, I do."

"Good, because I promise you, if you stay down, I'll make sure you come up when all this is over."

I smiled and picked up the glass of wine I'd been neglecting since he'd showed up at my door.

"You was workin' on somethin' before I got here?" he spoke quickly.

"Yeah."

"Well shit, sing something for me. It'll make me feel better."

"It's nowhere near finished."

"It's cool. Let me hear what you got so far. I'm sure it's dope."

I took another sip from my glass before clearing my throat and pressing play on the instrumental beat I'd been vibing to for the past couple of hours.

Yeah, yeah, ooh.

You say you love a girl who likes to fuck.
Well, baby, tonight you're in luck.
You like the way I ride it.
Jump on it, spin around, watch you cum inside it.

You ain't never had a love like this,
Boy, tonight you've met your match.
Come get this lovin' one on one,
And I promise you'll be attached.

"That's all I have so far," I told him.

"Damn, now that was sexy as hell. You sure you got the skills to back all that up you was singin' about?" he asked.

I chuckled. "No cappin' over here."

"You tryna finish your next verse?"

"Are you sure you're up to it?"

"Making music always makes me feel better."

"I know something else that'll make you feel better, too," I told him.

"Oh yeah? What's that."

"Wait right here," I told him, hopping off the couch and running down the hallway to my bedroom.

I came back with a small box and sat it on the coffee table in front of him.

"What's this?" he asked.

"Open it."

Jaron reached forward and opened it, revealing my weed stash, complete with blunts, loud, and lighters. His eyes lit up as his grin softened into a genuine smile. "Bet. You already know what the vibe is."

He wasted no time rolling a fresh blunt and sparking it up so that we could smoke and fall into the zone of our impromptu music session. I stood to my feet and let my hips catch the rhythm of the melodic beat.

Jaron looked at me and laughed. "Fuck cloud nine, you on cloud nineteen right now, ain't you?"

"Oh, absolutely." I grinned.

"Sing somethin', c'mon let's go."

I opened my mouth to sing and instantly felt the cobwebs associated with dry mouth. "Hold up, I need somethin' to drink."

"Make that two," he told me.

I okayed him and made my way into the kitchen. "I got water and gin," I announced with my head inside the refrigerator.

"Nothin' dark?" he asked.

"Nah."

"How you a part-time bartender, and only got one type of liquor in your crib?"

"I work around so much liquor that I don't want to deal with it too much at home. I just keep a little here and there."

"Well shit, you know what they say about gin, right?"

"What?" I asked, popping my head up and looking in his direction as he walked towards me.

"They say gin will make you sin. That's why a nigga sticks to dark."

I chuckled. "Well, it's either sin or water tonight." I pulled the liquor bottle and a water bottle out of the fridge and placed them both on the countertop. "Pick your poison."

Jaron flashed a hellish grin at me before reaching for the bottle of gin. "Shit, the way I'm feelin' I'd be a fool to pick anything else."

"Yeah, liquor was definitely made for nights like this," I said as I pushed up against him to grab two glasses out of the cabinet, partially for stability, and partially because I wanted to.

"Here, pour your own troubles," I said, handing him his glass.

Even though my body was still slightly pressed against his, he didn't budge. It wasn't as if he didn't have the space to either. He hadn't moved, and I didn't want him to.

"Bottoms up," he said, putting the glass up to his soft lips and taking it to the head.

I smiled and followed suit.

"Now sing."

"Right here?" I asked.

"Yeah, let's go," he piped, clapping his hands together as if he was a coach.

You're addicted to my lovin',
Like a moth to a flame.
Hands gliding down my hips,
Love it when I scream your name.

You ain't never had a love like this,
Boy, tonight you've met your match.
Come get this lovin' one on one,
And I promise you'll be attached.

I opened my eyes, not even realizing they'd closed and felt Jaron's breath gently blowing against my face. He was in my space...my bubble...my aura. I stared at the facial hair traveling down the side of his face, stopping right at his neck. We stood close enough to press our foreheads together, taking in everything about the other's presence, from the passion flickering in his eyes to the faltered rhythm of my heartbeat. I gently lifted my head, and he pressed his juicy lips against mine. My intuition was right; they were soft as fuck. Kissing him was like kissing a cloud or a freshly fluffed pillow. As much as I wanted to be sucked into the moment, I knew better. I could feel the shadow of shame clouding over me, raining on my true desires.

I ripped away from him. "We shouldn't," I told him.

He took a couple steps back, resting his back against the edge of the countertop. "You're right," he said, wiping his lips with the back of his hand. "I'm sorry."

"Don't apologize..."

"Nah, I know there are lines, especially between the two of

us, and I feel like I crossed it."

"We more like long jumped over that shit." I chuckled, trying to lighten the mood.

Jaron smiled. "My fault though, I just got caught up with the song and shit. I ain't mean to make you feel no type of way. I can go if you want."

I reached out and grabbed his arm. "No, you don't have to go."

"You sure?"

"Positive. I like having you here."

"You do?"

"I mean, you know—for the music and shit," I clarified. "What just happened was a mistake, but we're good."

He nodded, letting the silence wedge itself in between us. "This may be the gin talkin', but if it was such a mistake then why do I wanna do it again, and again, and again..."

My eyebrows lifted halfway to my hairline. His honesty was killing me softly, gently. The angel on the right side of my shoulder had been replaced with a second devil, and with him came all of the desires I'd been suppressing. If I didn't act, I'd surely explode.

"Then do it again," I announced boldly.

Jaron licked his lips and wrapped one hand around my waist. "Say please."

I smirked. "Kiss me, *please*," I whispered.

He slowly slid his hand through my hair and gazed into my eyes before bringing his lips to mine again. I immediately moaned in his mouth and wrapped my arms around his neck. Even though I knew we were dead wrong, it didn't stop me from kissing him, touching him, or feeling him in every way I'd dreamed about. I would never know why sinning felt so good, and I wasn't going to stop to find out.

Jaron stepped forward until my back was pressed against the cool, stainless steel refrigerator door. The more his hands blindly roamed my body, the more my pussy leaked like a faucet. His fingertips tugged on the hem of my tank top, pulling it down to expose my naked breasts. My tits were a perky B-cup on a good day, so I hadn't bothered to put on a bra. He cradled each breast in his hand before sucking them into his mouth.

"Mmm," I moaned just before he came back up to kiss me. "Let's go to my room," I told him.

With his hand in mine, Jaron followed me down the hallway to my bedroom. As soon as my back hit the bed, he snatched my leggings down, parted my thighs like the Red Sea, and began sipping from my private fountain. My body convulsed with pleasure.

"Goddamn, your pussy is wetter than water," he announced as his tongue flirted religiously with my inner thigh. "I'ma drown in this shit."

I flexed my mini ab muscles to prop my head up and look down as his tongue rippled through my soft folds. "Ooooh shit."

His fingertips squeezed the indent of my hips as I thrusted forward. "That's right, cum for me, Bellamy."

"Mmm, here it comes! I—I'm cumming!" I shrieked at the top of my lungs.

Jaron shoved his tongue deeper inside of me, licking me clean from the inside out. "Mmm, shit. I'll never let a drop of you go to waste," he said, brushing his fingertips against my hard nipple.

I tossed my head back against the bed, feeling complete, yet wanting more. The second I heard his belt jingling, I knew what time it was. My elbows propped me up as I watched him pull a condom out of his wallet before stepping out of his jeans and peeling his shirt over his head. He looked good with clothes on, but even better with them off. His hard chest was covered in light body hair and adorned with a six pack of abs. From the base to the tip, his dick curved upwards like a ripened banana. I licked my lips before sitting all the way up on the edge of the bed. Jaron stepped up to me while holding the base of his dick. There was a look on his face that said, *You gon' suck it or not?* without even one word slipping off his tongue.

I grabbed the sides of his hips and began licking the tip of his dick like a lollipop. The palm of my hand was cupped around the base of his dick, slowly gliding up and down in a twisting motion.

Raspy groans emerged from his diaphragm. "Mmm, you sure you know what you doin'?"

I flashed a smile up at him just before sucking the soul straight out of him. With the night he had, I knew he needed the release, and I was happy to provide it.

"Yo, turn the fuck over," he demanded, ripping the condom wrapper with his teeth and sliding the rubber on.

I obliged, ready to be penetrated. He slid me off the edge of the bed and onto my feet before wrapping a handful of my hair around his fist. His humid breath grazed the nape of my neck as he pushed past my walls that had been neglected for the past ninety-four days, but who was counting?

"Fuckkkkkkkk!" I screamed, standing on the tips of my toes.

Jaron grabbed my hand and shoved my fingers into his mouth before placing them on my clit. "Let me see you play with that pussy."

His curve managed to hit my G-spot with every stroke, and that's when I realized why Tati's ass had been so crazy over him. The dick was too damn bomb. He locked his right hand across my throat while gnawing on my neck. Thrust after thrust, he smacked my ass, coaching me to throw it back against him as he gripped my curves to keep me in place.

"Fuck! Mmm, yes! Right there! Right there! Right there!" I cried.

Jaron continued to fuck me deep until our bodies collapsed on top of one another from pure exhaustion. The next time I opened my eyes, the bright sun was peeking through my blinds the next morning.

"Shit," I mumbled.

Jaron

As much as I'd enjoyed my night with Bellamy, reality sunk back in as soon as the sun came up the next morning. Once I left her spot, I headed to get a new phone and not soon after getting it set up, my phone rang with the words *Unknown Caller* displayed across the screen. I blew out a deep breath and pressed accept, already knowing who it was.

"Yo."

"You've been a hard mothafucka to get in contact with these last twelve hours," Devil said on the other end of the phone.

"Yeah, I know. I was going to call you."

"Oh, yeah? When?"

"Look, there's something I need to tell you."

"This a secure line, nigga. Speak."

"I got robbed last night before you and I were supposed to meet up. I was leaving the studio and four niggas ran up on my truck and took everything. My chain, my money, my phone…"

"Don't you mean *my* money?" Devil corrected me.

I rolled my eyes. "Yeah."

"How much did you have on you?"

"Fifty stacks."

"And the product?"

"I had a brick tucked underneath the spare tire in the back. They didn't get it."

"Do you have any left?"

"I do. It's safe...but I'm gonna need more to make up for what I los—what they got a nigga for."

"You got any idea who robbed you?"

"Nah, probably some young, dumb niggas lookin' for a come up or somethin'. They ain't seem like they were affiliated with anybody you got beef with. They were just probably watchin' me and decided to try their luck."

Devil fell silent on the other end of the phone for a few seconds. "So not only do you owe me money, but you're also now asking me to lend you more of the shit you just let some young, dumb mothafuckas take from you, you rappin', singin' wannabe Drake so bad ass nigga?"

I chewed the inside of my bottom lip, trying my best not to clap back at his ass. The retaliation he'd reap would be more than I was willing to pay, and I'd been through enough bullshit already. "I know shit is fucked up right now, but don't worry about it. I'm already on it."

"Yo, you lucky you even share a drop of the same fuckin' blood as me, or I swear I'd have niggas split your shit for bein' so fuckin' stupid, nigga."

I gritted my teeth. Family or not, I wasn't going to beg Devil for shit. "I already admitted to fuckin' up, aight? Trust me, I'ma get it back," I assured him.

"I'll be in touch, *little* brother," he said before ending the call.

"Fuck!" I fussed, punching my steering wheel.

Devil, nor anybody he rolled with, were to be crossed or fucked with. When it came to street business, it didn't matter that he was my older brother. He felt the need to remind me that he was my brother and the fact that he didn't give a fuck about me all within the same conversation. I hated feeling like someone had the upper hand on me, but he did. I had to think smart and most importantly, I had to think fast because I knew if I didn't make back what I lost, Justin "Devil" Mitchell would make sure he was the only Mitchell boy left. I was going to have to put in work to make back everything those niggas took from me. The most important thing was to get the stash out of my crib and over to Bellamy's just in case those niggas tried to run up in my shit.

As soon as I pulled up in front of the studio, I killed the engine and let me thoughts distract me. I still couldn't believe I'd been caught slippin' right in that very spot. I was always careful about how I did my business because I knew the streets were watching Devil. Being that he was my blood, that meant niggas were watching me just as hard. I couldn't help but feel I'd been set up, but I was cautious not to bring it up to Devil until I knew for sure. With my keys in hand, I jumped out of my ride and headed straight for the back room to watch the security footage from the night before. After fifteen minutes of watching random cars drive up and down the street that night, I saw an unmarked car pull up behind my truck and a black Honda Accord pull up on the opposite side of the street five minutes later. The man in the unmarked car got out and walked over to the Accord and leaned his head into the driver side window. I watched him reach into his back pocket and pull out a folded manila envelope before handing it to the driver. Seconds later, the Accord sped off down the road and the driver of the unmarked car shuffled back over to his vehicle and drove off. Thirty minutes later, the Accord pulled back into the same spot it had been in and shut off the lights.

"What the fuck..." I mumbled as I kept watching.

An hour and fifteen minutes after that, I watched myself walk out the front door only to be ran up on and robbed by whoever the fuck was in that Honda. My blood was boiling hot. I made sure to save a copy of the footage on a USB flash drive as proof that I'd been set up. I just needed to know who paid them niggas to do it, and what the fuck they wanted with me. Once the copy was made, I made a mental note to myself to put it in the bag with everything I was gon' let Bellamy hold onto. That way, I knew that shit would be safe for whenever I needed it.

Chapter Eight

Two weeks later.

Gotti

I was still upset with how things ended between Dash and me. It was almost as if we'd ended before really even having the opportunity to get started. I was ashamed to admit how thirsty I was over him. So much that I'd purposely press the button to his floor and step out to see if I'd catch him in the hallway. I also tried to look through the blackout windows anytime I saw his car parked out front. I even Googled him and searched every mainstream social media network for a Dashiell Graham. *Nothing.* He was as stubborn on social media as he was in real life.

"Fuck it," I mumbled to myself while pressing his name in my phone to call him.

The phone only rang twice before I heard, *You have reached…* and I ended the call. "I know this nigga did not send me to voicemail!"

Feeling rejected and enraged, I called again only to hear no rings and straight voicemail. The only logical next step was to delete his entire existence from my phone and refocus my attention on something that really mattered, my thesis paper. I sat my laptop on my lap and opened up the document I'd been working on for what seemed like a decade. Moments after I typed my first sentence, my phone rang. My heart thrashed in my chest, as my brain willed the caller on the other end to be Dash. I frowned when I realized Bellamy was calling.

"Hey, girl," I answered with not an ounce of enthusiasm

in my voice.

She sighed. "What is it about something you can't have that makes you fall twice as hard?"

It seemed like she was speaking my life, and she hadn't a clue about what had gone down between Dash and me. Instead of flipping the conversation over to my own life, I tried my best to answer her question.

"Maybe we just like the thrill of it. It's like we always want something until we don't. But damn all the hypotheticals, girl, what are we really talkin' about?"

A loud groan escaped her lips. "You cannot judge me for what I'm about to tell you."

"Okay, go for it," I said, closing my laptop.

"Jaron...and I, we—well, we have this crazy deep connection, and I—"

I frowned. "Hold up, Jaron? Like...your sister's man, Jaron?"

"I thought you said you weren't gon' judge."

"Technically, I didn't, but go ahead," I told her.

"I know it sounds crazy, but I can really see a future with him, Gotti."

"It wouldn't sound half as crazy if he wasn't already dating your fuckin' sister, Bells. I mean, damn. How much colder can you get?" I knew I was laying it on thick, but it was the truth. Never mind the fact that I was still stuck in the web of my own feelings about how things ended between Dash and me.

She sucked her teeth. "You just don't get it."

"What is there for me to get? By the way you talkin', I'm not even gon' ask if you fuckin' him because I already know."

"He cares about me just as much as I care about him."

I rolled my eyes. "Mmhm. I bet he does. You've said it a million times, you can't believe shit a nigga say when his dick is hard."

"I know, but he's...different."

"How?"

"He just is, Gotti! His body is like the orchestra to the song in my heart. His arms the string quartet, his voice is the bass. He makes me feel things I never imagined. On top of that, the nigga is a musical fuckin' genius! I've never been able to connect with nobody like this before. That's gotta mean something, right?"

I chuckled. "Okay, Miss Poetic Justice. Damn, you've fallen extra hard."

Bellamy was a serial lover in my opinion. I didn't know Jaron from a hole in the wall, but his actions proved that he was messy as fuck and was probably nothing but a serial liar. I loved my best friend, and I didn't want to see her get her heart broken over someone who clearly seemed to want to have his cake and eat it too. She deserved the best, and I just didn't feel like he was it.

"I have...it's so crazy that it's scary."

"And did you come to this revelation before or after the dick down?" I chuckled.

Although I couldn't see her, I knew she was rolling her eyes at the phone. "Did you not hear all that I just said about this man, girl? Trust me, the good dick is just the cherry on top."

"So...what are you going to do about Tati? Is he going to break up with her? Are you going to tell her?"

"To be honest, we haven't talked about her. I mean, we've talked about her, just not in regards to us and next steps."

"And you're cool with that?" I probed.

"Everything is just so new right now, Gotti. I'm just taking it—"

"One dick stroke at a time?" I asked, cutting her off.

She cackled. "You get on my fuckin' nerves, you know that?"

"I wouldn't be your best friend if I didn't."

"A part of me does feel bad for Tati though. I don't want to be the reason why she gets her heart broken again. I don't think she ever really got over her last boyfriend and how that ended."

"Yeah, when Trey committed suicide, that shit was tragic."

"As fuck! Jaron and I both know she can't handle another

blow to the heart like that, at least not right now."

"So, your plan is to keep fuckin' him and fallin' deeper for him while he's still sharing a bed under the same roof as your sister?"

She sighed. "Well, when you put it that way..."

"There's no other way for me to put it, Bellamy. That's the reality of it. Don't get me wrong, I want you to be happy. You deserve that shit, but is all of this worth it? It just seems super messy and it doesn't have to be."

"Love is rarely ever clean cut, Gotti."

My lips twisted. I knew she was right. Love was nothin' but a messy ass bitch. "Can you at least take a step back until he figures out what he's gonna do about your sister? It's not your place to fix the mess he created for himself."

She huffed. "I know, I know. You're right. The shit was wrong and that's that. No matter how BOMB the dick is, Tati is my sister...and yeah."

"And yeah, what?" I asked, coaxing her to finish her statement.

"And...until he figures things out with that situation, I'll fall back on the personal shit and keep things strictly professional."

"Do you really think it'll be that easy to just turn your feelings for him off like that?"

"Hell no, but what other choice do I have? I'm not giving up on my music all over a one, two, three-night stand."

I rolled my eyes. "You're hopeless, you know that?"

"Enough about me, bitch...what's goin' on with you and the nigga that live in your building? He still got your ass climbin' up the walls?"

"Not exactly."

"What the hell happened?"

"Nothing, we just haven't seen that much of each other lately. I've been busy with work and writing this paper, and he's been, you know, busy doing his own thing."

"Mmhm."

"What?" I questioned.

"Nothing. I know you lyin' and it's cool. I guess, I'm the only one in this friendship brave enough to get judged."

"Ugh, we had a difference of opinion, okay? And he hasn't spoken to me in two fuckin' weeks, and it's driving me fuckin' crazy, Bells! Crazy!"

"Yeah, you definitely sound like a lunatic right now, but good dick will do that to a bitch, trust me, I know."

"I call and he sends me straight to voicemail. I text and he leaves me on read…I don't know what's up with him."

"What the fuck is the issue between y'all, Gotti? Like, what happened? Spill the tea."

I sighed. "Long story short, we went out to dinner and it was great. We both agreed that we were cool with getting to know one another outside of the sex shit and then on the way back to the apartment, he got pulled over."

"Oh shit. Did he get locked up or somethin'?"

"No, but they were harassing him, so I stepped in and called the cops out on their shit, and then they asked to see my I.D. Once they ran my name and found out who my father was, they let us go, and he got upset!"

"Mmm."

"That's all you have to say?"

"I mean, think about it…you can look at him and tell he don't get his money direct deposited to his account every two weeks like a normal nine-to-five nigga. It's not a surprise that niggas like him don't like the police. Just because you were raised in a household with law enforcement, you gotta realize that everybody doesn't hold the same respect for them that you do."

I groaned. "I fuckin' hate it when you're right, but what am I supposed to do now? Apologize? I've tried that."

"If you still feel a way about how things ended, which I know you do, then keep reaching out until he hears you."

"Fine. I'm going to call him again, but I promise you if I don't get an answer, I'm deleting his entire existence from my life for the second time today!"

Bellamy chuckled. "Yeah, if only it was that easy."

"Ugh, I know. Okay, I'll talk to you later and let you know how shit goes."

"Good luck, bitch."

"Bye."

I ended the call and went right into my call log to press the number I'd recently deleted. To my surprise, the phone rang twice and then he picked up. "Yo, why you keep callin' my phone?" he answered.

My forehead wrinkled. As much as I wanted to pop off, I was so sick over the distance he'd put between us, I decided to let it slide. "Look, I've been thinking about what you said to me, and I was childish before and I don't know, maybe I was scared, but…"

"But what?"

A sigh escaped my lips. "You wanna come over tonight? You know, to—to talk?"

"Don't you got school shit to do?"

"Yeah, so?"

"Nah, do your school work, G," he said and ended the call.

"H—hello? Argh!" I screamed, tossing my phone across the living room.

He had some nerve talking to me like that. Who the fuck did he think he was? I folded my arms tightly across my chest while opening my laptop and staring at the blinking cursor on my computer screen. It was almost as if it was begging me to write the next word, sentence or paragraph, but I just couldn't. My eyes then transferred to the time in the top right corner, and I sighed. I was only fooling myself if I thought I was going to actually get my paper done. Dash had fucked up my entire mood. Instead of sulking in my loneliness for a second longer, I decided to throw on a pair of sweats, my UGG boots, a hoodie, and my coat and head down to the late-night spot down the street that had the best fried wings I'd ever tasted. If I couldn't get dick, food was the next best thing to bring me comfort.

Litter and debris skittered across the sidewalk as light

flurries of snow fell silently from the night sky. I shoved my hands deep inside my pockets for warmth as I shuffled down two blocks to the after-hours spot. The closer I got, the more I could smell the fried chicken grease, and my stomach began to growl. Just as I approached the door, I froze. Not only was Dash standing inside, but he was also standing with his arm flung over the shoulder of another bitch. My body was at a standstill as rage heated up my cold extremities. There was no chill in my step, my tone or my temperament as I swung the door open and stepped into his space without being granted an invitation.

"Wow, so this is the shit you on?" I asked, smacking my lips.

He frowned. "Yo, you stalkin' me now?"

"Don't fuckin' flatter yourself, nigga! I just think it's funny how one minute you on my line and the next you tryna act like you care about my education just so you can be out here with the next bitch!"

"*Bitch?* Who the fuck you callin' a bitch?" his yellow-bone date questioned, inserting herself where she obviously didn't belong.

He reached out for me. "Yo, G, you need to chill. You embarrassing yourself."

"Don't tell me what the fuck to do, nigga!" I yelled, swatting his hands away.

"I said chill the fuck out," he thundered, hovering over me with a grimace across his face.

"Nah, I'm good. I got it now. Thanks for letting me know what this shit really was. Just don't get pissed off when you see me with another nigga!" I told him and turned to walk out of the restaurant.

I hadn't gotten ten steps from the door before I felt his strong hands wrapping around my waist, exploiting his stout gravitational pull to bring me back towards him. "Stop fuckin' playin' with me, G."

His deep voice vibrated my nerves. It annoyed me to the fullest that I was so hypersensitive to everything about him. I'd only been in his presence for a matter of five minutes, and I could feel myself unraveling like a spool of yarn.

"Get your hands off me, Dash! I'm good! I'm done!"

"Yo, what's your fuckin' problem?"

"Oh, I don't have a problem. Shit is more crystal clear to me tonight than it has been in two fuckin' weeks! You wanna act like you wanted to stop talkin' to me over some police shit, when you just really didn't have the balls enough to tell me you wanted to fuck other bitches!"

"You about to get me tight, G. Get in the fuckin' car. I'm not doin' this shit with you with all these mothafuckas standin' out here."

"Fuck you, Dash! Go back to your date or whoever the fuck she is!" I yelled.

"Fuck outta here. Get in the car. I'm taking you home."

I could see the igloo from the grill in his mouth whenever he talked. Goddamn, I never knew how much I loved a boss ass nigga. "I walked to get here, and I can walk back! Don't worry about me. Take your black ass back inside!"

"It wasn't an option. Get your ass in the car before I put you in there myself."

I flashed my eyes up at his, instantly seeing the anger and annoyance in them. Instead of responding, I waited for him to unlock the doors and then carelessly let my body crash into the passenger seat. The engine purred with the press of a button, and he pulled out of his perfectly parallel parked spot. After a couple minutes of silence, I glanced over at him. He was steering with one hand and still wore a scowl etched so deep into his facial features that I feared it was permanent.

"Yo, don't fuckin' look over here," he told me.

"Excuse me?"

"Nah, you buggin' right now. Don't ever come out your face disrespectin' me like that. We could've talked about this shit like adults back when I was feelin' more forgivin', but that shit you pulled back there was reckless and childish. That's not how I move, G."

"Have you forgotten that I tried to fuckin' talk to you? I was the one calling and texting. You were the one who chose not to respond. If anybody is being childish, it's you!"

"I'm not a fuckin' kid, G. All that cursin' and screamin' and shit to get my attention won't work. I saved you from yourself back there, trust me."

"I wouldn't have to scream and yell if you'd just talk to me! That's all I wanted was to fuckin' talk to you, Dash. That's it! You don't have to lie to me and tell me to focus on my school like you're doing me some sort of favor when you really lying just so you can be out in the streets with the next bitch."

"One thing I already told you about me, G, I don't give a fuck enough to lie."

"What's that supposed to mean?" I frowned.

"I ain't lie to you about shit. You think I give a fuck about that bitch back there? You see where she is and you see where you are, right?"

"Yeah, so?"

"So? All I'm saying is don't entertain what you don't want."

"What if I do want it?" I queried. When he didn't respond, I spoke up again. "Look, I'm sorry, okay? All this uncertainty between us is turning me into someone I don't like. I just want to know what's up. I'm a big girl, Dash. I can take whatever it is you throw at me."

"Tell me what you really want then, G."

I sighed. "I want you."

Dash was so raw that he left a mark where ever he went. He was my favorite mistake that I would keep making over and over and over again. The two of us went together like fireworks and rain or ice cream cones stacked three scoops high in the middle of a heatwave. He pulled me out of myself and turned me inside out to the point where I didn't know who I was half the time. Yet, I couldn't stop myself from wanting to turn the page to the next chapter in whatever it was that life was going to throw my way. As long as it involved him, I was going to be good.

"You don't know what you're saying," he said, while shaking his head.

"I do."

"We live two different lifestyles."

"I won't judge you from your past or your present. I'm willing to be more open minded, but I just need you to promise me two things."

"What's that?" he asked.

"That you'll try to be more open-minded too, and that you won't hurt me."

"You in the presence of a real nigga now, G. I won't let you fall without bein' there to catch you," he told me.

Dash

G had become my ultimate obsession. I still didn't know if it was a good thing or a bad one, but not speaking to her for two weeks had a nigga lowkey buggin' out. It felt good knowing I wasn't the only one. Neither of us knew what we had between us, all we knew was that it was somethin' worth holding onto. I stepped out of the car, and we walked back into the building. Instead of allowing her to press the button to her floor, I blocked her hand and pressed the button to go up to mine.

"Is this your way of inviting me up to your spot?" she asked.

"Yeah."

"What's the occasion?"

I looked down at my phone that hadn't stop vibrating since I left the after-hours spot. I quickly pressed the sides of the phone to turn it off and looked up at her. "You."

As soon as I opened the door, I didn't even bother flipping on the light switch before pushing her back against the wall and firmly pressing my lips against hers. My tongue snaked its way inside her warm mouth. "Damn, I missed you."

"I missed you too," she echoed, moaning between her words. G gently pulled away from me and rubbed the tip of her nose against mine. "Wait, shouldn't we talk more? You know, about our disagreement."

"We ain't gotta agree on shit for me to fuck you," I whispered as I nibbled on her earlobe.

A devilish smile creased her face. We may not have always seen eye-to-eye on everything, but we were both definitely in the mood to fuck, even if it meant sweeping whatever conversation that needed to be had under the rug for the next few hours. I kissed her neck while pressing my thumb against her clit. I could feel it throbbing as strong as a heartbeat through her sweatpants.

"You said you wanted a nigga, right?"

"Mmm, yeah."

"You want me to beat that pussy up?"

"Mmm, shit. I want you to homicide it," she whispered against my lips.

"I know it's oozing for daddy, ain't it?"

"Mmhm," she purred.

G had an ass so round it was hard not to want to reach out and grab it. I gripped it tight and lifted her up so that she could wrap her legs around my waist. She hastily let her hands roam all over the back of my head, neck, and shoulders as she pressed her warm lips against mine. I'd never been the type of nigga who enjoyed kissing, but I could kiss every part of G all day long. I walked us down the hallway to my bedroom and let our bodies crash against the bed like waves at high tide. She straddled my lap while pulling off her coat and hoodie. I followed suit and lifted my hoodie and T-shirt over my head at the same time. G blew into her hands and then ran them down the center of my chest.

"Take off your pants," she told me.

The tone of her voice alone was enough to have my dick standing at attention. She sluggishly removed her body from on top of mine and watched me unhook my belt while she slid off her shoes, socks, and sweats. I sat up to take off my Timbs and watched as she got up to stand in front of me. She dropped to her knees and slid off my socks one by one and put my boots to the side of the bed. Without saying a word, I stood in front of her and let my jeans fall around my ankles. She held them down as I stepped out of them and then pulled down my boxer briefs so that she could stare at the dick that she'd been missing for a couple weeks.

"Ooh shit," I groaned as she started licking up the base and then sucked on the tip to get it soaking wet.

She massaged my length with both hands while going as deep as her throat would allow. I watched her swirl her tongue around the tip and then tighten her lips around the head. She was trying to make a nigga cum quick. I reached down to push her hair out of her face so I could get a good look at her. The only light shining in was from the streetlights outside my window. With my fingers spread wide, I palmed the back of her head like a basketball to draw her lips deeper onto my rod. She flashed her warm brown eyes up at me, showcasing the spit bubbling out of the sides of her mouth and dripping onto the tip.

"Goddamn, G."

I knew if I didn't stop her soon, I'd bust right in her mouth. Although it took everything in me to gently pull away from her, I did.

"Is there something wrong?" she asked with a string of saliva hanging from her lips to the tip of my dick.

"Not at all," I said, grabbing her by her shoulders to pull

her up to her feet. The warmth of my body hovered over hers as I laid her down on the bed and slid her panties off. I slid my fingertips over my tongue and then gently placed them between her sticky, wet thighs. As wet as she was down there, it seemed like she'd came just from suckin' my dick. That's when I knew I had a freak on my hands.

"You gon' let me open you up?" I whispered against her neck.

I watched her legs spread like butter as she accepted. I ain't have a rubber on me, and I didn't even give a fuck. I was still gon' hit. I grabbed her hips and slid every square inch of my dick inside her. I wanted her to feel all of me with each long, deep stroke. Her breasts bubbled up to the top of her bra, threatening to spill over with every thrust.

"Ooooh shiiiiiiiittttttt, Dash!" she moaned.

"Mmm, say my name, G. No one alive can do your body like I do."

I was only a few strokes in, and my dick felt like I was in the middle of a tsunami. As wet as she was, she was tryna fuck around and make me a father. G rested her hand behind her head to prop her neck up so she could watch me long stroke her to climax.

"Yessss, right there! Right there!"

I propped her legs up on my shoulders and locked my hands underneath her ass to plunge deeper inside of her while quickening my stroke. Soon enough, I had the headboard banging like a marching band at a HBCU homecoming.

"Ooooh fuck! I'm fuckin' cumming!" she screamed while digging her nails into my warm flesh.

As soon as the words fell off her lips, I felt a gush of liquid engulf my dick and smiled to myself. She'd squirted and probably didn't even know the shit was happening. I quickly pulled out of her and dove in between her thighs to taste the sweetness that was dripping from her lower set of lips. Her body convulsed with pleasure as I flicked my tongue against her throbbing clit. G propped herself up on her elbows and began thrusting the lower half of her body towards my lips. She wanted more from me. She wanted everything I fuckin' had to give her.

I replaced my tongue with my thumb and began massaging her clit before pushing the tip of my dick back inside her waterpark. She tossed her head back against my king size pillows, arching her back with desire. With her body close to mine, I rolled over onto my back so that she could ride me. She wasted no time finding the rhythm as she bounced up and down on my dick. I reached up and slid her bra straps over her shoulders to expose her chocolate milk drop nipples. I liked to watch them bounce. G pushed her body forward while holding her weight up on both arms. She leaned forward and kissed me while bouncing her ass up and down as if she was trying to flip a SOLO cup on her lower back. My fingertips palmed the back of her neck while my tongue pushed past her lips to play hide and seek with hers.

"I fuckin' missed you," she whispered against my lips.

"I missed you, too," I assured her before sliding her off of me.

I got up and pulled G to the edge of the bed before flipping her tiny frame upside down so that I could eat her pussy standing up. Her pussy was sweeter than iced tea and a nigga had a fuckin' sweet tooth.

"Ooooh fuck!" she squealed.

I buried my face so deep, I had both of her pussy lips parted like the Red Sea. Instead of relaxing and letting herself be the only one receiving pleasure, she grabbed my dick and ran her tongue over the head. I gave her ass cheeks a tight squeeze before letting my tongue trail from her pussy to her asshole. I'd never met a bitch that made me even think about eating her ass, but with G there was no question. I *wanted* to do that shit. *I wanted to eat that peach.*

My face was a sticky wet mess by the time I put her back down on the bed. G was the type you needed to put a towel down for. She was a certified Super Soaker. She stayed on all fours, ready for me to break her back. I kissed her ass cheeks and smacked them. She looked back and popped it for fun just to watch it jiggle. I could see the stickiness of her love juices splattered against the back of her ass and pussy as I pushed back inside her warmth. I had no idea how, but her pussy felt wetter than before. She reached around and spread her cheeks, forcing me deeper inside of her.

"Say my name when I'm hitting this shit!" I demanded while jiggling her ass in the palm of my hand.

"Mmm, fuck yes, Dash! Fuck this pussy!" she screamed while tossing her hair to the side.

G began gyrating her hips in a circle and throwing her pussy back against me. She had every one of a nigga's senses wide open. I loved watching the way her tight pussy cupped my dick like a balled fist. I loved hearing the way her skin sounded smacking against mine and vice versa. I loved how soft her hair felt balled up in my hands as I fucked the shit out of her. I loved the way she tasted sweet like a fresh candy apple from Coney Island. I even loved the scent of sex that filled the room.

"Look back at me when that ass in the air, G."

She arched her back into a full curve before looking back at me while biting her bottom lip. I smacked her ass as she slid up and down on my rod. After a few more strokes, I gave in to the tightness of her pussy and let it drain my dick. I let out a low groan from deep within me and fell against the bed with my heart beating over a hundred beats per minute.

"Goddamn."

I slowly turned to my side and looked into her eyes. She was still holding onto me like she wanted me to camp out in her pussy all night long. "You still wanna talk?" I asked with a smirk.

She flashed a smile at me as her voice squeaked, "Shut up."

I'd fucked her until her entire voice was raspy, which let me know I'd done my job. Whatever we needed to talk about could wait until the sun came up. All I wanted to do was keep her tangled up in my sheets for as long as I could.

Chapter Nine

Tatiyana

I'd been feeling like shit for the past few days and chalked it up to me stressing over the status of my relationship with Jaron. He'd been more than distant. It was like I was in love with a damn ghost. Instead of moping around and eating my feelings, I decided to throw on some workout clothes and get out of the house and go for a jog. Our apartment complex was only a few blocks away from the park with a running trail, and I figured the cold, brisk air would do me some good.

I pushed my Air Pods into my ear and slid my phone into my armband before locking the door behind me. As soon as I got onto the street, I pressed play on my phone and started shuffling down the sidewalk to warm my body up. The longer I ran, the better I started to feel, which put a smile on my face. I had gotten so close to the park that I could see it in the near distance and decided to go ahead and cross the street. I looked both ways as I stepped off the curb and started jogging across the street when I heard the honking of a car horn. It was so close that I could feel the heat from the engine radiating right next to my body. I quickly darted out of the street and fell to my knees onto the sidewalk, panting like a dog in the middle of the summer. The driver of the car didn't even bother to stop to see if I was okay. Instead, they continued to speed down the road like a bat out of hell.

"Are you okay?" a random woman asked me while holding her hand out to help me up.

My hand trembled as I placed it in hers. "I think so." I

nodded. "Thank you."

"No problem. That was crazy! That car came out of nowhere!"

"I know!" I agonized, dusting off my knees.

"You sure you're okay? Do you need me to call the police?"

"No, I'm fine. Thanks again." As soon as she started to walk away, I tried to take a step forward and immediately realized I couldn't put my full weight on my left leg. "Shit!" I groaned.

I slowly limped over to the nearest park bench and sat down to try and steady my breathing. I still couldn't believe I'd almost been hit by a careless driver in broad daylight. My mind was so out of sorts that I couldn't even focus on jogging anymore. All I wanted to do was call Jaron and have him waiting for me when I walked through the front door. I rubbed my sore wrists before reaching for my phone and pulling it out of the arm band to call Jaron.

"What up?" he answered on the fourth ring.

"Where are you?" I inquired, still trying to settle my nerves.

"I'm busy right now. What's up?"

"I need you."

"What's wrong?"

"I need you to come home right now."

"Tati, what's wrong?"

"I—I was jogging to the park and when I went to cross the street, a car came out of nowhere and almost hit me. I had to dive onto the sidewalk."

"Are you okay?"

"I'm okay. I'm just rattled as fuck, and my ankle is probably going to be the size of a watermelon in an hour if not sooner."

"Okay, good. Take an Uber back to the crib and put some ice on it. I'm gonna call and check on you later."

My eyes widened with shock. "Jaron, I just told you I almost got hit by a fuckin' car in broad daylight and you're telling me that you'll call me later?"

I stood to my feet and immediately felt my body go warm all over. My mouth immediately began to moisten, and I knew what was about to happen. Before I could even wait for his response, I dropped the phone and turned to throw up on the side of the bench. My head began to spin as nausea set in within seconds. I had to get home and fast. I picked up the phone and realized he'd hung up. I didn't even care. I ordered an Uber instead of staggering all the way back to the apartment, trying my best not to throw up again. *Just get home to lay down, Tati. Just get in the house,* I told myself over and over as I waited.

As soon as I unlocked the door, I bolted for the bathroom and tossed up what was left in my stomach. When I was done, I crawled into the shower with my clothes on and doused my entire body in the warm shower water. Thirty minutes later, I got out and tossed my wet clothes in the washing machine before venturing back out into the living room to find wherever I dropped my phone in my haste to the bathroom. The moment my eyes looked at the screen, there was a notification from my period tracker app, letting me know my period was late by almost two weeks.

"What the fuck," I mumbled out loud.

I'd been so wrapped up in Jaron that I neglected to realize my period hadn't shown up. Aunt Flo came like clockwork every month, stressed or not, so I knew something wasn't right. I didn't have it in me to venture back outside to grab a pregnancy test, and there was no way I was going to persuade Jaron to grab one from the store on his way home, so I decided to have one delivered to the house with a couple other groceries to make the trip worthwhile.

My delivery came two hours later, and I hurriedly sifted through the bag for the test and darted to the bathroom to take it. I washed my hands and sat on the edge of the toilet seat to wait for what felt like the longest three minutes of my life. As soon as the alarm on my phone dinged, I swiped the test off the bathroom sink and saw two bold lines on the test screen staring back at me.

"Oh my God…"

*****

I WOKE UP the next morning to the sound of shuffling and rustling near the living room. I quietly snuck out of bed and crept down the hallway to see Jaron with his body inside of the closet, stuffing something inside of a black duffel bag.

"What are you doing?" I asked him.

"Nothing, Tati. Go back to sleep."

"I haven't really been sleeping that well lately."

"Why not?"

"What do you mean, why not? It's been weeks, and I've barely seen anything except for the back of your head! You don't answer your phone when I call, you don't do shit but spend your time anywhere else but here with me! I've been worried about you!"

He grimaced as if I'd offended him. "You don't need to worry about me."

"Well, as your girl that's easier said than done. I mean, look at you," I said, acknowledging the dark circles underneath his eyes. "How long has it been since you slept for more than a couple hours at a time?"

"Tati, I'm good, aight?"

"Stop lying to me and tell me where you've been spending your time and who you've been spending it with!"

"I've been stayin' in a hotel, aight? Alone."

"A hotel? Jaron, what the fuck? Why waste your money at a hotel when you have an entire home here with me?"

"I just needed to blow off some steam, aight?"

"Some steam? Do you hear yourself? I don't even know who you are right now. You literally just switched up on me overnight. Look at what you're doing to us! You're distant! All we do is argue. We can't even have a normal conversation without me raising my voice!"

"And whose fault is that, huh? You tryna be my mother

118

more than you tryna be my girl and a nigga don't need all that."

"What's in the bag?" I asked, switching gears.

"The less you know the better," he said, tossing it over his shoulder.

I sighed. Talking to Jaron was like beating a dead horse. He'd put up a wall bigger than the Great Wall of China, and I couldn't climb it, knock it down, or bulldoze my way through it. He'd gone from being the man of my dreams to a complete nightmare.

"Please just talk to me, baby. Tell me what's going on with you," I pleaded.

He shook his head. "I said I'm good, Tati."

"Stop telling me you're okay when I can clearly see you're not!"

Jaron let out an annoyed sigh as he pushed his way down the hall and into the bathroom in our room. He walked back out seconds later with the surprise I'd left him on the counter in his hands. "What the fuck is this?" he asked.

I frowned. "What does it look like?"

"I don't know, you tell me."

"Jaron, I'm pregnant..."

"What?"

"I just found out yesterday..."

He scoffed. "Wow..."

"Wow? So, that's it? That's all you have to say?"

I'd be lying if I said I expected for him to give me the reaction he did. I was his fuckin' girl, and he was lookin' at me as if I was some one-night stand and he had a whole other family to get home to. It was me who washed his clothes, cooked the meals that he was never home to eat, and cleaned the apartment day in and day out to make sure his house always felt like a home whenever he did decide to return.

"Tati, a baby...now just isn't the right time for us to be starting a family."

My heart sunk to the soles of my feet. "Excuse me?"

"Just hear me out."

"No, fuck that! Are you fuckin' kiddin' me, Jaron? I'm your fuckin' girl, and you really gon' stand here and tell me that now isn't the time to have a baby like I'm some fuckin' side bitch?"

"It's not that, Tati. I swear it's not like that at all."

"Then, what is it like? Tell me the truth for once, Jaron! You at least owe me that much."

He sighed. "I just got some things I need to make sure are handled first. Once I know shit is good, then we can revisit this conversation."

"And what conversation is that? You know what, never mind. Let me make it simple for you. I'm NOT getting an abortion."

He twisted his lips to the side as if he was preventing himself from saying something he knew he'd regret in hindsight. His eyes flashed up at mine with rage before he tossed the test on the bed and walked past me.

"Where the fuck do you think you're going!" I yelled at his back.

"You made your decision, so I'm making mine."

"So, that's it? You're just going to leave me here pregnant with your child?"

"I fuckin' told you I got shit I need to handle, Tati! If I don't handle this shit the right way, you and that baby gon' be livin' in this mothafucka without me for life!"

My eyes widened. It became crystal clear to me that whatever Jaron was into was more than just music. I could hear the uncertainty in his voice. Something or someone had him shook, and I was determined to find out what the hell was really going on.

Bellamy

I'd decided to take Gotti's advice and put a lid on my feelings for Jaron at least until he figured out what was going on between him and my sister. But after the night we'd shared together, it was hard. Shit, it was harder than hard. Trying to find peace of mind was like trying to find fuckin' Carmen San Diego. Flashbacks of the night we'd spent together just kept playing in my head like a song on repeat.

I was in the bathroom throwing some loose curls in my hair when my phone vibrated against the bathroom sink. Low and behold, Jaron was calling. At that point, I was convinced he knew exactly when I was thinking about him because he always seemed to just pop up out of nowhere.

"Resist the urge, Bells," I mumbled to myself.

The phone continued to vibrate for a few more rings and then stopped. A minute after that, I got a text message.

Jaron [2:42 p.m.]: Damn, so you ignoring a nigga now?
Me [2:45 p.m.]: Chill. My phone was in the other room. I'm doing my hair.

Instead of responding to my text, my phone vibrated in my hand. I sighed, knowing he wasn't going to stop until he actually heard my voice on the other end of the phone. "Hello?"

"I take it you at the crib, right?"

"Yeah, I'm here."

"Good. I'm 'bout pull up on you."

"When?"

"Now."

"Now, like right now?"

"Yeah, is that cool? I got somethin' for you."

"Yeah, it's cool. I've got a couple hours before I need to leave for work, but um, what is this gift?"

"You'll see it when I give it to you." The way those words fell off his tongue made my spine shiver. He knew what he was doing, and he was so damn good at it. "I'll see you in a minute."

I quickly ended the call and finished tossing a few more curls into my head before running my fingers through them to loosen them up some more. Luckily, I'd already showered and had done my makeup for work, so I didn't have to worry about him catching me slipping.

"Yo, my bad for that last situation a couple of weeks ago..." Jaron said as he walked through the door ten minutes later.

"It's nothin'."

"Nah, it's more than nothin'. You really looked out for a nigga."

"You looked out for me with the music stuff, so this was just me returning the favor."

"You didn't open any of the bags I gave you, did you?"

I shook my head. "No. They are still tucked away in the back of my closet where you put them."

"Good. Thank you."

"So, where is this so-called gift you wanted to give me?" I asked, holding out my hand. "If you're wondering, I wear a size gold in jewelry," I snickered.

He chuckled. "Damn, my fault." I watched him pull out his phone and press a few buttons before mine vibrated against the coffee table. "Go ahead and check it out."

"What is this?" I asked, opening up my unread text from

him.

"Play it and find out."

I pressed play on the MP3 file and almost immediately burst into tears. "Oh, my God!"

"You like it?" he asked.

"Like it? I fuckin' love it! Oh my God, I can't believe that's me...singing my own fuckin' song!"

"Yeah, I mixed and mastered it for you a few nights ago. Sorry it's taken me so long to get it to you, but I wanted to make sure I could see your face when you heard it for the first time. That shit is fire, right?"

"It's everything, Jaron! Like, you don't understand. This is the best fuckin' gift anyone has ever given me in my life!" I beamed, smiling from ear to ear.

"I'm glad I could be the one to put a smile on that beautiful face."

"You always do," I babbled, immediately regretting the words as soon as they fell past my lips. "I mean, you know...with all you've done for me with the music stuff."

He flashed a smile at me. "It's cool. I knew what you meant."

"So, how have you been?" I asked, changing the subject as quickly as I could.

"Shit, maintaining. When I'm not in the studio, I've been stayin' in a hotel."

"Wait, you haven't been home? What does you know who have to say about all of that?"

"You already know how your sister is...but it is what it is, right now. It's better that I stay away until shit cools down and I can really figure out my next move."

"It's been weeks, Jaron."

He shrugged. "I know. Shit gotta play itself out, no matter how long it takes. I'm just not tryna put you or Tati in a bad situation. It's better that I just keep doin' what I been doin' and layin' low as much as I can."

"I know...I just want you to be safe," I advocated.

"I am. You ain't gotta worry about me."

I scoffed. "Who said I was worried?"

"You ain't have to say it. It's cute though." He chuckled. "Oh shit, I almost forgot. What you doin' next Thursday night?"

"Uh, if I'm not working at either of my jobs, I'll more than likely be right here in the house."

"Meet me somewhere."

"Where?" I quizzed.

"Just look good and be ready to rock the mic."

I shook my head. "You know how most people claim they hate surprises, but lowkey really love that shit? I'm not one of those people, Jaron."

He smirked. "It's an open mic night down at this club I hit up a lot to scout out new talent."

"An open mic night? So, you want me to sing?"

"Yeah, sing this dope ass song we just created."

"I don't know...do you think I'm ready?"

"I wouldn't have brought it up if I didn't think you were. Besides, I won't take no for an answer."

"And why is that?" I asked, playfully folding my arms across my chest.

He smiled. "Because I already signed your lil' ass up, so get ready."

Every single time his ass flashed his smile in my direction, I could feel my knees go weak. He was the epitome of sin, and I was caught smack in the middle of a love-binding, toe-curling forbidden romance.

"Stop it."

"Stop what?" he asked, closing in the space between us.

"You know what."

"Nah, tell me."

"You already know how you make me feel...and I need you to stop that shit. You and I both know that you belong to a certain somebody else," I reminded him and myself at the same time.

"Right now, I belong to you," he said, pulling me into his

arms.

I instantly melted like a popsicle sitting out in the sun. He was too much like a fantasy to be real. The more I stared into his eyes, the more I could hear Gotti's voice replaying in the back of my head. *I hope he's worth it, girl.*

"Jaron…"

"Yeah?" he asked as he began to nibble on my ear.

"Look, the truth is, I can't stop thinking about you…and everything about that night constantly plays in my head like a broken record, and as much as I don't want to think about you, I do. I crave everything about you and it's driving me fuckin' crazy that I can't have you the way that I want to," I admitted.

He looked me in my eyes while licking his lips. "I know shit is fucked up right now, but I promise you, it ain't gon' always be this way."

"So, what exactly does that mean?"

"It means, I'm gon' talk to Tati about us and everything involving our future, but I'm just
tryna do shit the right way."

I nodded. "I think you may just be here to break my heart."

"I would never do that, at least not intentionally. You've become a weakness to me, just like I've become one to you, Bells, no cap. As much as you over here in your feelings, you gotta nigga *so deep in my feelings*," he sang like Ella Mai and then let out a hearty laugh.

I couldn't help but smile. "Shut the hell up, fool."

"What time you got to be at work?" he asked while gripping my hips.

"I got time."

He smirked. "You got time, huh?"

"Yeah, I do," I agreed before tilting my head upwards to kiss his lips.

Off went his shirt.

Off went mine.

Until there was nothing but moist metaphors between us.

We'd gotten to the point where I just knew that every time we saw each other, he was going to give me the wood. There was no use in me even trying to put up a fight. I had no willpower when it came to him or the hearty piece of meat swinging between his high-yellow thighs. In the moment, neither of us had any shame about it until my phone started ringing.

"Oh shit," I mumbled as he placed warms kisses against the nape of my neck.

"What?"

"It's Tati. What should I do?"

"Answer it and put it on speaker. And if she asks, you haven't seen a nigga," he told me.

I cleared my throat before answering and took a couple steps away from Jaron's grasp to help me collect my thoughts. "Hello?"

"Hey, you got a minute?"

"Uh, I'm kinda in the middle of somethin' right now. What's up?"

"I'm about to pull up to your building in like ten or fifteen minutes. I really need to talk to you. I just…please tell me you're home."

"Yeah, I'm, uh…I'm here. I was just about to hop in the shower though."

"Okay, I'll text you when I'm on my way up."

I quickly ended the call and looked at Jaron, who was already putting his shirt back on. "I'll talk to you later," he said before kissing my lips goodbye.

I nodded. "Yeah, okay."

Fifteen minutes later, Tati was standing at my front door. She looked a mess as if she'd been doing nothing but crying all night long.

"Tati, what's wrong?" I asked her.

She walked in without saying a word and crashed her

body into the couch. She sat with her arms wrapped around her body as if she was in need of a hug. Either that, or she was trying to warm herself up from the cold weather outside. Either way, she looked like she'd been through some shit.

"Are you going to sit there all quiet or are you going to talk to me? You said you needed to talk when you called, so spill the tea. What's got you lookin' like this? I haven't seen you look this bad since..."

She cut her eyes at me, daring me to finish my sentence. "Have you seen or spoken to Jaron lately?"

I sighed. "This again? What am I? His keeper or something?"

"It was a yes or no question, Bellamy."

"Yeah, he dropped by here a little while ago and gave me this," I verified, picking up my phone and scrolling so that she could see the song file.

She huffed. "So he's still doing music, huh?"

I frowned. "Ain't that his job?"

"To be honest, I don't know what his job is anymore."

"What's that supposed to mean?"

"It means the nigga has been actin' different for weeks now. He's not coming home. I'm always alone. What the fuck am I supposed to make of that? He's got to be fuckin' somebody else, right? I mean, what else could it mean? Plus, he said some shit that really got me feelin' some type of way."

"What he say?"

"I don't remember his exact words, but it sounded like he was in some sort of trouble or something. I don't know. He's just...different."

My eyes widened a bit, but I tried my best to play it cool. "Tati, have you tried asking him before taking the leap off the cliff of conspiracies and conclusions you're making up?"

"What are you trying to say?"

"I'm saying, maybe it's all in your head and maybe it's not, but you should be able to talk to him about anything. He's your man, right?"

She attested with a nod. "Yeah, but communication isn't one of our strengths."

"Then, maybe you need to get real with yourself and realize that if you can't talk to the one nigga that's supposed to have your back, then maybe he's not the nigga for you."

I watched her swallow hard before wiping premature tears from her bottom lids. "Maybe you're right, but things are more complicated now..."

"Complicated? How?"

"Well for one, there's a ninety-nine percent chance that the man I love is cheating on me, plus I almost had a near death experience! And I'm—"

"Hold up, rewind. What? What near death experience?" I asked, cutting her off before she could finish her full sentence.

She huffed. "I went out for a run and went to cross the street and this car came out of nowhere and literally ran me off the road. I had to jump onto the sidewalk just to avoid being fuckin' roadkill in broad daylight!"

"Did you call the police? Were they speeding? Did you get their license plate?" I asked, bombarding her with a million questions all in one breath.

She wobbled her head from left to right. "No. I didn't do any of those things. I was so shaken up about it I couldn't fuckin' think straight."

"Did you tell Jaron?"

She scoffed. "He was the first person I called, and he didn't even give a fuck."

"I don't believe that," I defended, shaking my head.

"Well, believe it because he doesn't, which again leads me to believe he's fuckin' somebody else. Hence why shit is just... complicated as fuck."

I sighed. "So, what would make things uncomplicated? Him breaking up with you? You breaking up with him? Because it doesn't sound like that's what you want."

"It's not."

"Then what do you want, Tati?"

"I want him! I want us to be a family! I want him to bring his ass home and stop having me stressing all day and all night wondering when he's going to walk his ass through the front door. I want to be in a normal fuckin' relationship for once in my life, but I just don't think that's going to happen..."

"And why not?" I asked.

"Because I just can't shake the feeling that he's out here fuckin' around on me with somebody else, Bellamy! I can just feel the shit deep in my gut."

I chewed on my bottom lip as my heartrate quickened. The last thing I needed was for Tati to follow some breadcrumbs that would lead her right to whatever it was Jaron and I had going on. "So...what do you plan to do about it?"

"I've asked him numerous times and all he does is brush me off like I'm a fuckin' crazy person or something, but I know something is up, and you're going to help me prove it."

My forehead creased in confusion. "Huh? How?"

"He told me he's been staying at a hotel, so I spent hours calling around the area, and I finally found out where he's been staying."

My eyes widened. "Tatiyana, are you fuckin' crazy? Do you hear yourself? You on some real stalker shit right now, and I don't want nothin' to do with none of this. Nope, none of it," I disputed, shaking my head and waving my hands in the air.

"Please, Bells. I don't have anyone else, and I can't go alone."

"Then don't go at all! I'm telling you, if you go looking for shit, you're going to find shit. Can you really handle that?"

"I'm not as weak as all of you think I am, okay? Yeah, some fucked up shit happened to me in my past, but the past is the past. I'm fine!"

"Are you really? Because I can recall having these same types of conversations with you about..."

"Don't you dare say his name!" she yelled.

I sighed. "See, there it is right there. You can't even bear to hear the man's name, and Trey's been dead for years, Tati."

"Shut the fuck up, Bellamy!"

"No, your ass needs to hear this! It's time everybody stopped walking on eggshells around your ass when it comes down to you, your relationships, and your mental fuckin' health. You were so fuckin' paranoid about what Trey was doing every day and every night, when all the man was doing was trying to battle his demons in private with a fuckin' therapist!"

"So, you're saying it's my fault that he killed himself?" she screamed through a face full of tears.

"I would never blame you for something like that. Trey had his own demons, and we all knew that. All I'm saying is the paranoia that you have comes from something deeply rooted within you! You manifest that shit onto whoever the fuck you're dating and start accusing them of shit, whether they are really out there doing something wrong or not. You need professional help to deal with your own shit."

"Fuck you, Bellamy!"

"The truth hurts, but it's what the fuck you need to hear!"

"I don't even know why the fuck I came to you with any of this shit anyway. This is exactly why I keep shit to myself! What the fuck do you know about bein' in a committed relationship? You don't know shit about a nigga but how to suck and fuck him until he gets tired of you and moves on to the next bitch!"

Her venomous words struck a chord in me that I didn't even know I had. Tatiyana could be a true bitch when she wanted to be, but I couldn't say I saw her coming at my neck the way she did. I'd placed a mirror in front of her, and in return, she'd done the same to me.

"You know what, I gotta get ready for work, so you can see yourself out," I told her before turning my back and walking down the hallway to the bathroom.

Seconds later, I heard the front door slam behind her. I walked back down the hallway just to make sure she was gone and then pulled out my cell to call Jaron.

"I take it she's gone," he said when he answered.

"Yeah, and shit got pretty heated between us."

"What all did she say?"

"She knows where you've been staying, Jaron. So, if you were serious about keeping her away from whatever bullshit you're in, then you need to make plans to make some new moves and soon. I think she's planning on doing a pop-up just to make sure you're not there with some other girl."

He sighed. "This the shit I be talkin' about."

"I know. I tried to tell her to calm down, but she wasn't hearing me. Her mind is made up."

"Fuck it. She wanna pull up, let her ass pull up."

"Look, I'm truly not trying to be in the middle of y'all shit, but you two need to talk."

"I know we do. That's all she told you, though? That she knows where I've been staying?"

"Yeah, that's it. Why?"

"No reason. She just sounded like she was about to give you an ear full when she called you."

I exhaled. "Nope. You were the topic of conversation just like always."

"My fault about that shit, yo."

"It is what it is. Just watch yourself. Tati is..."

"Say no more, I already know. Thanks for the heads-up."

"Oh, wait, she did mention something about being run off the road recently when she was jogging. Did she tell you about that?"

He sighed. "Yeah, she did. To be honest, I think she's being more dramatic than she needs to be. You know how niggas in New York drive."

"So, basically you think it was a cry for attention?" I quizzed.

"Basically."

"Hmm, okay. Listen, I'll talk to you later. I'm about to head out to go to work."

"Enjoy the rest of your day."

I smiled. "You too."

It was clearer than crystal that I'd chosen a side and picked dick over blood. I'd fallen for Jaron in more ways than one, and I wanted the opportunity to love him freely and openly, not on some behind closed doors shit. Sister or not, Tati was a fuckin' basket case, and he needed to watch his back around her. All I could keep telling myself is that it would all blow over and one day he'd be where he belonged, with me. Until that day came, I was stuck wrestling with the fact that having even a piece of him for the meantime was better than having no piece at all.

Chapter Ten

Jaron

Bellamy's wild side was one of the things that attracted me to her the most. That, and the fact that she was more than just a pretty face with the smoothest skin I'd ever felt in my life. She looked out for a nigga, and she had talent. Not ordinary talent, either. The type of talent that could make her some big money one day if she played her cards rights. I could feel the attraction she had for me from our first one-on-one encounter in the studio but hearing her say the words hit differently. I fucked with her heavy, but I knew I had too much on my plate to give her what she truly needed. There were too many irons in the fire that I needed to take care of before I could even think about putting things to rest with her sister and honoring my feelings for her.

Truthfully, I was surprised that Tati hadn't told Bellamy she was pregnant, which made me question if it was even valid to begin with. I'd heard stories of women buying fake ass positive pregnancy tests online to try and trap a nigga, and if that's the shit she was on, I wasn't going to hesitate to tell her I wasn't on that type of time. Regardless as to whether or not I believed her, I knew we needed to talk. I'd been treating her like shit for weeks, and I knew I needed to be a man and right my wrongs. After Bellamy tipped me off about the alleged pop-up, I figured I'd make it worth her while and hopefully silence all of her suspicions, no matter how true they were.

I'd been in my room so long that the lit tapered candles were beginning to drip wax onto the nightstand. I had rose petals leading from the front door all the way to the bed and a bouquet of fresh red roses laying on top of the bed. I made sure to turn on my location sharing so that there would be no confusion as to what room I was in whenever Tati's crazy ass did decide to show up. A smile crept across my face when I heard my phone ring and saw her name pop up on the screen. I went ahead and pressed ignore to really rile her up. She called a total of five more times back-to-back before the ringing stopped completely. Ten minutes after that, I heard banging on the hotel room door.

I walked over and opened it nonchalantly. She shot me a grimace and pushed past me. "Where is that bitch, huh? Where is she?"

"Tati, what the fuck are you talkin' about?"

"Don't play with me, Jaron! Look! You got rose petals, flowers, and candles and shit. Where the fuck is she?"

"Tati, calm your ass down. Ain't nobody here but you and me."

"Bullshit! I know you're playin' me. Let me see your phone!"

"What?"

"You heard me! Let me see your phone! If you ain't got shit to hide, let me see it!"

"Tati, sit your ass the fuck down. We need to talk."

"I don't want to talk things out unless you're going to tell me the fuckin' truth, Jaron. The real truth!"

"Even when I do tell you the truth, you don't believe my ass. Ever since you moved in, all we do is fuckin' argue! I'm tired of this shit!"

She huffed. "Just tell me. Is there somebody else, Jaron?"

"No. I did all of this for you."

"Then, why have you been so secretive lately, huh? You haven't been home for more than an hour at a time. When are you going to stop lying to me? I'm not a child you can lie to about Santa Claus or the Tooth Fairy. I'm a grown ass woman, and I want the truth!"

Her eyes were begging for me to tell her the truth, but there was no way I could tell her that the car that almost hit her wasn't an accident. I couldn't tell her how much shit I was really in after getting robbed. It'd been weeks, and I still wasn't able to provide the cash for the drugs I'd been fronted. I knew it was only a matter of time before niggas started to retaliate to send a message. I chewed my bottom lip for a few seconds before letting out a long sigh.

"Look, Tati. Just know that whatever I'm doing, it's to keep you safe."

"Keep me safe from what?" she quizzed, giving me the side eye.

"I got robbed a few weeks ago and the shit that was taken from me wasn't mine, and now I'm responsible for it..."

"What did they take and whose was it, Jaron?" she asked, sitting down on the bed.

"What do you think they took?" I asked.

"Was it drugs? Money? Guns?" she asked.

I shot her a look that let her know she'd hit the bullseye.

She sighed. "Why didn't you feel like you could come to me and tell me that?"

"I didn't want you to worry. You're already on ten all the time."

"I—I know. I'm sorry. I just don't understand why I always have to beg for you to see me...to choose me, this baby, and our family. I know you say you love me, but you gotta stop loving me with one foot in and one foot out of this. You're either all in or you're not."

"It's hard to be all in when you're making this relationship toxic, Tati. You gotta chill, or else..."

"Or else, what?" she asked, cutting me off.

"Or else, I can't do this shit no more."

Tears welled up in the corners of her eyes. "What about our baby?"

"It seems like your mind is pretty much made up, and I'm not going to tell you what to do with your body. The only thing I will say is that now isn't the best time, Tati. That's just me being honest with you like you asked. You and I aren't one-hundred percent, plus all the shit I just told you I'm dealing with. Having a kid on the way isn't the icing on the cake for me, it's more like the straw that's gon' break the mothafuckin' camel's back," I admitted.

"Wow...I ask for honesty and you gave it to me."

"I'm sorry."

"Don't be..." She diverted her gaze away from mine and picked up the bouquet of roses lying beside her. The entire room fell silent for a few minutes. The only consistent sound was the heat pumping into the room and her sniffles.

"Tell me what's on your mind," I told her.

"I don't know...this just isn't what I expected. None of this is."

"And what did you expect?"

She shrugged. "I don't know. Maybe to be happy for once. Maybe to fall for somebody without waiting for the other shoe to drop. I just thought this would be different. I thought you would be different."

"So, what are you saying?"

Silence hung in between us again before she stood to her feet. "Dinner is at five o'clock at Mama's on Sunday...are you coming?"

I frowned for a few seconds, realizing she'd completely changed the subject. "Yeah, I'll be there."

"You promise?"

I walked over to her and kissed her forehead. "I promise."

She nodded. "Oh, and thanks for the flowers," she acknowledged, before turning to leave.

*****

SUNDAY ROLLED AROUND, and I pulled into the driveway at Tati's mother's house twenty minutes after five. My eyes immediately zeroed in on Bellamy's car, which brought a smile to my face. Although I knew we wouldn't be able to have our typical interaction, it was always a pleasure to be in her presence. She was simply unforgettable. I shut the engine off and hopped out of my truck. As soon as I walked inside, Tati was standing in the foyer waiting on me.

"Hey," I addressed her, while taking off my coat.

"Hey...um, everybody is already sitting at the dinner table."

"Okay, let me wash my hands, and I'll be in there in a minute."

I caught eyes with Bellamy for a split second before making my way into the bathroom to wash my hands. When I came out, I walked into the dining room and was surprised to see a few more faces than usual. I nodded to everyone and took my seat across from Bellamy.

"Let us bow our heads in prayer," Tati's mother announced. "Father God, we come to you today saying thank you. We thank you not only the abundance of food on our table this evening, Lord, but we thank you for the hands that prepared it. We ask that you bless this food to be nourishment to our bodies. In Jesus name we pray, Amen."

"Amen," everyone said in unison.

"So, who is this young fella?" the older man sitting beside Bellamy asked, breaking the silence as everyone packed food on their plates.

"Uncle Brendan, this is Jaron, my boyfriend," Tati told him.

"Nice to meet you, young man."

"Nice to meet you too, sir."

"This is my wife, Sandra, and our daughter, Jewel."

I nodded at both women before refocusing my attention to the food in front of me. Once my plate was filled with slices of roast beef, mashed potatoes with gravy, collard greens, and macaroni and cheese, I began chowing down. Halfway through my meal, Tatiyana stood up and placed her manicured hand on my shoulder. I turned to look up at her, analyzing everything from her fleeting breath to the dimpled smile across her face.

"Everyone, Jaron and I have an announcement to make,"

she said.

My face immediately went stone cold as I clenched my jaw. "Tati—"

"We're having a baby!" she blurted out.

While everyone around us clapped and cheered with smiles on their faces, Bellamy sat chillingly still with her eyes locked on mine.

"Did you hear what I said, Bellamy?" Tati asked while proudly resting her hand on her flat stomach.

"Y—yeah, I did. Um, congratulations," she said, still never removing her gaze away from mine.

"Thank you!"

"How far along are you?" her Uncle Brendan asked.

"Only a few weeks, but I was so excited that I just couldn't hold it in anymore."

As more of the news about the baby seemed to be unfolding right in front of her eyes, Bellamy was sitting at the dining room table doing her best to keep her composure, but her poisonous gaze made it clear that she was envious, broken, and enraged.

"Wow, that's really, um...exciting," she managed to mutter out. "Will you all excuse me for a second?"

She quickly got up from the table and darted out of sight. A couple minutes later, my phone vibrated in my pocket. I pulled it out to read the word *Garage* from Bellamy on my screen.

"Excuse me real quick, I gotta make a call," I advertised, excusing myself from the table. After throwing on my coat, I walked outside and made my way around to the side door where Bellamy was standing in the garage with her arms wrapped around her shoulders.

"Let me explain," I started.

"What is there to explain? I think a baby is quite fuckin' explanatory!" she snapped.

I chewed my bottom lip, knowing I deserved anything she was going to throw my way. "Look, I had no idea she was going to announce it in front of everybody like that. The last time we talked about it, I told her where I stood on everything."

"And where was that?"

"I told her that it wasn't the right time for a baby right now, but that ultimately it was her decision."

"Well, I guess we know what decision she made."

I could see her heart breaking through her eyes, which made me feel even worse about the entire situation.

"Do you tell my sister the same things you tell me?"

"C'mon now, Bellamy."

"I mean you two don't even have anything in common, at least not as much as we do. And now you're standing in front of me telling me that she's carrying your child? Even when you got robbed you didn't go home, you came to me!"

"I ain't never mean for none of that shit to go down like that, but I slipped up, aight? You said it yourself, her mind is made up. So, what you want me to do? My hands are fuckin' tied."

"What do I want you to do? I wanted you to leave her before it ever got to this point!"

"Calm down, why you talking all loud? People don't need to know what the fuck we got goin' on between us."

"And what exactly is going on between us, Jaron? Huh? Because at this point, it's beyond the sex and the music and all of that other shit. This is my heart we're talkin' about now. When I told you how I felt, I meant every word of that shit. I know you know that, but I can't keep this shit up, wondering if today is going to be the day that you break things off or not. And now you don't just have a baby on the way with some random bitch, you're having a fuckin' kid with my sister! She's in there right now carrying my niece or nephew inside her while I'm over here fuckin' their dad. How the fuck do you think that makes me feel? Huh?"

"I can't even front, I'm wishin' we could go back to before we crossed that line, but we can't."

She scoffed. "Yeah, well, you ain't the only one."

"I'm sorry, aight? Hear me when I say that shit."

"I fell in love with you, Jaron...you tell me what the fuck

I'm supposed to do with these feelings now," she said, wiping tears from the corners of her eyes.

"Look, Bellamy. I care about you. You know I do."

"So, you knew she was pregnant when you came over a few days ago with the song, huh?"

I lowered my gaze toward the ground before nodding. "Yeah, I did."

"And that's why you were wondering what she told me when she came over. You didn't want her to spill your little secret too soon. You would rather see me embarrassed in front of my entire fuckin' family. I looked out for you more than once! And you still sat there and let me get played!"

"You know that's not the type of shit I'm on. I wanted to find a way to tell you, I just couldn't bring myself to do the shit."

"Well, here we are, so we just need to be adults about the shit and cut ties while we still can," she told me.

I licked my lips. "Is that really what you want?"

She screwed up her face in disgust as tears poured out of her eyes like a fountain. "What kind of fuckin' question is that, Jaron? It's obviously not what I want, but it's what needs to be done."

I nodded. "Okay then."

I knew I was the reason for each tear that dripped down her heart-shaped face, but I was too deep in my own shit to dig myself out. The last thing I wanted to do was hurt Bellamy. I had every intention of doing the right thing by both of them when the time was right, yet somehow I still ended up the villain.

Gotti

I rolled over to the sound of my vibrating cell phone at two o'clock in the afternoon after pulling an all-nighter to finish my thesis paper. Using Dash as my muse, I changed my research to focus on the criminal justice system, its injustices against African Americans, especially males, and how those ideologies influence politics and power in America. Writing my paper only fueled my passion to get into the criminal justice system and fix it from the inside. Since I'd finally finished my paper, it was time for me to put school behind me and focus on finally turning my apartment into more than just a place where I slept, shit, ate, graded papers, and occasionally fucked. After spending the night entangled in Dash's sheets a few days prior, it was safe to say that I'd gone to sleep and woken up in love. I'd fallen for every square inch of Dash, from his voice to his personality, even down to his scent. A bitch was *spring, sprang, sprung* and there wasn't a part of me that was ashamed about it. As soon as I cracked open the first moving box, my phone rang.

"Hey, girl," I answered.

"Hey…"

"What's wrong, Bells?" I asked, sensing the sadness in her voice, although she'd only said one word to me.

She sighed. "You were right."

"About…"

"Everything…Jaron and I…the shit is a fuckin' mess. You told me to stay away and what did I do? The complete fuckin' opposite. Now, I'm over here lickin' my fuckin' wounds."

I hated to be the one to say, *I told you so,* but I knew his ass sounded too good to be true from the moment she started flapping her gums to me about him. The situation was a mess from the beginning, yet Bellamy went into it with her eyes wide shut.

"Tell me what happened."

"Tati's pregnant, Gotti. She's fuckin' pregnant with his baby," she cried.

I quickly sunk my teeth into my bottom lip to avoid speaking too quickly. "Shit, I'm sorry, Bells."

It had been a long time since I sat on the phone and listened to my best friend cry over a man. Usually, she remained in the driver's seat and cut ties with men before they even had the opportunity to try and hurt her, but from the sadness in her voice, I could tell that man had her hooked on him like a drug. I could definitely relate to the feeling.

"At least you found out before things got too deep."

"That depends on how you define *too deep*."

"Bells..."

"I fell in love, Gotti. I fucked around and fell in fuckin' love with the nigga who impregnated my sister. Just saying it out loud makes it sound like it should be the title of an episode of *Maury*."

"Or *Jerry Springer*," I added.

She let out a short laugh. "Shut your ass up!"

"I'm sorry. My bad, girl."

"I just don't understand why it has to be so complicated, Gotti."

I sighed. "I know, girl. But hey, chalk this shit up as a lesson learned. Love is almost never easy. My mom always used to tell me that sometimes, a man don't really love you, he just love how you love him."

"I don't feel that way though, at least I didn't before finding out about the baby shit. He was vocal about how much he cared about me, but now I don't know if it was all bullshit or if he was telling the truth but just got caught up in some bullshit."

"C'mon now, Bells. We're all grown, and we all know how the hell babies are made. He didn't get caught up in shit he didn't wanna be caught up in. Besides, it's not like she's some random. They were and I'm guessing still are in a relationship together..."

She huffed. "Yeah, yeah, I know. I just can't believe I played myself over a nigga already in a fuckin' relationship. What is this high school? His ass had me chasing fool's gold like I was the fuckin' leprechaun on the *Lucky Charms* commercial."

"Happens to the best of us, girl. Just try not to mull over it too long or you'll drive yourself crazy with regret."

"You wanna know what's fucked up?"

"What?" I asked.

"I don't even have the type of regret that I probably should have."

My forehead creased. "What do you mean?"

"I don't regret that it happened...I honestly don't know what I regret. Falling in love with him made me feel invincible, like nothing could touch me. Now I just feel..."

"Ordinary?" I asked.

"Empty."

I nodded, sympathizing with the feeling. I had gone through the same thing when Dash had broken things off with me after our disagreement. It was crazy the rollercoaster of emotions another human being could make you feel.

"You won't always feel like that."

"I hope not because this shit sucks. Everything about this nigga is glued to the forefront of my thoughts. I see this nigga when my eyes are closed. I can still hear his voice in my head. I'm just spiraling..."

I pulled the phone away from my ear when I felt it vibrate. I swiped to unlock my phone to read a text from Dash.

Dash [8:42 p.m.]: You busy? I'm about to grab food.

Me [8:43 p.m.]: I'm in the middle of unpacking my apartment finally.

Dash [8:43 p.m.]: Lol, it's about time.

Me [8:45 p.m.]: Shut up! Can we get takeout? You can help me unpack while we wait and then we can eat dinner and you can have me for dessert.

Dash [8:45 p.m.]: I'll see you in ten.

"Hello? Gotti? You still there?" Bellamy asked.

"My bad girl, yeah I'm still here."

"Am I interrupting something?"

"No, not at all."

"Must you insist on lying to me? I can practically hear your ass smiling through the phone, which means you must be talkin' to that black ass nigga, a.k.a. your boo."

"It's no big deal, he's coming over soon, and we're going to order some food while I unpack. I'm still here and available to talk shit about niggas with you for as long as you need me to," I assured her.

"Nah, that's okay with me. You go be booed up and shit."

I sighed. "I don't want you to feel like you have to go through this alone. You know I'm here for you."

"Nah, girl. I'ma be alright. Do your thing."

"Are you sure?"

"Yeah, I'm sure."

"I'll call you tomorrow, okay?"

"Okay."

"I love you, Bells."

"Love you more, Gotti."

We ended our call, and I went back to untaping boxes and pulling out all of the contents inside to try to make some form of organization out of the clutter. As happy as I was that Dash was coming over, I made sure to make a mental note to check in with Bellamy before I laid down to close my eyes. For the past few days, Dash had kept his distance from me to make sure that all of my focus was on my thesis paper and not on the wood that was dangling between his legs. I hated being away from him but admired the fact that he took my education seriously. My thoughts were interrupted when I heard a familiar knock at the door. I knew it was Dash just by the firm tap alone.

"Hey," I said, placing a quick peck to his lips. A smile creased my face when I saw a fresh bottle of Ace of Spades in his hand. "What's this for?"

"It's for you. We celebrating tonight."

"And what exactly are we celebrating?" I quizzed.

"You finally finished that long ass paper, didn't you?"

"Yes." I beamed.

"Then that's what the fuck we celebratin'. You decide what you wanna eat yet?"

"I don't know what I'm in the mood for. You?"

"I think we both know the answer to that," he answered, while moving some things off the couch so that he could sit down.

I giggled. "Stop. I'm being serious. Do you want Chinese?

Italian? Pizza?"

"Ain't pizza Italian?" he asked.

I sucked my teeth. "You know what I mean."

"What about Thai?"

"Mmm, yeah, Thai sounds good."

"You got a menu?"

"Check the drawer right next to the sink inside the kitchen. There might be one in there. People are always sliding shit under my door or in my mailbox."

"Bet."

Once our orders were placed, Dash opened up my refrigerator and stuck the bottle inside to keep it chilled.

"I can't believe it's taken me this long to unpack and really get my space in order."

"Yeah, you got shit strung out everywhere in this mothafucka."

"Shut up! It's my process. First, I pull everything out, then figure out where I want to put it and then place it there. It looks bad, but it's really not."

"Yeah, aight," he said, making his way over to the mantle when I'd just put up a few framed photos of my mother and I, me and Bellamy, and my favorite picture of my father and I on my seventh birthday.

"Like what you see?" I asked, interrupting his train of thought.

He swiped up the photo of my father and held it in his hands. "This yo pops?"

I nodded. "Yeah. That was taken on my seventh birthday. It was my first time going to Disneyland, and I had the best time ever," I told him, recalling every single detail about the photo without having to look at it.

My father had me scooped into his arms, and we were both cheesing hard as hell while wearing a matching set of Mickey Mouse ears on top of our heads with the castle perfectly nestled in the background. Instead of responding, Dash kept his eyes glued on the photo. "Earth to Dash. Did you hear what I said?"

He slowly turned his neck to me and then looked back down at the photo. The look on his face alone told me there was something he wanted to say, but just wouldn't allow himself to do it. "Are you okay?" I asked after another wave of silence crashed over us.

"Yeah, I'm good," he finally spoke up.

"It doesn't seem like it. You literally look like you saw a ghost or somethin'."

He put the photo back in its place and reached in his back pocket to pull out a one-hundred-dollar bill. "This is for the food. Tell 'em they can keep the change."

I frowned. "Why are you giving it to me? You can just pay them when they get here."

"I won't be here when they get here, G."

My forehead creased. "And why not? Where are you going?"

Instead of responding, he started making his way over to the door. I quickly darted past him and stood in front of it to block him.

"Get out the way, G."

"No, I'm not letting you leave until you tell me what's up."

"I said move, G."

"And I said no! Your whole mood switched up, and I wanna know why."

"No, you don't."

"I do. Now, tell me what the fuck is going on with you."

"Fine, you want honesty, I'ma give you that shit. When I was giving you your space to focus on your school shit, I was reminded how much I enjoyed bein' on my own."

"Okay, so…we don't have to spend every waking moment together. That's fine."

"It's bigger than that."

"What do you mean?"

He huffed. "Fucking with you is breaking my focus on other things."

"What other things require that much of your attention

146

all of a sudden?" I asked, folding my arms across my chest.

"Just know I'm fallin' back on your ass, aight?"

"What? You talkin' crazy and it's about to piss me off!" I barked, bossing up on his black ass.

He shrugged. "That's on you."

"None of this makes any sense! None of it!" I protested.

"Why is it so hard for you to understand a nigga need his space? Every day, I gotta deal with some bullshit and you wasn't supposed to fall into that category, Gotti."

"So, now I'm bringing bullshit because I want to know where the fuck all this shit you talkin' is comin' from all of a sudden?"

"It wasn't all of a sudden. I just told you that."

"Why are you trying to hurt me?"

He shrugged his shoulders. "I'm not. I'm just keepin' it real with you. If you can't handle that shit, then that's on you."

"Why the fuck did you even come here if you knew you felt like this?"

"I ain't gon' hold you, G. Respectfully, I only came to fuck and congratulate you," he admitted.

His words sent a cold shiver down my spine as tears stung my eyes. I couldn't believe my ears. There was a great deal of emotion behind the words he was speaking. In an instant. he made me feel small, like I was nothing more than a play thing. "You don't mean that."

"I don't know what you cryin' for. You knew what shit was between us from the very beginning. Your feelings should've never gone beyond physical attraction. Instead, you chained yourself to me, and for what?"

"So, I'm the only one with feelings here?" I asked as tears slid down my face.

"Why you grillin' me, G? I said what I said, and you still chattin' way too much."

"Can't we just talk about this?"

"Yeah, nah," he said, while shaking his head.

"Please?"

"You about to get me tight. Move."

"No!"

"Move out the fuckin' way, Gotti. I'm not gon' say that shit again."

His tone was cold and his expression was emotionless. Feeling defeated, I stepped out of his way and watched him leave without giving me a second look. His words had cut me to the bone, and I was left standing in the middle of my living room floor trying to pick up the pieces of my freshly shattered heart.

Chapter Eleven

Dash

The night I walked out of G's apartment, I planned to walk out of her life forever. I knew my words had cut her deep. That was exactly what I intended for them to do. I wanted her to feel the stinging pain of my rejection, but little did she know, I worshipped the ground her little ass walked on. Things between us were more complicated than she could ever imagine. We had ties deeper than just our feelings for each other. Whether she knew it or not, G was fragile. Not fragile like a champagne flute, but fragile like a nuclear fuckin' bomb. If she found out the truth, there was no tellin' how much hell she'd unleash.

"Sativa to change the things I can. Indica to accept the shit I can't," I mumbled to myself.

I had two blunts rolled and was riding through the city with the sunroof cracked and the heat on high. Every time my phone vibrated in the passenger seat, I turned the music up a little louder. Gotti had been sending me paragraphs on paragraphs for days, and I either left her ass on read or deleted them completely without even seeing what she had to say. I held the blunt in between my thumb and my index finger before lifting the lighter to the tip. One thing I knew for sure, a blunt would never have me in my feelings, and Mary Jane would never break my heart.

Flashback

January 1, 2012

It was the first day of the year, and the streets of New York were already on fire. Devil and I were at the top of our game and had no intention on slowing down. My cold hands gripped the Italian leather steering wheel of my cocaine white BMW. I was apprehensive as fuck about what we were about to do, but with my day one and my gun on the side of me, I was ready for whatever.

"You sure about this shit?" I asked, glancing over at Devil, who was riding shotgun.

"Trust me, we gon' be good."

"I do trust you. It's that mothafucka I don't trust," I told him.

We were on our way to meet with a dirty fuckin' cop. The bigger we got, the louder the streets whispered our names, and we needed the right connections. A monthly monetary arrangement made sure we got to do our thing and ensured that the NYPD would look the other way.

"This ain't shit but a little conversation to make sure we got an understanding, that's it. Besides, after we do this, we goin' to celebrate."

"What we celebratin'?" I asked.

He chuckled before stroking the few day's growth of beard on his face. "Life, mothafucka."

I cut my eyes at him before chuckling alongside him. "And a good one it is."

"It's about to get even better because…"

"Because what, nigga?" I asked, tilting my head toward the window.

"Yara is pregnant."

My eyebrows heightened with excitement. "Word?"

"Yeah. She carrying my seed."

"When'd you find out?"

"A couple days ago. She due this fall."

I extended my hand to dap him up. "Congrats, mothafucka!"

"Thank you! So, we goin' out after this and celebrating the fuck outta what is gon' be a beautiful mothafuckin' year, you hear

me?"

I nodded. "Bet."

"Shit, we can't fuck up now. We finally at the top of the mountain, nigga. The air different up here. I'm not goin' back."

"Hell no," I agreed.

*****

WE PULLED UP to the meeting spot and parked beside the only other car there. A man was leaning on the trunk, smoking a cigarette. Even in the dark of night, I could see the moonlight reflecting off his badge. We'd been supplying him money every month for the past year to give us insight on any snitches that came in singing our names to the NYPD and to make sure our names stayed off any paperwork. Unfortunately, the nigga had gotten too comfortable with the money that he forgot to do his part. We'd noticed unmarked police cars tailing us throughout the city for the past few weeks, so if he wasn't going to do his fuckin' job, the deal was off.

"You're late," he barked as soon as we got out of the car.

"It's New Year's, the traffic in the city is bananas," Devil replied.

"You got somethin' for me?" he asked.

"Here," Devil said, pulling an envelope out of his back pocket and tossing it on the table.

He snatched it like the greedy feign he was and proceeded to open it. "It's all there," Devil assured him.

He looked up at us and scoffed. We watched him pull the stacks out of the envelope and stack them one by one on the trunk as we all stood around. "You know what I l fuckin' love about money? I mean, besides the smell, of course. This shit is real. I can sort it, stack it, buy whatever the fuck I want with it."

"Well, you better make it last because I also called this meeting to let you know that we ain't your fuckin' puppets no more, mothafucka. The deal is dead," Devil gritted out.

He belted out a hearty laugh before it turned into a cough. "Are you sure that's what you want? No me, means no protection."

"I'll take that risk. Stick a knife in this shit. We done."

"How about this...you double my next monthly payment, and I'll do my best to forget the lack of respect you've shown me since I got here. Or, I could put a bullet it your boy over here and send your ass to Rikers for the rest of your miserable ass life. Ah, what the hell? I'm a nice guy. I'll put a bullet in both of you. What's it gonna be? It's up to you."

I grimaced. "You talkin' real tough for a mothafucka that's outnumbered."

"You think I've survived twenty plus years on the force by following all of the rules? No. I survived by looking out for myself. I'd be an idiot to think I'd be the one to wipe all you fuckin' drug dealers off the street and there would miraculously be no more crime. I'm just here to get my just due," he admitted.

I scoffed. I knew better than anyone there that the strongest army didn't always win the war. Shit, the bigger he was, the harder he'd fall when the time came. "Add up all the money you've gotten over the past year, it's more than your fuckin' childish ass salary. You've gotten more than your fair share, especially when you been layin' back gettin' paid and you ain't been doin' your fuckin' job. You supposed to feed us information and make sure our names don't come up on no shit with the fuckin' NYPD. So, why the fuck me and my niggas been gettin' tailed by unmarked cop cars and shit lately, huh? Fuckin' explain that!"

"I think you've forgotten that your upward mobility in this game has a ceiling. I'm the fuckin' ceiling, boys. I don't work for you. Like I said, I'm here to get my just due. You think I give a fuck about what happens to you when I leave here? You wanna keep your business goin' then you fuckin' pay me. If not, it's back to the pissy hallways in the slums for the both of you!"

Devil reached out and grabbed him by his shirt. "Niggas know what type of time I'm on. My name is sanctioned in these streets.

Everybody, including you, eats at the end of the day because of me. Put some fuckin' respect on my name, mothafucka! Yo, Dash, tell this nigga to stop disrespectin' me, deadass!"

He flashed a heinous grin. "You think your street talk intimidates me? That shit may work in the streets, but I have the government backing me. I'm the one wielding the power. You'd be wise not to forget that!"

I pulled Devil away while pulling out my gun at the same time and aiming it at the cop's head. "Fuck all this talkin'. I told you I ain't trust this mothafucka. We said we done, so let's put a bullet in him and be fuckin' done!"

"So, that's your plan? To kill a fuckin' cop? You mothafuckas will be rotting in a jail cell being somebody's bottom bitch by the end of the fuckin' week!" he threatened.

I released the safety, ready to splatter his brains all over his back window. Just before I squeezed the trigger, bright headlights popped over the hill at us. He shoved me back and darted off. Devil ran after him while I fired a few shots toward the car.

"Freeze! NYPD!" a cop yelled, hopping out of the vehicle and running toward us with his gun aimed.

Turning our attention to him, I aimed my gun, ready to shoot first and not ask one damn question.

"What the fuck is goin' on here, Cecil?" he barked, turning his rage to his fellow brother-in-arms.

"I've been undercover! Help me get these two mothafuckas in cuffs!" Cecil yelled out.

"Bullshit! Tell that mothafucka what you really been up to. He might put a bullet in you for us!" I yelled.

"Shut the fuck up!" the other cop yelled to me.

"Fuck this, let's body 'em both," Devil suggested.

Before Devil could pull the trigger, the other cop fired shots our way, hitting Devil in the side.

"Ahh, shit!" he yelled.

He fell on his back, and I shot back while pulling his body out of the way. I fired three rounds at Cecil before his partner jumped in front of a bullet that sent him flying to his back. I slung Devil into the passenger seat before jumping into the driver's seat and speeding off, never looking back.

"Just hold on, nigga! I'ma get you to the hospital, and they gon' stitch your shit back up in no time. You gon' be good!" I assured him.

I dropped Devil off at the emergency room, and he blended in as just another person who came up on some bad luck on the first day of the year. Once the word got out that there had been a shootout and a member of law enforcement was down, cops swarmed the cold streets like bees.

Less than forty-eight hours later, I was on my way to pick Devil up from the hospital. The bullet he'd been hit with went straight through his side and luckily didn't pierce any vital organs. As soon as I parked and got out, Devil was walking out through the doors. Before we got close enough to dap each other up, the feds came charging at us from all angles with their guns drawn.

"Get down on the ground! Get the fuck on the ground now!"

We slowly raised our hands up over our heads and slowly kneeled on the ground. They surrounded us, pushed our faces into the curb, and cuffed us. As much as we hated it, Cecil Warren was our only move. We were fucked if we couldn't convince him to pull some strings on his end. After all, with both of us gone, he would have to curve his spending habits because his monthly payments would dry up. Before we even spoke on it, I'd made my decision to take whatever charges they threw my way. Devil had a baby on the way that he needed to be there for, so I had no problem taking that weight.

I pleaded guilty before the Chief U.S. District Judge to drug trafficking. The district attorney said that over the span of five years, I'd been a part of a drug trafficking organization that was responsible for selling cocaine and that I was involved in the illegal possession and distribution of narcotics. There was no mention of the cop that died on New Year's. I didn't know if Cecil thought he was doing me a favor by leaving that out or holding it over my head as leverage to keep doing business with Devil when news of our arrest died down.

So, although the murderer of Gotti's father was unknown on paper, I sat down and did my time for the crimes I'd committed and ones I didn't. If I learned anything about dealing with cops, is that they had more similarities with drug dealers than they thought. We were all sold the same dream. Everybody wanted to be the hero.

Hero in the streets.

Hero in the precinct.

What they left out was that heroism comes with a price. The balance between good and evil had faulted. The bad guys came out on top, and the most innocent one of us all took the fall. The hero that night was Cecil Warren. The victim, Gregory Louis Evans, Gotti's father.

Flashback ends

Fast forward a little over eight years later, and we didn't seem to be any wiser because Devil and I were on the way to meet with the devil himself, Detective Cecil Warren. After I went in, he forced Devil to continue working with him, threatening to give the police our names as the ones responsible for killing Gotti's father. But this time, I planned to put a bullet in Warren for taking away eight years of my life. While I rotted away in a cell, he'd climbed the ranks, raising from a low-level cop to a well-regarded detective and protector of the city. He wore his badge like a Superman cape, yet he was dirtier than the sewer rats. As dangerous as it was meeting with him after all these years, I was willing to do anything to take my mind off G. She'd been blowing me up, and I was finding it harder and harder to fight from answering or responding. I couldn't bring myself to block her. Deep down, there was something inside me that liked that she was chasing me.

"Yo, Dash. You good? Where your head at?" Devil asked, glancing over at me when he pulled up to a red light.

"I'm good."

"Don't look like it. Plus, your phone been blowin' up like crazy ever since you got in this mothafucka."

I shook my head at the sound of my phone vibrating for the fourth time since I'd gotten in the car with him. I didn't even bother to look down at the screen because I knew it was Gotti on the other line.

"Yo, that's your girl?" he asked.

"Nah."

"Why you got that sad ass look on your face then, D?"

"Trust me, I'm good. I'm not fuckin' with her no more."

"Why you not fuckin' with shorty no more? She a bird or somethin'?"

My forehead crumpled. "She far from a bird. She makes a nigga mad happy. G is dumb smart, too. You would've thought shorty was all up tight and shit, but nah, she wild funny."

"Say that. She got your nose wide open, so what's the problem?"

"She's the daughter of a fuckin' cop, nigga."

His brows shot up to his forehead. "Oh shit."

"Yeah, exactly."

"And you ain't know before?"

"I did. I just didn't know who he was."

"Who is he? Somebody we need to be worried about?" Devil asked. Instead of responding, I pulled up his name on my phone and showed him a photo. "Get the fuck out of here. What you gon' do?"

"What you mean what am I gon' do? Ain't shit I can do but keep my fuckin' distance from her ass. I gotta disappear. It's gotta be like I never existed."

He sighed. "If you say so. You always were colder than me when it came to that shit."

I nodded. "I know."

Niggas who didn't know Devil on a personal level would never know how much of a family man he was. It didn't matter who he was in the streets; he never took the shit home. His girl and his two sons were his heart, so he kept them as far away from who he really was as he could. Anybody else was collateral damage in his book. That's where we differed. Money had always come first and foremost for me. Against both our better judgements, I couldn't surrender my heart to her. In the streets, everything was about survival. There was no good or bad, or right or wrong. It was only life or death. Every morning I woke up to face another day; I was at war for my life. I did what I did to make sure that I lived to see another twenty-four and never atoned for it by choosing not to get too wrapped up on the lives I'd taken. But seeing his face after all those years with G's right next to it, shook me. I never expected to see him again. I was responsible for taking the life of someone close to the only woman I gave a fuck about. I wasn't ready for Gotti to know the truth because I knew if she found out, forgiveness would never be on the table. All I could do was pray the Lord showed me enough mercy to let me take that shit to the grave.

Devil pulled up to the meeting spot and turned his head toward me. "You good?"

"Been good," I fired back, showing him my gun.

"Nah, nigga. Not tonight. This is straight business. You stay in the car. I don't even want you to see him."

I shook my head. "I ain't trust his ass all those years ago, and I still don't. You know my body, nigga. His days are numbered."

"Shit, I believe you. I'm sick of this mothafucka, too. You know the only reason I'm still workin' with him is because of what happened that night. Mothafucka blackmailing me and shit."

"That shit is ending soon. I don't give a fuck. His life will be the last one I take."

"You over there lookin' like the Hulk and shit right now, nigga. You definitely stayin' in the car. Shit, you look like you got even more swole since the last time I saw you. What, you live in the fuckin' gym now, nigga?" he asked, trying to lighten the mood.

"Gotta keep my ass busy."

"What's got you runnin'?"

"What makes you think I'm runnin'? I ain't never ran from shit and you know that."

He bobbed his head. "Facts, chill. I'll be right back."

*****

THE NEXT DAY, I was headed out to the barbershop to get a shape up when my phone started vibrating. "Hello?" I answered, while swiping my keys off the kitchen island.

"I gotta take care of Jaron."

"What happened?"

"The little fuck got hit, and he owes me money," he said, clenching his jaw.

"What you wanna do about him?"

"I know you just got home from school, nigga. I wouldn't ask you to get your hands dirty this quick. I just want you to keep an eye on him."

"You don't trust that he really got robbed?"

"I don't trust shit a mothafucka say, ever, especially when it comes to my money. Family or not."

"Where that nigga stay?" I asked as I closed the door to my apartment. "I'll go see about him."

I headed down the hallway to the elevator to head out to my car.

"I'll text you his address," Devil told me.

"Bet, I'll pull up on 'em and talk to the nigga."

"You a better one than me."

"I know." I chuckled. "Shoot me the address, I'm about to get in the car now."

"Bet," he said before ending the call.

The elevator dinged and just as I was about to step off, I saw her. She locked eyes with me and for a split second, I could've sworn time stopped. In the time it took for me to quickly press the button to close the door, I read her with my eyes. Gotti was a fuckin' mess. She was wearing a mask of exhaustion and heartbreak. Sadness filled her puffy, red-rimmed eyes with dark pouches beneath them. She looked like all she'd been doing was crying. From the wrinkled shirt on her back to the matted curls in her hair and chipped polish on her nails, she didn't look like the G I knew. The G she was before I broke her.

"Dash? Dash! Wait!" she yelled on the other side of the elevator door.

I didn't let my finger off the button until I was back on my floor. Knowing she might decide to come up to my apartment, I took the stairs all the way down to the alleyway exit. I didn't give a fuck if I had to pack up my shit and move, but I was determined to never allow myself to have a run in with Gotti again.

Chapter Twelve

Gotti

I'd been sulking in the dark as if someone had died for the past week, unable to get back into a stable mindset. I missed everything about Dash. Both my heart and my body ached for him. I'd fallen into the sunken place of my feelings, unable to get out. Either I was sleeping all day and eating all night, or I would go days without showering, eating, or proper rest. I'd become a brokenhearted, couch surfing, bedhead wearing hot ass mess, and the light at the end of the tunnel was nowhere in sight. The phone rang five times before I heard Bellamy's voice on the other line. I'd allowed myself to fall into a depressive state and had been intentionally neglecting one of the only positive relationship I did have in my life.

"Hello?" she answered.

"Are you mad at me?"

"I'm not sure. I spent the last week thinking you were dead, so keep talkin', and I'll see if I'm happy to hear from you or not."

I nodded. "I deserve that."

"What's been going on with you, and where have you been? I've been needing to debrief with you for days about all the shit going on in my life and you've been M.I.A."

I let out a loud sigh. "You're right, and I know I've been on some other shit, but that's only because I've been going through some bullshit of my own."

"What's wrong? Things not going good with Mr. Sexual Dark Chocolate?"

"Nah, it's over."

"Huh? What do you mean it's over? What happened?"

"I wish I knew, girl. One minute we were good, shit, we were better than good, and then all of a sudden, he came over and started acting outside himself out of nowhere. He called it all off, said he was only in it for the sex, and walked out. I haven't heard from him since," I admitted.

I could feel fresh tears welling up in the corners of my eyes. As tired as I was of crying, my body still had more pain to exude.

"Have you tried hitting him up?" she quizzed.

"I'm ashamed to say how many times I've called and texted. I've left voicemails. Shit, I probably would've sent that nigga an email if I had it."

She snickered. "Ooohwee, you got it *bad, bad*, girl."

"I know. And the worst part about it all is that I fuckin' ran into his ass the other day. He was about to get off the elevator and then when he saw me, he quickly pressed another button to close the door."

"Girl, what? Why that nigga duckin' you all of a sudden like you the police?"

"Exactly! It's so fuckin' weird, I don't get it. I keep replaying the last night we spent together over and over in my head, searching for an inkling of a detail that would make any of this shit make sense. I'm falling apart over here because of this nigga, and he doesn't even have the decency to tell me why!"

"It's not like you don't know where the nigga live, girl. Why don't you do a pop-up on his ass? Knock and if he answer, ask that nigga what's really good, or ask his ass for a cup of sugar, whatever you feelin' at the time."

I paused. Popping up uninvited on Dash could be risky, yet the thought never crossed my mind. Bellamy had planted the seed, and I couldn't get it out of my head. He'd caught me slippin' the last time, and if I popped up lookin' like myself, I wasn't going to let up on him until I got the answers my heart desired.

"Shit, you might be on to somethin', girl. A bitch may just have to take a page out of your book and pull up on his ass."

"Because you know I'm the pull up queen! And as much as I'm all for some ghetto love bird shit, just know that I'm not condoning it."

"Not condoning it? You literally just put the idea in my head, Bells."

"I know, I know, but you and I both know poppin' up on a nigga unannounced is risky as fuck, and you can't afford to take your third L from this man. Don't give him the satisfaction!"

I groaned while tossing my head back against the pillow. Truth was, I didn't know what the hell I was going to do. I just wanted to be put out of my misery.

"But um, just in case you forgot, I'm going through shit too though, remember?"

Feeling like a horrible friend, I sat up on my elbows and made sure I gave her my full attention. "My bad, girl. What's been going on since, you know? Have you talked to Jaron at all?"

"He's been reaching out, but I've been leavin' his ass on read. I don't have time for his shit anymore."

"You definitely sound like you're out of the sad phase," I told her.

"Hell yeah, now I'm just angry as fuck! I feel like I fuckin' played myself, and for what? A fuckin' song that probably won't go anywhere?"

"I mean, you never know about the song shit. At least you got that out of it, I'd at least see what I could do with it if I were you."

"I don't know. A part of me doesn't want shit to do with him. I don't want him to have a hand in any of my music. You know music is my one true love, and that nigga broke my heart, so fuck him and that song."

I bobbed my head in agreement. I was on some fuck niggas and feelings shit just like Bellamy was. There we were, heartbroken over two men who clearly didn't deserve our love, hearts, or time, and they were out running amuck like we never mattered at all.

"Yeah, girl. I feel you. Fuck that nigga and that song! You

are filled with so much fuckin' talent, and you're only going to go so much further without him and his drama holding you back from being the badass fuckin' bitch that you are!" I cheered.

"Hell yeah, queen! Hell yeah! And you too, bitch! Shit, you smart as fuck! The smartest bitch I know, okay? You about to get your master's degree, bitch! All I got is a mothafuckin' associate's and shit, okay? You the brains and the beauty, Gotti! That nigga is probably somewhere sick right now over you. He's a coward and you're a boss ass bitch! You don't need that nigga, periodt!"

"Periodt!" I repeated.

Bellamy had hyped me up right back, and I felt adrenaline begin to pump through my veins. It was the first time I'd felt the spark of life inside me since Dash had *dashed* right up out of my life, but she was right. I was a bad ass bitch who was about my business. I had a strong future ahead of me, and I'd lost sight of that by allowing myself to succumb to my depression. He may have knocked me off my square, but he was not about to get the fuckin' best of me. I was going to get myself together and pop up on his ass and demand he give me the answers I deserved, and I wouldn't leave until I got what the hell I came for.

"Well, I don't know about you, but I feel much better." Bellamy chuckled.

"Hell yeah, I'm hype as shit right now. I'm about to take a fuckin' shower, get my shit together, and pop up on his ass, Bells! How dare he fuckin' treat me like I don't mothafuckin' matter!"

"Whoa. We back on this shit again? You don't listen, Gotti."

"I know what you said, and I don't care. What's the worst that can happen? I see him with another girl? He's already stripped me of my heart, Bells. He can't take nothin' else from me," I admitted.

She sighed. "You know what, I feel you. You on some brokenhearted girl, scorned woman, let's put Angela Basset *Waiting to Exhale* on repeat type shit. I respect that shit, but like...okay, if you gon' do the shit, make sure you're ready for whatever. Like, what's your end game?"

"Well, when he answers, I'll demand that he give me an explanation as to why he's ghosting me. Once I get that, I'll have my closure, and I'll be done."

"And what if he doesn't answer?"

"Then, I'll take that as an answer too. I've been asking the universe for a sign since he left. I guess him dodging my ass on the elevator was a sign, but I still need more. So, if he doesn't answer, then I'm done for good. I'll walk away."

"You sure?"

I nodded. "Yup. Sure as I'll ever be."

"Okay, then. Do you and let me know how it goes."

"I will. Love you, Bells."

"Love you too, Gotti."

*****

TWO HOURS LATER, I was showered and squeaky clean from head to toe. It felt good washing all the heartache and stench off me. I even felt lighter because of it. With fresh curls bouncing all over my head, makeup on my face, and designer on my back, I walked out of my apartment with my head held high. Marching straight to the elevator, I pressed the button for his floor and waited to arrive. My adrenaline was pumping so hard that I didn't have time to be nervous or think about what I was even going to say. I was just going to let whatever was supposed to happen, happen. I stepped up to his apartment door and noticed he was one of the only apartments on the hallway that didn't have a welcome mat outside his door. My balled fist collided with the door, knocking for a few seconds and then stopped. I waited and I waited. Nothing happened. I knocked for a second time. Still nothing.

"Dash, are you in there? Please just open up," I requested. "I—I just want to talk, that's all."

I sighed while resting the palm of my hand against his door. I was again hit with another deafening wave of radio silence and defeat. I asked for a sign and the universe had delivered. It was time to wipe Dashiell Graham out of my life forever.

Bellamy

As much as I was anti-Jaron, I did need him to come get the shit he'd asked me to keep at my place for him. We weren't lovers and we definitely weren't friends, so I was done doing favors for his ass. I whipped out my phone to text him when there was a knock at the door. I quickly hit send and walked over to see who had decided to show up at my spot unannounced. Jaron was the king of pop-ups, but I was for sure he wouldn't be that bold. I looked through the peephole to see no other than my sister standing on the other side of the door. My face soured. *What the hell does she want?* I thought to myself before unlocking the door for her.

"Tati, what are you doing here?" I asked with a confused look on my face.

"Well, hello to you too!" she said, while giving me the biggest eye roll she could muster up.

"I mean, hey and all that, but what's up?"

"Why you actin' funny? You got somewhere to be?"

"Actually, I do. I picked up an extra shift down at the bar tonight. I have to be at work in a few hours."

She didn't need to know I was lying through my teeth. Truthfully, I didn't want to be around her. I felt so dirty and could barely keep my eyes off her stomach. I knew the moment she started to show, my heart would shatter all over again.

"Boo! You suck! I just really wanted to talk about the baby! I mean, can you believe it? Everybody was so shocked, right?"

"Everybody was definitely shocked," I agreed.

"What do you think? Are you excited?"

"Why does it matter what I think, Tati? It's your life. Are you excited?"

She bobbed her head. "Yeah, I am. I mean, aside from the initial shock and you know, all that shit with Jaron, but I think this is going to make us stronger."

"A baby rarely ever saves a relationship, Tati. You know that, right?"

Her face soured. "I mean, why not? If we both love the baby, then we'll both have love for each other. That will only get stronger over time."

I shook my head, dead set on dropping the conversation right where she'd left it. She was more naïve than I thought, and I wasn't about to go back and forth with her stupid ass. "Okay, Tati."

"I hope it's a boy. I know he does, too."

"Do you really think y'all are going to be this one big happy family?" I blurted out, completely ignoring whatever the fuck she'd just said.

"I mean, why wouldn't we? People deserve second chances, right?"

I rolled my eyes internally. She and I both knew this was not Jaron's second or even third time. There would always be more fuckups, and Tati would give out more chances like tickets at an arcade.

"I just don't want you going into this blind."

"Blind? What am I blind about? Jaron isn't perfect, and I'm well aware of that."

"Okay, Tati. Whatever you say," I said, throwing up my hands.

"No, say whatever you feel like you need to say, Bellamy. We're both grown. Say what's on your mind."

I could feel the truth edging to the tip of my tongue. As much as I wanted my sister to know the truth, she was still my sister, and I wanted her to have a healthy pregnancy. The news I would have to share would break her mentally, which I knew wouldn't be good for her physically. I couldn't live with myself if anything happened to the baby and it was because of me. In that moment, I made the decision to hold onto my truth at least until after the baby was born.

"It's nothing. You've said it yourself, you two have had your issues and he's not perfect, but I just don't want you to think that the baby you're carrying is the magic potion to fixing something that's already broken. Baby or not, Jaron just may never be who you want him to be."

She scoffed. "Oh, I see what this is. You're jealous. I can see it so clearly now!"

I frowned. "Jealous? Okay, Tati. This is what always happens when somebody tries to keep it fuckin' real with your ass. You say you can handle it and then you turn everything around on the other person because the truth is something your fragile ass could never handle!"

"Fuck you, Bellamy! I'm sorry I'm living the life you want, but guess what, baby sister? You can't have it! You can't have my life, or my man, or my baby, and you can't be me!"

The words, *Bitch, I've had your man all up and through this very apartment*, were seconds away from flying off my lips. I clenched my jaw tight while sinking my teeth into my tongue. "How about you do us both a favor and get the fuck up out my spot, before we both say something we regret."

"I don't regret shit! You've always been a hater, Bellamy, and I don't want your hating ass anywhere near me for the rest of this pregnancy. You're a mood killing cancer, Bellamy, and I don't need you fuckin' up my shit when I can be around more positive people!"

"Good, because I could give a fuck less about you, your dumb ass relationship, or your dumb ass little family! Now get the fuck out!" I yelled.

She left in a huff and slammed my door behind her. Every time her ass came to my spot, we ended up in an argument that got her ass kicked to the curb. I just knew Tati had to be the biggest bitch in the city, if not the entire East Coast. If she knew what I'd just saved her from, she wouldn't find it so easy to disrespect me. If anybody was the mood-killing cancer, it was her. Her telling me that she didn't want me around during her pregnancy was like music to my ears. The more I could distance myself from her and Jaron, the better off all three of us would've been.

*****

A FEW DAYS LATER, Jaron was at my door ready to pick up his shit. I made sure I had Jazmine Sullivan's *Pick Up Your Feelings* playing on repeat so loud that it could be heard throughout the entire apartment. He needed to know he didn't have a friend in me.

He walked out of my bedroom with a duffel bag flung over his shoulder. "Thanks, Bellamy. For, you know, holdin' a nigga down."

"Make sure you get it all. I don't want you to think of a reason to come back," I told him.

"Damn, it's like that now?"

I scoffed. "Been like that and will be like that."

"How'd the open mic night go that I signed you up for? I'm sorry I couldn't make it...I honestly didn't know if you wanted to see me, so I stayed away."

"It was fine, and you're right, I didn't want you there," I snapped.

"Did people like the song at least?"

"I don't know, I didn't sing it."

He frowned. "You didn't? What'd you sing?"

"Why does it matter? You weren't there."

"Look, I understand that you still feel a way, but I don't know how many times I can say that I'm sorry. I never meant for shit to—"

I threw my hand up to silence him. "Save it, Jaron. What's done is done. I'm over it, and I'm over you."

"But what if I'm not over you?" he asked.

"Seems like that's some shit you need to figure out, but from the other side of that door," I said, pointing to the exit.

He looked at me with sadness in his eyes, and I quickly tore my eyes away to look at whatever commercial was playing on mute. I refused to be a weak ass bitch in front of him. He wouldn't get the satisfaction of seeing me drop another tear. As much as I loved and cared for him, I couldn't play the role of the fool any longer. I went into the shit knowing I was the side bitch, and I foolishly thought that he'd leave my own sister for me.

Jaron headed to the door and turned back to look at me one last time. "For what it's worth, I—"

I exchanged one last glance with him before swinging the door closed. "Goodbye, Jaron."

The moment the door collided, I fell to my knees in a puddle of tears. My ears were bleeding to hear what he had to say and slamming the door in his face anyway was the hardest shit I ever had to do.

*****

LATER THAT NIGHT, I was sitting in the back of a small café, waiting for my name to be called. After getting over my fear of singing at the open mic night Jaron had signed me up for, I was determined to sign up for more appearances and chances to share my talent with the world. I was going to get my name out there with or without Jaron's help. Most recently, I'd signed up to sing at the Black-owned café's amateur night competition and because of the mood I was in, I was going to sing the hell out of K. Michelle's *Can't Raise a Man*. I figured if I let it all out and left it on the stage, then I'd feel better about letting Jaron go for good.

After I stepped off the stage, I made my way over to the nearest waitress to get an order of hot lemon and lavender tea. Not long after taking my first sip, I was approached by a man with milk chocolate skin and large, pouty lips.

"Excuse me, but I just had to approach you and personally tell you how good you were up there. Best in the building tonight, hands down," he praised, before licking his soft lips.

I looked him up and down before bothering to respond. He was wearing tailor-fitted dress pants and a black button-up shirt with the first three buttons undone to show off his neck tattoo. He wore a Cartier bracelet on his right wrist and a Rolex on his left. His fresh cut complemented the diamonds shining in his ear.

"Thank you," I replied.

"You sang those words like you know her pain."

I shrugged. "Maybe I do."

He took a seat beside me. "Damn, queen. Who hurt you?"

"Nobody important."

"That's good to hear. I'm Rome, by the way," he said, extending his hand to me.

I shook it. "Bellamy."

"It's an honor to be in your presence, Bellamy. You've got pure beauty and raw talent, you don't see much of that these days."

"You talk like you've been in the music business for decades, but you don't look older than twenty-five," I told him.

He flashed me a wide smile, showing off the dimple in his left cheek. "I'm actually twenty-nine, and I've been in the music business officially for the past five years, unofficially, all my life. My father owns Complex Records."

My eyes widened with surprise. "Hold up, *the* Complex Records?" I asked for clarity.

"Yup. So like I said, I've been in the game as an official music producer and talent manager for Complex Records, and I definitely like what I saw tonight."

"Wow, I—I don't know what to say. Thank you! Thank you so much!"

"Are you working with anyone?"

"Uh, it's complicated," I groaned before shrugging my shoulders.

"I see, well, if you're interested in uncomplicating things, send me some of your music, and I'll see what I can do to get it in the right hands," he said, reaching into his shirt pocket to pull out a business card.

My eyes glazed over the matte black business card with the name Jerome Massey written in gold script. Below his name was his job title, cell number, and email. I made a mental note to do some real research when I got home, but for the time being, he seemed legit. I thought back to what Gotti said about using the song Jaron had given me, and I didn't want to block my own blessing.

"Thank you. Yes, I do have something I can send you, but please don't think I'm limited to just that. I have an entire notebook of songs I've written," I assured him.

"Oh, word, so you take this music shit real serious, huh?"

"So serious. It's all I've ever really wanted to do."

He smiled. "I feel you. Well yeah, Bellamy, send me what you've got, and we'll talk when I have something for you, sound good?"

I smiled wide. "That sounds great."

"It was nice meeting you."

I bobbed my head while still cheesing. "Yes, yes! Nice to meet you too!"

I walked out of the club with a smile so wide, I was for sure my face was stuck that way. The moment I got to my car, Jaron called. I quickly hit decline and got inside. Before I lost my nerve to pursue the opportunity Rome had dangled in front of me, I pulled out the business card he'd given me and held it like a golden ticket. I pulled up my song on my phone and emailed it to him with a smile on my face.

"Here's to new beginnings," I mumbled.

Seconds after starting the ignition, Tati called. I ignored her bipolar ass, too. If I was going to allow myself to heal and get over Jaron and all the drama he'd brought straight to my doorstep, I needed to protect my mental health first and foremost. I put the car in drive and turned off my phone to ignore any future disturbances from them both. As far as I was concerned, they could both kick fuckin' rocks.

Chapter Thirteen

Three months later.

Gotti

It had been ninety-seven days since I'd seen or heard from Dash. There were no more accidental elevator run-ins. No blacked-out Mercedes parked out front. Nothing. It was almost as if he never existed. I'd been spending most of my time applying for jobs, going on interviews, and making sure I had all my ducks in a row for graduation. Although I'd managed to defeat my depression, I was going stir crazy in my apartment alone, and I desperately needed to rebalance my space. My graduation day was rapidly approaching, and my mother had been pestering me to spend some quality time with her. Since I literally had nothing else to do, I reached out to set up a spa day.

"Well if it isn't my long-lost daughter," she answered.

I smirked, happy to hear her typical cheerful voice, although I'd been dodging her like the plague for weeks on end. "Hey, Ma."

"Hey, Gotti. What are you doing?" she asked.

"Nothing much, how's your day going?"

"Eh, I'm bogged down with work as usual, how are you today?"

"I'm okay, I was uh, wondering if you could tear yourself away from your work long enough for a spa day this week. My graduation is this weekend, and my nails and toes could use a little TLC," I confessed.

"Of course I'm down to spend time with my favorite girl.

You know I've been trying to get on your busy calendar for weeks now."

I sighed. She'd finally addressed the elephant in the room. "I know, and I'm sorry. I've just been dealing with a lot."

"A lot like what, honey?"

Not wanting to get into it, I decided to keep things as high-level as possible. "Just school stuff, career stuff. I've been trying to apply for at least seven jobs a day, while still going on interviews and follow-ups, but it's daunting."

"Something will come through, baby. Never worry about that. Just know I'm so proud that you're about to get your master's degree, and I know your father would be too, if not more than me."

The mere mention of my father made my eyes travel over to the picture of us in my living room. "Speaking of Dad, his birthday is on Friday."

"Yeah, I know. It's hard to believe it's been another year without him."

Refusing to get down, I pepped up my voice and suggested, "Let's just make a whole day out of it on Friday, then. We'll get facials, massages, manis and pedis and then go grab lunch somewhere. Then, maybe we can go visit Daddy and put fresh flowers on his grave."

"I would really love that, baby."

"Good, then it's settled. I'll see you."

*****

A FEW DAYS LATER, my mother and I were kicking off our mother-daughter day with facials, completed with cooling cucumbers over our eyelids. After my deep-tissue massage, I could feel the tension and stress I'd been carrying around roll right off me. I was less than twenty-four hours away from getting my degree, and I wasn't going to let anything or anyone get in the way of that. After our bodies had been rubbed, plucked, pricked, and rejuvenated, we hit up a soul food spot in the heart of Brooklyn and then headed to the cemetery where we laid my father to rest.

"When's the last time you stopped by here, Gotti?" my mother asked as she laid her fresh bouquet of crimson red roses across his grave.

I shook my head. "I haven't been here in months. It's like every time I think I can handle coming again, I just psych myself out and never do it."

My mother swiped her manicured nails over her slicked down ponytail before looking down at the ground and sighing. "I understand. Over the years, I've gone through my phases where there are times where I wanted to pitch a tent and sleep here just so I could feel close to him again, but then there were other times where the mere thought of coming to see this cold, hard stone just sickened me, and I refused to come," she admitted.

"Wow, Mom. I—I never knew you felt that way. Why didn't you tell me?"

"I had to be strong for you, Gotti. At least I've always tried to be. You'll always be my baby girl no matter how big you get. I've always just wanted to protect you from everything and not being able to save you from the pain of losing the best man either of us have probably ever known...I just—"

I placed my hand on her shoulder before pulling her into a tight hug. "It's okay, Mom. You've been the best. You've been the strongest. You've always been real with me, and I love you for that."

She looked at me with a half-smile across her face. "Thank you, baby. I needed that. I really did."

"Anytime, Ma!" I said, kissing her cheek.

I walked over to his grave and laid down my bouquet of roses next to my mother's before slowly brushing my hand across the top. Feeling the cool, hard stone underneath my fingertips sent a wave of emotions coursing through my body. I remember not even being able to move my body after the funeral was over. It was like my feet had been rooted into the wooden floor in the church. I couldn't wrap my head around the fact that *this* was my life now. The life of my favorite person in the world had been taken, while his murderer had gone unscathed and there was nothing me or anyone else could do about it.

My mother stepped over and placed her hand on top of mine before leading us a couple feet across the grassy area to a bench for us to sit down. She never let my hand go as she locked her eyes on the roses we'd just left and started talking.

"It never fails, you know? Every year around this time, I replay the events of that day in my head down to the second I got the phone call. He woke up late that morning; a quarter past six. We argued about whose turn it was to refill the dog's food and water bowl while we were brushing our teeth. I remember the warmth from his lips against my forehead when he kissed me before leaving the house. Not even thirty seconds after he walked out of the door, I heard the engine to his patrol car grumbling in the driveway. Twenty seconds after that, I heard his keys jingling the lock again. He'd forgotten his lunch. I knew it, though because I knew him. I was standing right there at the door with his lunchbox in my hand. His smile was different that morning. It spoke to me without a word falling from his lips...he *knew*. He knew he wasn't coming home to us that night. He just didn't have the heart to tell me.

Later that afternoon, when I was on the way back from picking up your birthday cake from the bakery, he called me. It was the middle of the day, so I knew it wasn't the typical time for his lunch break. He said he just called to tell me that he loved me and not to be upset with him because his name had gotten picked to work an additional shift that night and that he wouldn't be home to celebrate your birthday with us. Still, I could hear it in his voice. It was more than disappointment. It was more than sadness. It was the sound of a man holding it together while knowing something wasn't right in his spirit.

By the time I got the phone call that night, I already knew. He'd been preparing me for it all day. He'd been preparing us both. But no matter how much you try to prepare your mind, you can never prepare your heart for the death of someone you love..."

By the time she finished her last sentence, we were both sitting with faces drenched in tears. She was right; losing my father never got easier. In fact, the pain only seemed to intensify when a memory would randomly pop into my mind and consequently seep out of my eyes. I missed him more than anything.

Fresh tears sprang out of my eyes like a toy Jack-in the Box. "Do you know if the NYPD is still looking for the coward who killed him?" I asked.

She shook her head while dabbing her damp cheeks with the back of her hand. "They closed the case after the third year. I had the option to keep it going but your godfather insisted that it was time to just deal with the closure we had and to use those department resources to do what your father would've wanted, which was to make sure that the other bad guys on the street were brought to justice."

"I haven't spoken to my godfather in a while either. I need to reach out to him."

"Yeah, and now that you're about to get your degree, maybe you can ask him to pull a few of his strings since he's a detective now. He may have people in higher places that can help to get you where you want to be," she suggested.

I nodded. "You're right. I'll reach out to him next week after all the rage from graduation dies down."

"Sounds like a plan. Are you ready to get out of here?" she asked.

"Yeah, I'll meet you at the car. I just want a quick moment alone with Dad."

"Sure, honey. Take your time."

I walked back over to my father's grave and ran my fingers across the engraved letters of his name, Gregory Louis Evans.

"Hey, Daddy. I know it's been a long time since I've come to visit. I'm sorry about that. It's just still really hard, you know? And I don't know when or if it'll ever get easier, but uh...I just wanted to say that I'm graduating tomorrow. I'll have my master's degree in criminal justice, and I swear I'm going to do something great with it. All I ever wanted to do was make you proud—and I know you'd be proud of me following in your footsteps. Mom said that they closed your case, but I swear, I'll do whatever I can to find out who took you from us, so that your soul can fully rest in peace. All I need is a clue or a breakthrough, that's all I need."

I sighed and closed my eyes for a few seconds, knowing the window of time I had before I started to cry again was closing.

"Just know that I love you, Daddy. I'll always love you," I said before walking away.

Tati

I was four and a half months pregnant with Jaron's baby and starting to show. Ever since my impromptu announcement of my pregnancy, I'd expected for Jaron to be colder than ever towards me. Instead, I'd gotten the complete opposite. He'd been coming home more often and was even helpful around the house when I didn't have the energy to cook dinner or clean up.

"Mmm, it smells good in here," I said, walking up on him as he stood over the kitchen stove. "What are you making?"

"Spaghetti."

"It looks good."

"It's the only thing I really know how to make," he admitted, flashing his gray eyes over at me.

I smiled. Little did he know how much his efforts meant to me. He would usually just order something and go pick it up or have it delivered, but the fact that he took the time to cook a meal had me cheesing from ear to ear. I didn't know what had changed in him, but I was glad it did. Things had been better in the past three months than they'd been since the inception of our relationship.

"Do you need any help?" I asked.

"You can cut up the tomato over there if you want."

I nodded. "Okay."

I pulled out the cutting board and a knife and began to dice the tomatoes after I washed them. After cutting up the tomatoes, my shirt and leggings were covered in tomato juice and other spices.

"Gross. I'm going to go change. This new belly I'm starting to get is really getting in the way." I chuckled.

"If you're complaining of it getting in the way now, I don't know how you gon' feel in a few more months," he joked.

"Shut up! I'll be right back," I said, before heading down the hallway to the bedroom.

As soon as I pulled my shirt over my head and tossed it in the hamper with my leggings, I saw his phone light up. My heartrate quickened. Every alarm in my body began to sound off. There was the angel on my right shoulder telling me to put on a clean shirt and go back into the happy bubble I was just in minutes prior. The devil on the opposite side was drowning her out by screaming at me to check his phone before he came in looking for me or it.

I rushed over to the nightstand and picked it up. My heart dropped when I saw the message on his lock screen from an unsaved number.

"Come fuck me like you miss me."

Everything in me began to tremble. I tried to unlock his phone to see the full conversation but couldn't use face recognition, and I didn't know his passcode. I darted back over to my side of the bed to grab the iPad that I knew his cell was linked to and pulled it up on there. I stormed back into the kitchen with just my bra and panties on, red rimmed eyes, and the iPad in hand.

He turned to face me. The smile he was wearing quickly faded when he saw my face. "What's wrong, baby?"

"A 6-0-9 area code? That's Trenton, New Jersey, right? Somebody there wants you to come fuck them like you miss them, so I suppose that's why you're trying to butter me up with dinner and dick before skating out for your night cap with the next bitch, huh?" I yelled, flinging the iPad at him.

He blocked it and sent it crashing to the floor. "Yo, Tati. What the fuck!" he growled.

"I should be asking you what the fuck, Jaron! I thought we were past this bullshit! I swear, I'm done with all this shit! Every promise you made wasn't true!" I screamed, while balling up my fists and swinging at him.

Jaron caught the majority of my blows, trying to pin down my windmilling arms. "Yo, Tati! Chill the fuck out!"

"Fuck you, Jaron! Fuck you and all of your bullshit and your lies!" I let out a scream as loud as a train whistle just before lunging at him again.

He darted out of the way and shoved me back a few steps. "Calm your ass the fuck down, Tati. I don't want to put my hands on you!"

"I fuckin' dare you, nigga! Maybe that's what you wanna do, shit, you do everything else to me, why not add domestic violence to the list too? Go ahead, knock down the mother of your fuckin' child, Jaron!" I taunted him.

He pushed past me, and I pulled him back. "Get the fuck off me, Tati!"

"You ain't goin' nowhere! Tell me the fuckin' truth! Tell me who this bitch is and whatever else bullshit you gon' cook up in that fuckin' head of yours!"

"Stop comin' at me like a crazy mothafuckin' bitch, and I'll be real with you!"

I huffed, unable to catch my breath. "Be real with me? Why be real with me now? Because you got caught up? You put me in a situation where just when I was starting to trust you again, I don't."

"Look, I'm sorry."

My face soured. "You're sorry? Yeah, I bet you fuckin' are. You can't say you sorry and keep doin' the same fuckin' shit, Jaron! What the fuck is an apology if there's no action behind it? It's just words!" I yelled, exposing the pattern of his infidelity and lies.

"Look, I know you're upset right now, but shit ain't gotta get physical. Just let me get my shit, and I'll be out."

"You think I'm gon' let you leave to go run up under the next bitch? That's exactly what you want! To run away! I should've never trusted your, *for the streets* ass and those stupid fuckin' gray eyes!"

"Let's just give each other time to calm down, that's all I'm askin, Tati."

"No, we gon' talk this shit out right now! I can't believe you would do this to me!" I screamed while swiping up the same knife I'd used to dice the tomatoes with and aimed it at his stomach. There would be no more back and forth with him and no more broken promises. He was going to hear my war cry if it was the last thing he did.

"I swear to God if you keep fuckin' with me, I will gut you like a mothafuckin' fish!" I said through clenched teeth.

He lunged forward in an attempt to take the knife away from me, and I pushed the knife into him. He stumbled back into the stove, sending the boiling pot of spaghetti noodles crashing to the floor.

"Ahh!" he yelled. "T—Tati!"

I watched him hit the floor, screaming and squirming for a bit and then he stopped moving all together. I stood frozen in time as my hand slowly made its way over my mouth to muffle an echoing scream. "Oh shit. What the fuck! What the fuck did I just do!"

My hands trembled as I scrambled out of the kitchen in search of my phone. "What the fuck! What the fuck! What the fuck!" I screamed, unable to tell dream from reality.

The room began to spin as my heartbeat rocketed around inside my chest. Millions of thoughts raced through my panicked brain.

"What if he's dead?"
"I can't go to fuckin' jail!"
"What about our baby?"
"What the fuck am I going to do?"
"I have to call 9-1-1. Fuck, I can't call 9-1-1. What would they think"
"Who else can I call?"

The one and only person that came to mind was someone I hadn't spoken to in months, Bellamy. I quickly clicked her name and pressed the phone to my ear, prayerful that she'd pick up. I called three more times before she finally picked up.

"What? I'm working at the bar," she answered.

"Oh, thank God. Bells, I need you! I need you to come to my apartment right now! Things are bad! They are so, so bad!"

"What the hell is going on?"

"I just need you to get here as fast as you fuckin' can, please!" I begged.

"I thought I was a cancer that you didn't want in your life anymore."

"I know what I said, but I need you right now, Bellamy. I don't have anybody else."

"Call Jaron."

"I can't call him. It's about him. I fucked up, and I need to get here. Just please promise me you'll come," I pleaded.

Bellamy fell silent on the other end as I heard the clinking of glasses and rattling of dishes amongst the murmur of the patrons in the bar. "Let me see if I can get off. It's pretty busy in here tonight."

"Please do whatever you can. Please, Bellamy, you're my sister."

She sighed. "Okay, I'll be there in twenty."

I let out a relieved sigh. "Okay, twenty minutes. I'll see you in twenty minutes, Bells."

*****

BELLAMY ARRIVED THIRTY-TWO minutes later. I opened the door with blood on my skin and trembling hands. She walked in to see Jaron bleeding out and unconscious on the kitchen floor.

Her eyes widened with fear. "Tati, what the fuck did you do!" she screamed. "What happened?"

I walked over and picked up the iPad to show her the text message that made me snap. "I was right all along, Bellamy! He was cheating on me with some bitch in Trenton! Here's the proof!"

"Okay, and because of that you decided to stab him? Tati, what the fuck were you thinking!" she yelled at me.

"I wasn't. I—I grabbed the knife. I was angry. I was—I don't know. I didn't think he'd lunge forward and then I—I just. I—oh my God, Bellamy, what if he's dead? What if I killed him? I can't go to jail! I'll never make it! And what about my baby?"

"Did you call 9-1-1?" she asked.

I shook my head. "No. I—I didn't know what to tell them."

"What do you mean you didn't call, Tati? Look at him! He's bleeding all over your kitchen floor because of what YOU did! If you don't want to end up in jail for the rest of your life, you better try to save his!"

My eyes sparkled with tears. "What if they arrest me?"

Bellamy scrunched up her pointed nose. "Why did you call me if you weren't going to listen to anything that I fuckin' say!"

"Because you're the only one I can trust," I said, narrowing my eyes at her.

She exhaled dramatically. "Did he hit you first?"

"N—no," I admitted.

"Did he hit you at all?"

I shook my head. "No."

She looked at me with disgust in her eyes. "You're a fuckin' crazy ass bitch, Tati. I'm leaving. I don't want to be a part of any of this mess!"

I reached out and grabbed her arm. "No! You can't leave me! I need your help, Bells! I don't know what the fuck to do!"

"Call 9-1-1, Tatiyana! Come clean about what you did and pray to God he's not dead," she said coldly.

"Okay, I'll call, but when they get here we need to have the same story."

"We don't need to have nothin' because I'm leaving. I already told you that."

"You have to stay, Bellamy! You're the only person that can prove that he attacked me. Without you, it's my word against his."

"But you just said he didn't attack you at all."

My ears heard her words, but my brain was too busy cooking up a story. "We'll tell them that you were over here for dinner and saw him attack me and saw that it was self-defense. I'll tell them he has anger issues and that he's threatened me before, and finally acted on it today, so I grabbed the knife and what happened, happened."

She folded her arms tightly across her chest. "Do you fuckin' hear yourself? There's not a fuckin' mark on you, Tati! You need to tell the truth. Call the paramedics before I do and tell them exactly what I walked into," she warned.

Feeling defeated, I grabbed my phone while looking down at Jaron. "I should know how to pick 'em by now," I mumbled before pressing the nine and the one. Before I could press send, the front door flew open and dozens of men in sea of navy-blue attire and guns stormed in.

"EVERYBODY GET DOWN ON THE FUCKIN' GROUND NOW! WHERE ARE THE DRUGS? SHOW US WHERE THE DRUGS ARE!"

"Drugs? I don't know anything about any drugs! You have the wrong apartment!" I yelled.

*****

THE NIGHT ENDED with my apartment being raided for drugs, me and Bellamy in cuffs, and Jaron being rushed to the hospital. They split us up when we got to the precinct and put us in two different rooms. As much as I hoped Bellamy would have my back, we'd both said some hurtful things to each other, so I didn't know what she was liable to say when questioned.

I jumped a bit when I heard the door open. A male officer walked in and dropped a file on the table. "Hi, Miss Daniels, I'm Detective Cecil Warren. I'm here to get your statement about what happened when my team raided your apartment and found Mr. Jaron Mitchell with a stab wound in his stomach."

"Is he dead?" I asked.

"I'm not sure yet."

"I didn't mean for any of that to happen. I—I was scared," I admitted, tears sliding down my cheeks.

"Tell me what happened between you and your..."

"Boyfriend. We were making dinner and ended up getting in an argument. Things got heated, and he threatened me. He got closer to me, and he said that he would bash my face in. So, that's when I—I grabbed the knife and I—I didn't mean to. I didn't think that—I just don't want him to die."

"What did you argue about?" he asked.

"Another woman."

"You were arguing with your boyfriend about another woman, he got enraged enough to where you felt you needed to defend yourself and then you stabbed him…in self-defense?" he asked.

"Y—yes."

"Had he been abusive to you in the past?"

I shook my head. "No, only threats."

"What kind of threats?" he asked.

"You know, like threatening to put his hands on me or hurt me, and today, he finally acted on it."

He propped himself up on the edge of the steel table and looked over at me. "Were you aware of how your boyfriend made a living, Miss Daniels?"

"Yes, he produces music for artists all over, and he has a studio."

"And that's all you know about how he makes his money?"

"Should I know more?" I asked.

"So, I take it that you're not aware that Mr. Mitchell sells cocaine?"

My upturned nose crinkled in confusion. "Excuse me?"

"I'm going to keep it real with you, Miss. If he doesn't survive, you're looking at attempted murder. If he does, he can still choose to press charges against you and you could still be looking at time behind bars."

I shook my head. "I can't go to jail. I'm pregnant. I really just need all of this to go away."

"Lucky for you, we don't want you, we want him. Help us take him down or else I can't help you."

"Help you take him down? He's the father of my unborn baby," I reminded him.

"Miss Daniels, I've been in law enforcement for many years, and if there's one thing you can't do, it's bullshit me. I was nowhere near the incident, and I know exactly what happened. You found out your man was sleeping with some other woman and you got mad. You were tired. You'd had enough. You saw that knife and saw the opportunity to get him back for how he'd hurt you. You wanted him to hurt to, didn't you? Didn't you!" he yelled, slamming his fist down on the table.

"I—I..." I stammered, not knowing what to say.

"It's either him or you, Miss Daniels. And when I say that I mean it's either him or you raising your baby how you want while the other serves the sentence. It's either that or both of you in jail and a stranger raising your kid, it's your choice," he said before walking out of the room.

He left me with my thoughts and my anxiety at an all -time high. I'd never been the best liar, and I assumed that Bellamy hadn't corroborated my story, which really meant I was on my own. If I'd really killed Jaron, I knew I was done for. I'd been caught red handed. All I could do was pray he was alright.

Dash

I woke up drenched in a cold sweat. Gotti had invaded my dreams for the fourth night in a row. This time, she was pregnant and looking like she was ready to pop at any second. I tossed my head back against the pillow, staring up at the fan whooshing around and around above my head.

"You okay, baby?" Darrika asked, pressing her naked light-skinned ass against my side.

"I'm good, go back to sleep," I mumbled to her.

Darrika was a little yellow bone that had been around for the past six weeks and had no real importance to me. I only allowed her to occasionally occupy my space to pass the time. She could never be G, though. No one could. I may have had another woman in my bed, but Gotti still had full control over my heart.

Unable to find sleep again, I pulled myself out of the bed and went to take a shower. When I got out, I grabbed my phone and went into the living room to roll a blunt. I sat in silence, only hearing the flick of my lighter and the ambiance of the busy New York streets at three o'clock in the morning. There was something about living in the city that I would always love. From the sounding off of car alarms in the wee hours of the morning, to the busy streets and highways; there was nothing better. My phone lit up with a new email confirming that the gift I'd purchased would be delivered on time, which made me crack a smile.

For weeks, I'd known that G's graduation was coming up, so I'd already made arrangements to have my gift sent to her door. As much as I wanted to be there in person to see her walk across the stage and get the degree I knew she'd worked so hard for, I had to stay as far away from her as possible. If not, I didn't know what the fuck I was liable to do. Regardless, I couldn't stop myself from subtly telling her that she was still on my mind months later. I'd never been one to regret anything I'd ever done but being the one to end her father's life was something I wish I could take back. In a different world, I would've been proud to meet the man who raised the woman I was in love with.

Chapter Fourteen

Gotti

I woke up the morning of my graduation day feeling like I'd just gotten hit by a bus. The three o'clock in the morning wakeup call I received from Bellamy, asking me to bail her out of jail had thrown me for a complete loop. She'd kept me up half the morning, giving me the instant replay of everything that had gone down before crying herself to sleep on my shoulder as we sat on my couch. The annoyingly loud ringtone on my phone alarm let me know that I'd only been able to get an hour and a half worth of sleep. My hand felt around for my phone while my eyes remained shut. As soon as I had my phone in my grasp, I quickly scanned my lock screen for any text messages or social media notifications. There were several, ranging from close family members to distant high school friends congratulating me on my new degree. *A few days shy of 100 and still nothing from Dash.*

My freshly pedicured toes sunk into the plush bathroom rug as I stepped out of the shower. Drake's *Toosie Slide* was blasting through my Bluetooth speaker when Bellamy knocked on the door. I pulled the knot tighter on my robe before swinging the door open.

"It's your graduation day, bitch!" she squealed. Her voice was hoarse from crying and talking into the wee hours of the morning.

I smiled at her effort. "I can't believe the day is here. It feels like it took fucking forever."

"I bet, but you did it. I'm proud to call you my bestie!"

I outstretched my arms and pulled her into a hug. "Mmm, woah." I frowned.

"What? My pits stink?"

"Yeah, you definitely need to hit the shower before going anywhere with me."

She stepped back and tossed her left arm in the air before taking a big whiff of her underarms. "Shit, yeah that's fair," she said before lowering her arm.

The loud roar of our laughter gave the volume on the Bluetooth speaker a run for its money. I graciously gathered up my makeup and stepped out of the bathroom to let her get herself together. I was headed into the living room to get started on my makeup when I heard a knock on the door. I scurried over and cracked the door open to see a delivery man standing there with a bouquet of fresh red roses blocking his face.

"Hi," I said.

"Hi, I have a delivery for uh, Miss Golani Evans," he said.

"That's me. I'll take them, thank you."

"Where do you want me to put the rest, ma'am?" he asked.

"I'm sorry, the rest? There's more?"

"Dozens more," he said, pointing to the rows of red roses lining the hallway to my apartment door.

"Oh, my God," I said, covering my mouth, "yeah, uh, bring them in. Bring them all in," I said, waving him in.

Twenty minutes later, Bellamy stepped out of the bathroom and her eyes widened. "Uh, why does it look like the botanical gardens blew up in your apartment?"

I cheesed. "I know, right? Aren't they beautiful?"

"Yeah, but uh who the fuck are all these roses from, Gotti?"

I shrugged. "I don't know. There was no card."

"You know what that means, don't you?"

"What? You don't think, he—no, right? He wouldn't."

"Are you sure there was not one card in this sea of roses?"

"I didn't see one."

She scanned the room for a second. "Then, what the hell

is this?" she asked, swiping up a card from one of the twenty bouquets of roses surrounding us.

"Oh shit, I swear I didn't see that. I'm still tired! What does it say?"

"It says, G, *congratulations*."

"It's him," I confirmed, "it's fuckin' him."

"How do you know?"

"He's the only one that calls me G, Bells. I know it's him."

"Are you gonna reach out? You know, and say thanks or fuck you?"

"I don't know. I—I can't allow myself to think about him. Not today! He doesn't get to make today about him!" I declared. "Now, let's finish getting ready and go get me a degree!"

Between the both of us, it took over an hour to get ready from head to toe.

"You sure you got everything, Gotti? Cap?"

I nodded. "Check."

"Gown?"

"Check. Check."

"Lipstick, phone, purse, keys?"

"Quadruple check!" I told her. "Let's go!"

When we got in the car, Bryson Tiller's *Sorrows* started blasting through the speakers, and I immediately started drowning in my feelings. There was a time when I thought I'd be riding shotgun in Dash's whip as he whizzed us through traffic to get me to my graduation on time. There were times it seemed like he cared more about me furthering my education than I did. I envisioned all the cute couple pics we'd take together. He'd be holding me in his arms while I tossed my cap in the air.

"Fuck," I mumbled as I reached for the next button.

"Yeah, please change this shit. Don't nobody need to be in they feelings right now," Bellamy huffed.

I nodded. "I just want the pain to stop," I admitted. "I mean, it's not the same heart wrenching pain it was when it first happened. It's more like a dull ache, y'know? Most days, I can ignore it. I forget about it, even. But today...it's loud, Bells. It's so fuckin' loud," I said, choking back tears.

She reached over and patted my back. "I know, girl. Trust me…"

"Ugh, fuck! I don't know why I had to go and give my fuckin' heart to him! He was supposed to be a one-night stand! A blip on the fuckin' radar! Now, look at me."

"Mmhm, that's what that good wood will do to you."

I nodded. She was right as hell. Good wood was his superpower. It'd been months since I'd last felt him inside of me, and I could still feel the fire of passion burning in the pit of my stomach for that man.

"You know what you need, bitch?" she asked.

"What?"

"A good night out with a bad bitch and some good weed. Lucky for your ass, I got both," she snickered.

I rolled my eyes. "Whatever. You know I don't smoke."

"Who gives a fuck? You just graduated college…for the second fuckin' time, bitch! You need to let your hair loose and live a fuckin' little! Seize the day! Livin' la vida loca, bitch!"

I broke up with laughter. "Don't you mean, carpe diem?"

She rolled her eyes before hunching over with laughter, baring her gums. "You know what the fuck I meant! Now, all you need to do is shave those hairy ass legs of yours and get your ass in that closet and figure out what you're going to wear tonight. Oh, and make it sexy, bitch. Tonight's category is 'I'll steal your nigga,' feel me?"

I cackled. "You know what? Fuck it! You're right! I wanna shake my ass! No, I deserve to shake this ass! I'm about to get my fuckin' degree!" I yelled while honking my horn.

"Hell yeah! That's the spirit! Go on and challenge that hoe ass inner spirit, I know you got! After your graduation, we gon' go get dressed, I'ma grab my weed, and I'll be pullin' back up on your ass tonight!"

"Aight!"

"Don't bullshit me, Gotti! Getting your ass out of the house is like pulling fuckin' teeth."

"I'm not bullshittin' you. I'm going. We're going!"

"Pinky fuckin' swear it right now," she demanded while firmly sticking out her pinky finger.

I looped my pinky finger around hers and nodded. "Pinky swear, hoe! It's on tonight!"

*****

A CELEBRATION DINNER, hundreds of photo memories, and a much-needed nap later, I was inside my bedroom staring at my reflection in the full-length mirror.

"I deserve a fatter ass." I sighed.

Bellamy roared with laughter from my bed as she sealed the blunt she'd been rolling. "What the hell did you just say?"

"I'm just sayin', I follow the rules. I went to school. I'm trying to change the criminal justice system from the inside and for the right reasons. The least God could do is give me a fatter ass. I'm not talkin' about nothin' crazy, I'm just sayin' if I woke up with a little more ass tomorrow morning, He wouldn't hear a complaint from me."

She shook her head. "Are you high already?"

I chuckled. "Whatever. I'm not wearing this shit. Back to the drawing board I go," I told her while stepping out of the backless red dress I was in.

"What about the black one?"

"Which black one?"

"You know, the one with all the straps. You wore it on New Year's for your birthday," she told me.

I groaned internally. One mention of my birthday, and I immediately knew what dress she was talking about. It also happened to be the same dress I was wearing the night Dash had fucked my brains out for the first time. I couldn't wear that. It almost had sentimental value to it. I felt like a loser for even making the connection between him and a stupid dress. My ass for damn sure looked good in it.

"I see you goin' back and forth about somethin' in your

head, and I'm here to tell you to stop. Wear the dress, Gotti," Bellamy interjected before passing me the blunt.

I nodded. "The black dress it is."

*****

AN HOUR AND A HALF LATER, I was sitting on the couch in my black dress looking at the crumbs on the cushion from the edible brownie we'd consumed. Smoke hung so thick in the air that I could barely see Bellamy, and she was sitting a couple feet away from me.

"How you feeling right now?" she asked.

"Yo, I'm high as shit right now," I muttered.

I had never been that high before; I was almost afraid. I'd heard of people having bad trips off weed and shit, and I was not trying to be climbing up the walls all paranoid and shit. I had enough drama to deal with. Being high just made it seem like things were okay, if only for the moment.

I turned my head in her direction. "I got a question."

"What is it?"

"Why the fuck don't snakes have legs?" I asked.

Her forehead wrinkled as she looked at me. "Bitch, what?"

"I'm just saying!"

"Yooooo, your high ass is hilarious!" she championed, letting out a full-throated laugh.

I rolled my eyes. "That was a serious question! See, I never should've let you talk me into this shit. I should've stopped two blunts and one edible ago!"

"You high, right?"

My neck ticked to the side. "Too high. What kind of weed is this?"

"You havin' fun, right?"

I nodded. "Yeah."

"Then, it's the good kind, and I've done my job. Besides, if we never did anything we shouldn't do, we'd never feel good about doing the things we should."

I frowned. "Who the hell said that?"

"Girl, that white man on *House of Cards* made that shit up, not me." She laughed.

We were straight trippin'. They say laughter is the best medicine, and Bellamy had my side splitting open.

"If we don't hurry up and get going, I'm going to fall asleep!"

"To the kitchen we go to take a shot then!"

"Oh hell no. Ain't no way I'm gettin' drunk on top of how I already feel. I'm not trying to die tonight, B."

"One shot and that's it until we get to the club."

"Where are we goin' anyway?"

"You don't worry about that," she said while never looking up from her phone. "Boom! The Uber has been ordered and it's on its way! To the kitchen!"

Bellamy looped her arm in mine and led us into my kitchen. She poked her head in the refrigerator and pulled out the bottle of champagne Dash had brought over. I'd never bothered to open it. I'd never heard of anyone celebrating having a broken heart.

"Oh shit! Let's pop this shit open!"

I nodded. "Fuck it, do it!"

"Turn on some music for the occasion."

"I got the perfect song. Alexa, play *No Lames* by Kash Doll," I asserted.

"Yassss! Cheers to no lame ass niggas!"

"Hell yeah!"

"See, I'm tellin' you girl, we need to be on our Lori Harvey shit, aight? Fuck these niggas! A bitch is better off alone before agreeing to deal with another nigga's bullshit."

I knew her words were more of a self-reflection. The truth was, we'd both been unlucky in the love category. We needed to have one night without carrying the baggage of our past lovers on our shoulders. That shit was fuckin' heavy and it was clear we were both over it. We clinked our glasses together and let the wet champagne coat our dry throats.

*****

THE NIGHT HAD barely gotten started, and I was having a better time than I'd had in a while. Besides the fact that Bellamy had to drag me out of my comfort zone to experience it, I was finally in a good space. That is until the Uber driver pulled up to our destination. The club Bellamy had chosen just so happened to be the same club I'd met Dash in. I was immediately reminded as to why I hated going out.

"Can we go somewhere else?" I asked.

"Hell no. This club is poppin'. I always come here."

I sighed, knowing I'd lose the battle. Instead, I decided to submerge myself back into the Zen the weed had put me in if I was going to survive the rest of the night. I spent most of the night in a haze, staring at all of the people around me while Bellamy flourished in her element. She loved being the center of attention, whereas I was fine fading into the back.

"Are you ready to go yet?" I asked.

I was high as hell, and my growling stomach had enough room in it to house an entire large pepperoni pizza by itself.

"Girl, it's barely one o'clock in the morning. Shit is just starting to pop!"

"I'm so fuckin' hungry! How are you not hungry?"

"How about this, I'll buy you a shot, and you can chew it."

I rolled my eyes. "I hate you."

"Love you too," she said, blowing a kiss at me.

I began to let my eyes wander around the club again when I froze. "There's no fuckin' way..."

"You say somethin'!" Bellamy yelled over the music.

"He's here. He's fuckin' here!"

"Oh, shit! And he's comin' this way. Shit, act fuckin'

normal like you don't even see this nigga. Whatever you do, do NOT make eye contact with him. I can smell the despair pouring out of your skin right now. Hold it together," she coached.

I nodded silently while my internal thoughts thundered.

He's here.
I can't believe he's fuckin' here.

I needed to sober up. I needed to not be high anymore. The ride needed to end before I did something I'd regret. In the blink of an eye, Dash stationed himself in front of me, dark as night and sweeter than sin. It was closest we'd been to each other in months. Even through all of the mixture of scents in the enclosed space, he stood out. His scent was *that* intoxicating.

Say something!
Say anything!

Before I could draw in my next breath, he walked past me as if I were just another strange face in the crowded space. His walk was cold; callous even. He had to have seen me. He had to have known it was me. He had to have cared. Yet, with each step he took, he was putting more distance between us. Watching him walk away was like feeling my heartbreak for the second time.

"I gotta get out of here," I said in Bellamy's direction, unsure if she even heard me.

With my head low, I pushed through the mob of partygoers until I reached the crowded women's bathroom. I gripped the rim of the closest vacant porcelain sink and tried to steady my breathing. It was almost as if I'd been smothered and was seconds away from dying. My heart was thundering louder than the 808 bass vibrating the paper-thin bathroom walls. The nerve of him to just waltz back into my life after months without a warning or explanation. He didn't have the right! *He owed me.* I was going to let his ass know that I wasn't the one for his bullshit. We were both grown and too old for games. I was determined to get an explanation out of him and wasn't going to let his ass leave my sight without one. With the self-inflicted fire under my ass, I stormed out of the bathroom in search of answers. On my journey, I felt someone reach out and grab my hand, slowing me down.

"What's up, ma? Let a nigga buy you a drink."

I'm too high to cuss you out like I want to, is what I wanted to say. My mouth was just too dry to let a word slip off my tongue. I had to save every letter of every word for Dash's ears.
Before I could even open my mouth to say no, I heard a familiar voice command the attention from both of us.

"Tell your friend you good before I tell 'em," Dash whispered in my ear. *Time stopped.* The sound of his voice alone instantly lubricated my flower.

One look in Dash's eyes, and the stranger who initially wanted to buy me a drink had poofed into thin air. I frowned. "What'd you do that for?"

"Stop playing with me, G."

"Whose playing? You're the one whose been ghost for months now! At least he acted like I was worthy enough to be seen."

I turned away to point at the man who had immediately cowered away when Dash approached us. My eyes rolled as I slowly turned my neck in Dash's direction. He was staring at me as if I was the only other woman in the club. Neither of us dared to put a stop to the silence between us. I snaked my tongue out of my mouth to slowly lick my lips. *Fuck, my throat is so dry*, I thought to myself. The next song came on and without parting his lips, he gripped my hips. His strong hands felt like a love song wrapped around my body. I was seconds away from becoming a puddle on the floor. *Five...four...three...two...one.*

"Dance with me, G," he whispered in my ear.

Seconds felt like hours as they faded between us. I slowly swayed my hips to the bass, poking my ass out the moment he brushed up against me. *He's going to be the fuckin' death of me,* I whispered to myself. Halfway through the song, Dash's grip tightened around my stomach.

"Congratulations, again," he whispered against the nape of my neck.

"Thank you for the roses. I'm surprised you remembered."

"Important things never leave me, G..."

"Did it really need to be that many roses though? I think one bouquet would've sufficed."

"Twenty bouquets of roses isn't subtle?" He chuckled.

She huffed. "Look, Dash I—"

"Yo, on everything, my fault," he interjected.

I slowly shook my head. I'd almost let the feeling of him brushed up against me and my high, make me forget who the fuck I was. "You can't even say the words *I'm sorry!* You really don't give a fuck about me, do you? You were quick to tell me you wasn't into games and all you do is play 'em! Was I just a joke to you? Or was it that you just wanted something to control? Whatever it is, I'm not that type of girl," I said over my shoulder, stopping myself from fully facing him.

"You think I'm just a nigga out here thirsty for pussy? I've never come off like that, and I never tried to control you. I know you better than that."

I turned to face him, drawing back my fist, ready to drill it straight into his chest. "Bullshit! Stop with the games!"

He caught my fist, swallowing my fist inside his own. "I'm no good for you."

I frowned. "See? Control! I'm a grown ass woman! Let me be the one to make that decision for myself."

He nodded. "You're right."

"I know I am!"

"So, now what?" he asked.

"What do you mean, 'now what'?"

"I tried staying away from you, and I can't, so I'm askin' you now what?"

"I don't know. You don't get to run in and out of my life anytime you want, no matter if you think you're making the right decision for me."

"What you want us to be? And don't even say friends because a nigga could never be just your friend, G. You know that. But if you want to move on, I'll try to respect that."

I scowled. "Do I look like I've moved on? Before I agree to anything, you need to tell me why you ghosted me the way you did, Dash. I didn't deserve that shit."

"You're right, you didn't. I can tell you I'm sorry a million times and it won't make up for what I did or how I handled the situation. I'm man enough to admit that."

"Are you man enough to admit that you were a coward?" I asked.

"Chill, G."

"Tell me the truth then, Dash."

He licked his lips. "I don't want to talk about that shit right now, G. Can I just enjoy everything about you, tonight? A nigga missed you, and I never miss any fuckin' body," he confessed.

I huffed, exasperated and simply too tired to beat the dead horse any longer. It was clear I wasn't going to get the answers we both knew he owed me. Dash was a maze I hadn't mastered and probably never would.

"I missed you too," I announced.

He smirked. "How much?"

I could feel myself blushing even in the darkness of the club. All he had to do was slide his hands in between my thighs to find out just how much. I grabbed his hand and slid it in between my legs as I leaned against the bar.

Dash leaned into me as his fingertips glided against my hairless kitten. "You tryna make a nigga splatter cum all over your walls, ain't you?" he whispered in my ear.

I gasped as his thumb pressed against my throbbing clit. "D—"

"Is that what you want, G? You want daddy to cum inside you?"

I turned my head away from him, not wanting him to see me starting to lose my poker face. "You're *impossible*."

"And you're irresistible."

My teeth sunk into the cushion of my juicy bottom lip. "Walk me out?"

We walked out of the club hand-in-hand as if it was our first time meeting all over again. I quickly pulled out my cell to quickly inform Bellamy of what was about to go down via text. I was sure I'd hear about myself the next day, but that was a risk I was willing to take. Dash led us to his parked car and opened the passenger side door for me. He started the engine and put his hand on the gearshift.

"Stop," I told him.

"What's wrong?" he asked.

"I want it right now."

"G..."

"Right here, *right now*."

He killed the engine and looked at me a few seconds before letting his seat all the way back and pulling me onto his lap. His warm hands crept up my bare thighs, lifting the hem of my dress up to my stomach. The weed still had my head floating in the air like a trampoline, but there was no denying the vibration between my thighs. Dash cupped a handful of my ass in his hand as I leaned in to kiss and lick the tattoo around his throat. The rattling of his belt and the bulge in his pants let me know he was just as ready as I was. He quickly reclined his automatic seats before pulling my panties to the side and rubbed the head of his dick up and down my slit before sliding me down on top of his long, chocolate pole.

"Ahhhh!" I screamed out, gushing with ecstasy. It had never felt so good to be split in two. I slowly bucked back and forth, rocking my hips as if I was trying to put him to bed.

"Mmm, shit," he groaned, while smacking my ass.

I pressed my body tightly against the chiseled abs underneath his shirt while moaning in his ear. "Shit, I missed you."

"Mmm, did you?"

"Mmhmm," I whimpered.

"Then, wet this dick up, G, because he missed you too," he

said, thrusting upwards.

I bounced on top of him, screaming out as he gripped my waist. The repetitive sounds of my ass slapping against his thighs filled the car as the windows quickly began to fog up.

I moved my hips in cursive before switching it up and bucking forward; his rocket blasting me straight into an orgasm. "Yessss, Dash. Oooh yeah," I moaned as he pulled me up and down on his cream-covered dick.

I swear, I blinked and all I saw was unicorns, sprinkles, and other pretty shit. Between the dick and my high, I was on another planet.

"Mmm, yeah. Cum all over me. That's what I want," he commanded as he pushed my dress further up my back.

I tossed my head back, sending all of my curls cascading down my back. Dash cupped my breasts in his hand before pulling my dress over my head so that he could wrap his lips around my nipples and nibble at my sides. He tossed the top half of my body over the seat and bounced my ass up and down on him like a basketball. "Oooh shit!" I squealed as he licked his finger and slid one inside my ass.

"Mmm, you like that shit, right?"

"Mmhmm," I agreed, moaning with every stroke.

Dash and I made our way to the back seat where he buried my head into his raven-colored leather seats. He gripped the back of my neck and pushed into my guts from behind while vigorously rubbing my clit.

"Mmm, shit! You feel so good!" I squealed.

He locked his hand around my throat, snapping my neck back. "Bring me those lips," he commanded before sliding his tongue into my mouth.

"Oooh shit, I'm gonna cum!"

"That's it, baby, get every inch of this dick," he said, while pulling both my arms behind my back.

Dash drilled into me as sweat cascaded down our bodies. The moment I came, I felt his lips wrapped around my clit.

"Mmm, shit. Spit on it, baby."

He obliged before slurping his lips against my flower.

"Oooh shit, yes, get it nice and wet," I growled.

He flipped me over onto my back and tossed my legs up to the roof of his car. I spread my legs wide and grabbed my ankles. My body jerked with pleasure as my abs crunched forward. I tightened my grip on the passenger headrest, feeling myself about to cum.

"Yes! Yes! Yessss! Keep doing that right there!" I squealed, flicking my nipple with my thumb.

He refused to let up on my clit until I came. By the time I'd ridden out my climax, I was stuttering with my head hanging off the backseat. While waiting for me to catch my breath, Dash started planting kisses on the indent of my waist and sucking on my thighs for so long, I was sure he'd given me thigh hickeys.

He climbed on top of me and wrapped both his hands around my throat before pulling my lips onto his. My legs spread from the back window to the front seat, welcoming him back inside my warmth. Dash grabbed hold of my right foot and popped it out of my heel to suck my toes. I jerked, completely not expecting him to do that, but it felt so good. The car was filled light squeals and silent mouth gaping gasps as Dash leaned in close to me.

"Open your eyes and look at me, G. I want you to look at me when you cum," he said, fucking me faster and deeper.

I popped open my eyes to see him staring me in the face. I pressed my lips against his, sucking the traces of weed and my personal juices off his bottom lip. I enveloped his neck in my arms, tearing my nails into the tats on his back.

His body shook. "Mmm, goddamn you feel good. Got a nigga about to cum, G," he whispered in my ear.

I imprisoned his waist in my legs and held on for the final part of the ride. Nobody had ever put it on me like he did, and he made sure I remembered that with every stroke.

"Take me home," I mumbled against his lips.

*****

I WOKE UP the next morning with Dash staring right at me. The scent of his Tom Ford cologne still lingered in between my sheets. Conscious of my morning breath, I quickly tossed my hand in front of my mouth before speaking. "Good morning."

Instead of greeting me back, his forehead furrowed even deeper. He turned his back to me and swung his feet onto the rug.

"What's wrong?" I quizzed.

Somewhere deep down inside, I knew things between us still weren't right, but I was determined to push those thoughts to the basement of my mind for the moment. I was just glad to be back in his company. Dash was a beautiful creature; definitely a one-of-a-kind nigga with limited edition dick. The way he looked at me gave me goosebumps. I loved it. It was as if I was his. Like what we had between us was a forever thing. I'd never had anyone make me feel safe by just looking at them besides my father.

"You were right last night, G. There is something I need to tell you about why I fell out the way the way I did."

I sat up fully, resting my back against my headboard. "What is it?" I crawled up behind him and wrapped my arms around his neck. Dash removed my hands as he turned to face me. His heart was visibly in his throat.

"I respect honesty, Dash, I always will...just keep it real with me."

"What if the truth is going to hurt you more than anything?"

I frowned, not immediately knowing how to reply. "Whatever you have to tell me, I'll listen, Dash. Just tell me."

Dread flashed in his eyes and sadness clouded his features as he stared at me, which told me whatever words were about to fall off his lips next, weren't going to be good. They were going to break me; break us. I needed to prepare my heart for impact.

My mind began to race through a rolodex of all the possible scenarios that could come out of his mouth. *Did he get somebody pregnant? What if he's married? Is he going back to jail?*

"It was me," he said.

My eyebrows creased in confusion. "What? I don't understand. What was you?"

"It was me, G. I'm the one who killed your father..."

A long draw in of breath filled my lungs with the oxygen they desperately needed. I couldn't believe my treacherous ears. At that moment, two wives, a set of project twins on the side, and a life sentence would've been easier to digest.

"What the fuck did you just say?" I mumbled.

"Just hear me out, G."

"No! Say what the fuck you just said! Are you joking with me? Do you think this type of shit is funny!" I yelled.

There was no way I'd been yoked together with the man who'd killed my father. There was no fuckin' way Dash could be the man responsible for putting a smile on my face and breaking my heart at the same time.

"This isn't a joke, G. I know I just told you some crazy shit, but I just want the chance to explain myself. *Please*...it's been a long time since I said that word."

"Hear you out? Hear you out? You just told me you fuckin' took the life of the ONLY man I've ever loved besides YOU! And you want me to hear you out? Get the f—"

"G!"

"Fuck you! Did you know who I was from the very beginning? Was this some sort of sick fuckin' game to you? All that shit you were talkin' about with your hate for the police, I should've known then!"

"It was never like that. I didn't know you had anything to do with my past until I saw the picture of him in your apartment."

"The same fuckin' night you ghosted me?! So instead of being a man and telling me then, you let me suffer for months! Months, Dash! Had me thinkin' I was the fuckin' problem, and for what? Huh?"

All I could see was red. My heart rained tears, instantly turning itself into ice. He'd gone from a God to the Devil reincarnate in my eyes.

"Get the fuck out of my apartment! I never want to see your ass again!" I screamed, pushing him as far away from me as possible.

He grabbed hold of my swinging arms. "You don't mean that."

"Like hell I don't. Stay the fuck away from me, Dash, or I swear to God, I'll kill you myself!" I screamed before shoving my body into his chest with all of my might in hopes that he'd let my arms go.

"Let me fuckin' go! I should call the police on your ass right now! I swear to God if you don't let me go, that's exactly what I'm gon' do!"

Dash didn't utter a word. Instead, he looked into my tear-stained eyes and slowly lowered my arms down to my sides. I watched him grab his phone and shove it into his pocket before he stepped out of my bedroom and made his way to the front door. The moment I heard the door click behind him, I let out an ear-piercing scream. My knees crashed down to the floor, and I doubled over in tears. I felt like I'd been sleeping with the Devil. I was worse than dirty. I was disgusting. I was filthy. I was broken. I'd done the unspeakable; committed the ultimate betrayal. How could I have not known? There wasn't enough marijuana or alcohol to pull me from the jaws of my feelings. I was instantly submerged in a muddle of emotions and back into my depressive state all over again.

Chapter Fifteen

Dash

A week passed, and I still couldn't believe I'd told her *the truth.* They say if you loved something, let it go. If it comes back, cool, if it doesn't, you had no business with it in the first place. I knew G would never come back to me, and there was nothing I could do to change that. I'd been doing my best with trying to give her the space she needed to digest the news and process it however she wanted to, but I was afraid that if I gave her too much space, she'd forget all about me. I let three days pass before I started reaching out through texts and phone calls, hoping for a chance to explain myself. All my calls were sent to voicemail, and I received two long paragraph texts, basically telling me to stay away before she had me sent back to jail and to stay the fuck away from her. It didn't take long after that for me to figure out she'd blocked me. Oh how the tables had turned. Not so long ago it was her blowing me up, and now I was the one sweating her.

I stepped off the elevator on G's floor and headed down to her apartment. I knew I was taking a risk by showing up unexpectedly, but I didn't give a fuck if she had the President of the United States in there with her, I had to tell her everything.

My knuckle collided with her cold door. "Yo, G, open the door," I said, pressing my ear against the door.

I could hear the TV blaring on the other side. She was home. All she had to do was answer the door, so I knocked again. "G, don't make me cause a scene outside your shit."

She swung open the door with haste. "What the fuck do you want?"

"I just need you to hear me out," I said, blocking her doorway so she couldn't slam the door in my face.

"I don't want to hear a fucking thing you have to say to me because there isn't anything you can say that will change how I feel about you. I hate you."

"You don't mean that."

"Don't tell me what I don't mean. I trusted you! Y—you said you wouldn't hurt me and you ripped my heart out of my fuckin' chest. So if I didn't already make myself clear, get the fuck away from my door before I call the cops on your black ass!"

"Listen, all I want to do is explain to you what happened so you know the full story. After that, I'm gone."

"You have three minutes," she said, folding her arms across her chest.

"Can I come inside?"

She looked me up and down. "No. Now, talk."

"Aight, listen, we were there to meet up with a dirty cop. We'd been paying him to be our eyes and ears on the other side of the law. The nigga had been slacking, so we were cutting ties with him when another cop showed up with his gun out. Shots were fired, and then my boy got hit. All I was trying to do was get us both out of there alive. I fired shots at the dirty fuckin' cop, and the other cop got in the way. As soon as I got in the car, I sped off and didn't look back. The bullets I shot were never meant for your father, G. I swear to God if I could take it back, I would. I swear, I didn't know he was your father when I met you. I found out the night I saw that picture over there in your living room."

"And you just decided it was a better idea to ghost me for over three months, fucking me and then coming clean to me about the fuckin' coward you are!"

"I only told you the truth because I love you, G. If I didn't, I could've continued to lie to you for the rest of my life, but that ain't the type of nigga I'm tryna be. This was some shit I thought I'd take to my fuckin' grave. Never in a million years did I think the daughter of the man I killed would be the woman I gave my heart to."

"What did you just say?"

"I said I fuckin' love you, G," I proclaimed.

Checkmate. I was done. She had me. G was the queen of my heart and the type of woman you didn't meet twice. No man walking on earth could do anything to me. If I'd lost her for good, I wouldn't have anything left.

"So, what did you end up doing time for? Someone else's murder?" she asked sarcastically, completely disregarding what I'd just told her.

I huffed. "We got picked up soon after, and I went down for some drug shit."

"And who did you say you were there to meet the night my father..."

"Some dirty ass fuckin' cop."

"Name?"

"Cecil Warren," I told her.

Her eyes widened with fear as she frowned and stared past me. "And how many shots did you say you fired?" she asked.

"Three, why?"

She paused. I could see a million thoughts racing through her head before she snapped back to the present. "Nothing, it's nothing."

"G, did you hear what I said? I said I love you."

"I heard you, Dash."

"And?" I asked. It was as if her ears were immune to flattery.

"And what?"

"You don't have anything to say about that?"

She grumbled. "You killed my father on *my birthday* of all days, and now you're here telling me that although you did that shit, none of it should matter because you love me? Get the fuck outta here!"

I sucked my teeth. She was letting her emotions drown out her better judgment. "I'm not saying it shouldn't matter to you, I'm saying that I did it, and I can't take it back, but I'm still here tryna be everything you want me to be. I wanna be with you, G. I wanna love you. I wanna protect you."

"Protect me? And who's going to protect me from you, huh?"

I clenched my jaw tight. "Cut it out, G. You know who I am."

"I don't know shit about you. Everything I thought I knew about the man you are was wrong!"

"I know it's gon' take time for you to forgive me, and I'll spend every day for the rest of my life proving you wrong about the type of nigga you think I am. I love you and as much as I'm trying not to, I still fuckin' do. If you think I'ma give up on you, you're wrong. You're going to be my wife, Gotti," I said before walking away.

I never regretted anything in my life until meeting Golani Evans. Once I got a hit, I started to question everything I thought I knew about women, love, and myself. The hard exterior I portrayed on the outside was nothing compared to what I was feeling on the inside. I was sick without G by my side. I knew all of this would happen if she ever found out, and I foolishly told her ass anyway, breaking both our hearts in the process. As much as I wanted to avoid seeing the tears falling from her eyes and the betrayed look across her face, I couldn't look her in the eyes everyday knowing I was lying straight to her face. So if Gotti knowing the truth meant that she'd never be mine again, I'd have to take that loss. I'd seen a lot of shit in the streets, but I was certain that a broken heart would kill you faster than a speeding bullet.

Bellamy

"Don't act like you not happy to hear a nigga's voice!" Jaron's voice bellowed on the other end of the phone.

My heart plummeted to the soles of my feet, skipping beats on the way down. He must've crossed my mind a thousand times since the night I saw him bleeding out in the middle of his kitchen floor. I didn't know whether to be grateful he was alive or mad that he had gotten me wrapped up in all his mess in the first place. Regardless of the reason, I'd accepted the charges anyway and there we were.

I sucked my teeth. *Whatever.* "What do you want, and why are you calling me? We don't have anything to discuss," I informed him, with my game face on and poppin'.

The night Tati handed me the iPad, my eyes burned with rage. Jaron was nothing but a liar. He'd been lying to Tati, me, and God knows how many other women across the tri-state area. Although he was a liar, I didn't want to be caught up in my crazy ass sister's drama as an accessory to murder either, so I needed to play nice.

"Look, can we talk? In person. I want you to come see me."

"If it's that important, you should just say what you have to say now, Jaron, because I'm not coming to see you."

"I respect that."

"Do you? Because if you did, you never would've dialed my number in the first place."

"You answered though, right? Any why is that? Because you still fuck with a nigga, that's why."

"Even behind bars you're still as arrogant as ever," I told him.

"But am I wrong?"

"She showed me the iPad, Jaron. You were lying to me just like you were lying to her. Why would I ever want anything to do with you?"

"Because you're the only one that gets me, Bellamy. I knew

it from the first day I met you. You can't tell me you didn't feel that shit too."

"None of that matters anymore. You've got a kid on the way with a woman who literally almost stabbed you to death. I would have to be the stupidest person alive to go down this road any further with you."

"Crazy in love," he said, before belting out a chuckle.

"Nah, that's all Tati."

"Speaking of Tati, I'm pressing charges. Your sister is going to jail, Bellamy."

My eyes widened. That was one of the last things I expected to hear fly out of his mouth. "You're really going to send the mother of your unborn child to jail, Jaron? I mean I'm not saying she should've did what she did, but you're alive, and now I think it's clear that you both know that your relationship is toxic and that it's better to be apart."

"You think she'll really stay away from me while she's carrying my kid, Bellamy? She either wants me, or she don't want nobody else to fuckin' have me. She gotta go to jail. That's the only way I'll be sure things are done between us."

"What about the baby?"

"What about it?"

"Jaron..."

"Look, I'll raise the baby one hundred percent by myself if I have to. I'm just not doing shit else with her."

"You would be a single father and raise your kid alone?" I asked, hearing my voice soften in the process.

"I'll do what I gotta do for my seed, but I'm done with your sister."

I rolled my eyes. "You've said that before."

"I know, but I really mean that shit this time. She already tried to take my life. What else do I have to lose? And once she's out of our lives, and I'm out of here, maybe you and I could pick up where we left off."

"You've said that before too. You're like a fuckin' broken record, Jaron. All you do is talk the same shit over and over. So no, I don't believe you. Sorry, not sorry."

I heard him sigh heavily into the receiver. He'd shown me exactly who he was way too many times for me not to believe him, yet there was still a small piece inside me that wanted to believe him. Maybe he was a product of his environment that would be different if he was around something different, or maybe he was just a dog ass nigga.

"You have sixty seconds remaining," the operator chimed in.

"Look, Bellamy, you're the one I want, whether you believe it or not. And when I get outta here, you're the first one I'm coming to see."

"Yeah, but will I ever be the only?" I retorted. Before he could formulate a response, the call ended.

I lowered the phone from my ear and tossed it on the couch. It was the first time I really didn't feel much of anything when it came to Jaron. If anything, our conversation felt like all the ones we'd had in the past. I decided it was in my best interest to push any thoughts of him to the back of my mind and focus on the task at hand, cleaning my apartment. I glanced into the kitchen and saw my Swiffer mop and Clorox wipes staring back at me.

"Fuck," I groaned before turning on my music and getting to work.

*****

MARY J. BLIGE'S VOICE bellowed through my Bluetooth speaker as I sang alongside her while cleaning out my hall closet. I tossed bags of old jackets and shoes out into the hallway, determined to send them all to Goodwill without bothering to sort through them. In the midst of cleaning, I found a flash drive laying in the back of my closet where Jaron used to have his bags stashed. I swiped it up and put it on the kitchen countertop next to my laptop before continuing to clean. Twenty minutes later, I was mopping the kitchen floor. With half the floor left to go, I glanced over at the flash drive on top of the laptop, and my curiosity finally piqued. I leaned the mop against the refrigerator before sliding the flash drive into my laptop. Seconds after I hit play, I heard a thudding bang against my front door.

"Who the fuck is knocking like they the damn police?" I grumbled before walking over to answer the door.

I swung it open to see Gotti standing there, looking like a sad puppy. As soon as she flashed her glossy eyes up at me, tears sprang out. I pulled her into a hug. "Girl, what the fuck is going on?"

"I'm sorry for the waterworks. Did I catch you at a bad time?" she sniffled.

"I'm just taking a little break from cleaning. There's still a toilet and a shower back there that need scrubbin' if you wanna lend a hand," I said, hip-bumping her.

"I didn't come to clean, Bells. I came to vent. My life has literally blown up in my face recently, and I think I'm going crazy," she confessed before heading over to the couch.

"What the hell is going on, Gotti? And before you start, do I need to roll a blunt first?" I asked.

"Roll two," she said, plopping down.

"Damn, girl. Okay, okay. I'll be right back."

I came back out with a blunt in one hand and my stash box in the other. After plopping down right beside her and sparking up, I turned to face her. "So, what's up?" I asked, crossing my legs Indian style.

"It's about Dash."

"Mmm, I was waiting on this. I thought you were done with him."

"I was...and then I saw him the night of my graduation at the club and then the next morning, he dropped fuckin' Hiroshima down on me."

"What did he say? He got another bitch pregnant or somethin'?"

She smacked her watermelon pink lips. "No."

213

"Then, what?"

Her eyes sparkled with tears. "He killed my father, Bellamy."

My eyes widened as I began to cough repeatedly. "What the fuck did you just say, Golani Evans?"

"You heard me right. The man I fell in love with was the one who killed my father."

"Why the fuck would he say something like that? Was he joking? Was he—"

"He was telling the truth, Bells. He told me everything that went down the night it happened."

"It's like I wanna know what happened, but then I respect if it's too painful for you to talk about."

She shrugged. "Thank you."

"So, how do you feel? I mean, this shit is crazy as hell, Gotti."

"I don't know. After he told me what happened, he apologized and then he told me he loved me."

"Oh fuck," I said, passing her the blunt.

She shook her head and pushed it away. "Nah, I'm good."

"So, what did you do? Did you say it back?"

"Hell no, I didn't say it back. I can't love him anymore. Not after knowing what I know."

"You and I both know hearts don't work that way," I reminded her.

She huffed. "I won't lie, after my father had been killed, I wanted revenge for a long time. Jail time wasn't good enough. I wanted him dead, you know? Take one life for the other, but now that I'm finally able to put a face to the man that...I don't know what I want to do. Do I kill him? Do I turn him in? Do I let him live with the guilt alone for the rest of his life and completely push him to the back of my mind?"

"Girl, that's completely up to you, but I'm gon' support you whether you decide to fall back into his arms and run off into the fuckin' sunset or send his ass to jail for the rest of his life."

"Ugh!" she screamed. "It's so fucking annoying because it's

like he just wanted me to jump into his arms and forget about everything he said and everything he did. I need validation of my emotions, not flattery and apologies!"

"So, you don't believe he's sorry?"

"I don't know what to believe anymore," she admitted.

"You think that if he had the chance to go back and do it all over again, he would change what he did?"

Her shoulders hunched forward. "He says he would."

"Then, maybe you should believe him."

"Would you?"

I shrugged, unsure of my answer. "I don't know. All I know is, some people deserve second chances, and others don't."

"I just feel like going back to him is the ultimate betrayal to my father, you know?"

"How? It's not like you knew who he was from the beginning. There's no way you would've known something like that, and if he hadn't decided to say anything, then you still would be crazy in love with him right now."

"So, you're on his side now, Bells?"

"Hell no! What he did was fucked up. You have the right to feel however you feel about that, but all I'm saying is, he came to you and told you the truth when he didn't have to. I'd rather Dash be an honest sinner than a lying hypocrite like Jaron, who will try and finesse his way out of a situation only after he's gotten caught up in some shit. I just think that should count for something when you're deciding whatever you want to do."

She sighed before burying her face in the palms of her hands. "How can I hate somebody and love them at the same time?"

I completely knew the feeling. Love was a burden that neither of us wanted. "Girl, if I knew the answer to that, I'd be the richest bitch on the planet. But at the end of the day, your father would want you to be happy, Gotti. And if Dash makes you happy then..."

"You know what makes me happy? Chocolate. Chocolate makes me happy. It doesn't ask questions. It doesn't break my heart. Chocolate is the only fuckin' thing that understands me."

I was high as hell, and I was sure she'd caught a contact or something talking crazy like that. A laugh belted out of my mouth. "Girl, what the fuck? You gotta be high."

She smiled. "Maybe I am a little high. That shit you got is strong as fuck."

"That's how I like it." I cheesed.

"So, what's been going on with you since the whole Tati and Jaron thing? Have you spoken to either of them since?"

"He called today from jail."

"Saying what?" she asked.

"Talkin' 'bout he's going to end things with Tati and that he's going to press charges."

"Oh shit!"

"As much as I do want them to be done with each other for the good of the fuckin' universe and shit, I did try to convince him not to press charges. I may not like the bitch, but I don't want to see her pregnant and locked up. That's not a good look."

"Yeah, not at all. But um, do you believe him when he says he's done with her? And if she does go to jail, will that change things for you?"

"I've been trying not to think about that exact shit all day," I admitted, "but everything is complicated now. More complicated than it was before."

"I just don't understand why he dragged it on this long. Like, how hard is it to fuckin' say, *'Yo, I don't wanna be with you anymore?'* It's not like he's married to her."

I sighed. "I know. I've asked that question a trillion times."

"If it's one thing my mom always told me, it was no matter how much you think you can change a man, you can't. The only two things that can change a man are God or himself, and you'd be a fool to put your money on the second option."

"So, you think God changed Dash?" I asked.

She pressed her lips together tight, pausing for a few seconds. Shrugging her shoulders, she said, "Maybe I'm a fool."

I sighed. We were back to being love sick puppies all over

again. "Phew! This shit is gettin' way too heavy. You sure you don't wanna hit this shit?" I asked, offering her my blunt again.

She shook her head. "Nah, I'm tryna get a job, girl. My graduation has passed and it's really crunch time now."

"I feel you. Go ahead and be responsible and shit. I respect it. But as for me and my house, we will smoke the weed." I giggled.

"I will admit that I am feeling better than I was after seeing Dash again. I still can't believe that nigga told me he loved me."

I sucked my teeth. "Like, don't tell me you love me, nigga. Tell me you're outside with pizza and a blunt!"

"The next nigga that approach me, I'ma tell his ass I'm in a committed relationship with tacos and walk the fuck away."

We both burst out laughing, which drastically uplifted the mood in the room. I tossed my head back against the couch, and my eyes landed on the laptop sitting on the kitchen counter. "Oh shit, I almost forgot. I was cleaning out my closet when I found something."

"What?"

I jumped up and grabbed my laptop to bring it back over to Gotti. "It was a flash drive."

"What's on it?"

I shrugged. "I don't know yet. I had just started watching it when you showed up. It was in the back of my closet where Jaron had his stuff."

"Jaron had his shit here, Bellamy?! You never told me that."

I huffed. "Because it wasn't a big deal. It was just a couple of bags. I never touched them and now they're gone, but this was left behind."

"Well, are you going to finish watching it? I'm curious now."

"Fine, let's see what's on it. Knowing that nigga, it's probably a sex tape with some random bitch."

Gotti cringed. "Oh God, I hope not."

"We're about to find out."

I pressed play on the video. It soon became clear that we were watching the footage from the night Jaron had gotten robbed. We saw two cars pull up, exchange words and a package, and then drive off. After Jaron pulled up, one of the previous cars pulled back up and started jumping him. It matched everything he told me when he came over after it happened.

"Oh, my God, is—is that Jaron?" Gotti asked.

"Yeah, that's him."

"Rewind it really quick." I pushed the back button and brought it back to the beginning. "Pause it right there!"

"What?"

"Oh my God, I—I know that man right there," she said, pointing at the man, who was driving an unmarked car and was seen handing over a package to the driver of a blacked out sedan.

"Who is it?"

"He's my godfather...he's a detective, Bellamy."

I frowned. "You don't think he had something to do with Jaron's robbery, do you?"

"I don't know why he would, but this is the second time this week I'm starting to question his motives."

"What do you mean?" I asked. "What's going on?"

"I'm starting to think he had a lot more to do with my father's death than I thought."

"You think he knows it was Dash?"

"I don't know, but I'm going to find out. Can I take this flash drive?"

"I—I don't know. What are you going to do with it? Should I tell Jaron I found it if he calls back?"

"No, don't say anything. I'll take care of it, I promise. I just need to hold onto it," she told me.

I sighed before pulling the flash drive out of the port. I could see the wheels turning in her brain. She was calculating her next move right in front of me. "Okay, here," I said, handing it to her.

Gotti

I left Bellamy's apartment more conflicted than I was when I got there. My conversation with Dash had been playing over and over in my head for days. And after seeing my godfather on the surveillance footage doing some shady shit, I didn't know what to think about him or the night my father was killed. For years, I'd been hanging to his every word about what happened that night, but with Dash's recollection, it was clear things didn't add up. I didn't remember all the minute details of the case; since I was younger, my mother decided it was best to keep me away from as much of it as she could so that I could have a "normal" life. But one thing I remembered for sure was that my father suffered from *four* gunshot wounds, not three. My godfather was also the one who encouraged my mother not to keep the investigation open, and Dash had called him out by name as doing business that went against the law he was supposed to uphold.

As soon as I got into my car, I pulled out my phone to call my godfather, or Uncle Cecil, as I had him saved in my phone. The phone rang four times before he picked up. I could hear the ringing of multiple phone lines and murmurs of various conversations in the background.

"Hey, there. Long time no speak!"

"Hey, Uncle Cecil. How are you?"

"I'm good. I've been missing you. I'm sorry I wasn't able to make it to your graduation. I've been swamped with case after case."

"So uh, speaking of work, are you down at the precinct now by chance? I was hoping I could drop by and talk."

"Talk? Talk about what, Golani?"

"Well, now that I have graduated, I've been trying to land a job and nothing has come through yet, so I was hoping that maybe you could um—"

"Say no more, I'd be happy to put in a word for you. How about this, come on down and when you get here, I'll treat you to lunch, and we can talk job stuff."

I smiled. "Okay, sure. I'll uh, I'll be there in thirty."

*****

MY GODFATHER AND I met up at the small diner a half a block away from the precinct. He flashed me a warm smile before pulling me into his arms. "Look at you!"

I smiled back. It had been close to a year since we'd seen each other. Between school and dealing with my own shit, I rarely found the time to check-in with him. The patches of gray hairs sprinkled across his head and beard showed he'd aged a bit more. I could see the tiredness in his chocolate brown eyes as we took a seat at a booth and started to look over the menu.

"Good afternoon folks, what can I get ya?" the middle-aged waitress asked while pulling out her pen and pad.

"Yeah, uh. Let me get the uh, Reuben with a side of fries and a sweet tea."

She quickly jotted down his request before turning to me. "And I'll have the bacon cheeseburger with a side salad and a sweet tea as well," I told her.

After she walked away, I found myself staring at the large clock on the far wall shaped like a black cat. The tail swung from side to side as I watched the long hand make its way over to the five, while the shorthand was settled onto the number twelve. The bells on the door jingled against the glass as two more patrons entered the establishment, taking their seats at the counter.

"So, you wanted to talk to me about a job, right? What are you looking to do?"

"Change the world," I told him.

He chuckled. "I've always admired your spunk, Golani, but I'm going to need you to be a little more specific."

"Well, to be honest, I think I might be starting to consider law school, but I just need a break for like a year or two, and I wanna get in the field. So, at this point, I just need something that pays the bills and something that's really going to give me the experience that I want and need."

"Following in the footsteps of your father," he said.

I nodded. "Yeah, I guess I am."

"Well, I'd be happy to help in any way that I can. Send me your resume, and I'll pass it along to a few of my connections, and we'll see what happens. Sound good?"

"Yeah, that sounds great, thank you! Because I seriously don't know how many more interviews I can go on. I'm feeling burnt out."

"It's okay to take a break once in a while. You're always running and doing something and never taking the time out to just breathe before you're hit with something else, right?"

I blew out a long breath. "Yeah, that's exactly how I feel."

"I know because I'm the same way," he said, reaching out to place his hand on top of mine.

I looked up into his eyes and remembered seeing his face on the surveillance video. Chills instantly ran through my spine as I slowly pulled my hand away from his. "Look, Uncle Cecil, I've got to be honest with you. I didn't call you to just talk about helping me find a job."

We both turned our attention to the waitress as she sat our plates down in front of us. "Thank you," we said in unison.

"Let me know if y'all need anything else. I'll be back to check on you in a few," she said.

"So, what else did you want to talk to me about?" he asked, before shoving a French fry in his mouth.

I slid my straw into my glass of sweet, iced tea and took a long sip. "What if I told you I knew who killed my father?"

"Gotti, we've gone over this a hundred times. We both know it was some low life hoodlums that got away."

"His name is Dashiell Graham, and I want you to arrest him," I blurted out.

His eyes widened. "How do you know him?"

"That's not important."

"Like hell it isn't. You need to stay away from him! Promise me you'll stay away from him!"

"How do you know him?" I asked, testing him to see how he would react. His responses had made it clear that he knew more than he was letting onto.

"I know the names of a lot of criminals, and his has come across my desk on multiple occasions throughout the year. Now, you need to tell me how you know him, Golani."

"We were…friends."

"Friends?"

"Yeah, and he told me that he did it."

"He told you that he killed Greg?"

"Yes, and I want him to spend the rest of his life in jail for it."

He wiped his mouth with his paper napkin. "Gotti, I wish it was that simple, but it's not."

"How is it not? He confessed. Arrest him, and I'll testify to it."

"What else did he tell you about that night?"

"Nothing. He only told me what I just told you. So, are you going to arrest him or not?"

"Like I said, it's not that simple."

"Why isn't it?"

"Golani, I—you're an adult now, and I think it's time you knew the truth about your father."

"The truth? What don't I know?"

Once again, he reached out to grab my hand. "Dashiell Graham didn't kill your father."

"What? Why would he lie to me about something like that?"

"I'm your father, Golani. Your *real* father."

My limbs started to fail me as I sat paralyzed in place. "W—

what did you just say?"

"It's the truth."

"How long have you known?"

"All your life. I've always wanted to tell you, but your mother wanted to keep it a secret, especially after Greg's death. She just thought it was best to keep things how they were, so out of respect for her, I obliged."

"Out of respect for her? What about your respect for my father? Where was your respect for him?"

"Golani, what your mother and I have, is special and it's complicated, and it's—"

"Hold up, have? As in presently still going on?"

"Yes," he admitted.

"But you're married! I—I grew up with your sons and treated them like cousins. I—no. No! There's no way! You're lying!" I said, pushing myself out of the booth seat.

"Gotti, it's the truth! I know it may be a lot to take in, but I am your biological father. I've played the background long enough, and now I really do want us to have the relationship we should've always had."

As much as I didn't want to make a scene, I could feel people staring at the tears pushing out of my eyes. Suddenly, it felt like the walls were closing in on me, and I couldn't hear anything else he had to say. Without saying another word, I swiped up my purse and ran out of the diner.

*****

MY FIST COLLIDED with my mother's front door, rattling the spring-themed wreath hanging over it. She quickly swung open the door with her cell phone attached to her ear and tears in her eyes. It was obvious he'd gotten to her before I did.

"She's here, Cecil. I have to go," she said before ending the call. "Come in, Gotti."

I walked in, and the smell of the apple cinnamon candle she had lit wafted past my nose. "Sit down, baby."

"I'll stand. It's obvious you know why I'm here, so…"

"What do you want to know?"

"Tell me the truth! For once! Someone tell me the fuckin' truth!" I screamed.

"I never wanted you to find out like this, Gotti. I—I just thought it was best if you—"

"If I what? Died never knowing the truth about who my real father was? How could you lie to me all of these years? Every year I cried over him, mourned over him—and you just…"

"I'm sorry, baby. I—I thought what I was doing was best. I loved you father with all my heart. He was good to me, and I knew he would be an amazing father to you."

"And yet you cheated on him with his best friend!"

"What Cecil and I have, it's complicated. It's always been complicated. We first met when I was working in records management down at the precinct. I loved him first, but he was married to Cathleen. I spent a lot of years chasing him, being his second choice, and I got tired. I got tired of waiting around and hoping and wishing, so I moved on. I'd just started seeing your father when I found out I was pregnant with you. I knew you weren't his, but I also knew that Cecil wouldn't leave Cathleen because she was due with his twins. I didn't want to be a single mother, and I knew your father was interested in me, so I did what I thought was best for everyone involved. So, although Gregory wasn't my first choice, he was the *best* choice."

"So, you set him up to think that I was his daughter when you knew the truth from the very beginning. Wow, you're disgusting!"

"Gotti, please just forgive me. I'm sorry for lying to you all these years, and I'm sorry I chose not to tell you. I just never wanted to see the look on your face that you have right now!"

I shook my head while staring silently at the candle flames dancing against the wicks. She'd betrayed my father and our family. There was nothing she could say to justify what she'd done or reverse the trauma she'd caused. I didn't know if I'd ever forgive her for that. I pushed out a long sigh.

"How many times was my dad shot?"

She frowned. "What? Um, four times."

"And where were the bullet wounds?"

"Why does any of this matter right now, Gotti?"

"Because it does, so just tell me!" I demanded.

"One was in his leg, two in his right shoulder, and the other in his chest."

Once again, the room started to spin. "A—and his wounds, were they all something he could heal from?"

She sighed. "I—I don't know. The autopsy report said that he died from the bullet in his chest and out of the four gunshot wounds he sustained, it was the last one."

I cupped my hand over my mouth. "Oh, my God."

"What? What's wrong, Gotti?"

"Were the bullets all from the same gun?"

Her brows hinged together. "What is going on that's got you suddenly so interested in the details of your father's death? You've never wanted to talk about it before."

"What? I always wanted to talk about Dad, but you never wanted to and now I see why! If you're not going to tell me the truth, then at least give me the report so I can read for myself."

"It's been years, Gotti. I don't even know where I'd look for something like that. But, no. The bullets weren't from the same gun, but that's because there were two assailants there that night that got away."

"It all makes sense now."

She wore a mask of confusion on her face as she reached out to grab my wrists. "Gotti, what are you talking about?"

"The fact that they never caught who got it, the fact that Dash went to jail in the first place, and the fact that he got you to call off the investigation into what really happened to him that night!" I yelled, snatching my arms away from her.

"Dash? Who is Dash? Gotti, slow down. You're talking too

fast, I can barely keep up!"

"Let me make it simple for you, Mom! Your lover killed my father!"

She shot her worried eyes down to her feet. "W—what? Why would he do that? He would never do that!"

"He killed him because Dad found out that he was doing some dirty shit. He was probably going to stop him, and he put a bullet in him to make sure that nobody ever found out! That's the man you fell in love with! A fuckin' murderer! Are you happy now? My father's death is on your hands! You're going to have to live with that for the rest of your life!" I berated her.

"You don't think I know that?!" she yelled back. "You have no ideas the secrets I've kept or the amount of skeletons in my closet, Golani, but everything I did—everything I've always done is for you!"

"Bullshit! Everything you did was for yourself and you know it," I told her before storming toward the front door.

"Golani Marie Evans, sit down!" she demanded.

"No! I'm done with your lies! I'm done with you!"

"Sit down, and I'll tell you the truth. The *real* truth," she confessed.

I stomped back over to the couch and plonked down onto it. "Fine, I'm sitting."

"The ballistics report showed that three of the bullets were from one gun and one was from another."

My eyes widened. "Y—you knew? You knew this whole time, and you didn't say anything?"

"Listen to me, Gotti, if it was as simple as telling you the truth, all those years ago I would have, but it's not. Am I proud about the role I played in it all? No, but I just wanted to protect us."

"Your role? What do you mean your role? What did you do?" Her cryptic language wasn't doing anything but annoying me more.

"I deleted the ballistics report because it showed the different bullets used at the scene, the gun model, when it was fired, how your father was positioned when he was shot, everything that could've taken Cecil down for what he'd done, but he was just trying to protect us."

"Protect us from what?"

"The night that your father was killed, Cecil was the one who caught him dealing with some bad guys. It wasn't the other way around, Gotti. When he confronted him about it, he aimed his gun, and Cecil did what he had to do. If anybody ever found out that Cecil really did it, he'd have to turn your father in and tell what he knew. We would've lost his pension, life insurance, everything. How was I going to afford to put you through college or make sure you continued to live comfortably? So, Cecil and I did what we thought was best for you, Gotti. Everything has always been for you," she affirmed.

"No, he manipulated you! He's been manipulating you for my entire life. You were just too stupid in love to see it."

He'd been using her for years, ordering her steps to cover his tracks. There was no telling how many others were involved to help cover my father's death, but one thing was for sure, Dash didn't kill my father. He would've lived from the wounds he suffered from Dash's gun. It was the bullet to the chest from my *"Uncle"* Cecil that ended things. I was exhausted but wired. I was unable to pause my brain or turn off the revolving thoughts of Dash or the overload of information that had been dumped on me. I had to reach out to Dash and tell him the truth.

Chapter Sixteen

Dash

Seeing Gotti's name and picture pop up on my phone was a welcomed surprise. I quickly swiped to accept the call and heard her sobbing on the other end as soon as I put the phone up to my ear.

"Hello? What's wrong, G?"

"I—I need to see you right now."

"Where you at? I'll come straight to you."

"How soon can you get to Prospect Park?"

"What you doin' at Prospect Park?"

"I'm just trying to clear my head and there's something I really need to talk to you about, Dash. Can you please just come?" she requested.

"Yeah, I'll be there in twenty," I told her.

As soon as I laid my eyes on Gotti, I immediately gave her a once-over, assessing her mood from afar. She had a flutter in her step and a tucked lip with weary, swollen eyes.

"Thank you for meeting me," she sniffled. "Sorry, I feel like all I've been doing today is crying."

"Tell me what's wrong, G."

"There's something I need to tell you. Something that is probably going to change your life forever."

I straightened my posture while positioning myself in front of her. "I'm listening."

"Do you remember the cop's name that you met with the night my father was killed?"

"Yeah, Cecil Warren. What about that dirty mothafucka?"

"One thing I didn't tell you when you first told me his name is that he's my godfather, Dash."

I clumped my eyebrows together in confusion. "What?"

"And I went to him to try and get you arrested for killing my father. I told him I was willing to testify and everything."

As I stood in front of her, my mouth instantly went dry as my heart cartwheeled in my chest. I knew she'd probably hate me for the rest of her life for what I'd done, but I never thought she'd take it to the next level to try and get me sent back to jail.

"So, did you ask me here to meet you to watch me get arrested?" I asked coarsely, widening my stance.

She shook her head as I looked over my shoulder at the people walking by. "No, because you didn't kill my father, Dashiell."

"What? What do you mean?"

Gotti let out a long sigh before leaning her head back in an attempt to stop the tears from sprinting down her cheeks. "After I told him I'd testify, he kept feeding me bullshit about how complicated things were and then out of nowhere, he decided it was the perfect time to tell me that not only did you not kill my father, but that he's my actual biological fuckin' dad."

I grimaced. "Goddamn, G."

"Oh wait, it gets better. So, I go to my mom for answers, and she confirms everything and tells me that she knew that my godfather was actually the person who killed my father and that she helped cover it up by deleting evidence! My entire life has turned into some reality fuckin' TV script overnight, and I just can't—the betrayal...it cuts so, so deep," she bawled.

"After I told you what I did, what made you dig deeper to find out the truth?" I asked.

"You told me you shot your gun three times. My father was shot *four* times, Dash. All the shots that he sustained from your gun, he would've survived from. It was the bullet to the chest that killed him."

"I remember him yelling out that he'd been undercover, trying to say whatever he could to save his own ass. Cecil fuckin' got caught up and silenced your pops to make sure his own shit didn't blow up in his face. Your father didn't deserve that shit, G."

"I don't know what pisses me off more, that my mother lied to my father all these years about me and her secret life with this man, or the fact that she willingly helped cover up her own husband's murder. How could she be so stupid to help him? He's been lying to her for years, telling her the exact opposite of what really happened that night and feeding her bullshit to help him cover up his mess!" she fumed, swiping tears out of her vision.

"People do stupid shit for love all the time," I told her.

She vigorously shook her head. "Love or not, I don't want anything to do with either of them anymore. I'm washing my hands with everyone. My whole life is based off a lie, Dash. I don't even know who I am or whose I am anymore."

I wrapped my arms around her and to my surprise, she didn't try to push me away or put up a fight. Instead, she embedded herself into my arms deeper. "They'll get what's coming to them, especially him," I warned, "and you're mine, G. I already told you that."

"I swear I'm going to make sure everyone knows who he really is. And if that takes my mother down, too then so be it. I'm so fuckin' tired of the lies. I don't think I've ever been this emotionally drained in my entire life."

"What exactly is your plan to take him down?"

"I have proof that he's dirty."

"What kind of proof?"

She sat up to reach inside her purse and pull out a flash drive. "This is proof that Cecil is a dirty fuckin' fraud. He's on here handing off something to some guys and then those same guys come back and rob someone outside of a studio."

"Outside of a studio?" I asked, as Jaron instantly came to mind.

"Yeah."

"And when was this?"

"I don't know the exact date. I'd have to watch it again."

"I wanna see what's on it, too. Because if it's what I think it is, then I'm pretty sure Cecil orchestrated the whole fuckin' thing."

"But why? What did he have to gain out of someone getting robbed?" she quizzed.

"A hell of a lot. We've been fuckin' with that nigga for a long time, and he's always trying to stir some shit up. I wouldn't be surprised if he tried to put one brother against the other and use that shit as leverage for his own personal gain. He's a dirty, greedy mothafucka, G, and you need to promise me you'll stay away from him," I warned her.

She scoffed. "He said the same thing about you."

"Well, now you know which one of us you can actually trust. Let me hold onto it, watch it, and then I'll get it back to you."

"I think I should hold onto it. We can go back to my place and watch it, but I'm not letting this out of my sight."

"Aight, that's cool."

As relieved as I was to hear the news that I really didn't take the life of her father, my blood was still boiling after finding out how long Cecil had been playing us. For years, he'd been threatening to drop our names in connection to Gotti's father's murder and lining his pockets in the process while knowing he was the one who pulled the trigger in the end. Because of him and his lies, I carried guilt and grief that wasn't mine to carry for years, and I almost lost the only person who meant everything to me because of it. I'd stayed off his ass long enough and his time had run out. Cecil Warren had to die. The readjustment of Gotti's head against my chest brought me back into the moment, and I had to ask the question that was burning the tip of my tongue. "So, what does this mean for you and me?"

She shrugged her shoulders before giving me an answer. "I honestly don't know. Emotionally, I'm all over the place, and I just don't want to—"

"Fuck all that other shit, G. I love you."

"Dash, I love you, too, I just—"

"If we love each other, then fuck everything and everybody else, G. It's just you and me against the world."

She shot her eyes up at me, studying my face in silence for a few seconds. "*If* I decide to do this with you again, it's got to be for real this time, Dash. No more ghosting each other, no more tit for tat or petty games. We have to promise that we'll always be up front with one another and always tell the truth, no matter how much it hurts."

I flashed her a warm smile. "Anything you want, I got you."

*****

THE MOMENT I stepped into Devil's presence, I could smell the blood in the water. After watching the video inside G's apartment and recording it on my phone, I sent it straight to Devil. He called immediately, and we set up a time to go to the jail and talk to Jaron about everything that had gone down with the raid of his apartment.

"You comin' in?" I asked as we pulled up to the jail.

"Nah, you go talk to that mothafucka. I don't want to see his fuckin' face."

"Why not? I thought we wanted to figure out what the fuck happened," I reminded him.

His wide nostrils flared. "I changed my fuckin' mind. I gave that nigga chance after chance, and he keep spittin' in my face. He's not a kid no more, and he damn sure ain't got our fuckin' bitch ass father protectin' him no more. That mothafucka wanna be a gangsta so bad and look at the fuckin' mess he made. And who gotta clean that shit up? Huh? Me!"

"Nigga, chill, you beastin' right now," I said while unhooking my seatbelt, "just chill, I got you."

*****

I FOUND MYSELF zoning in and out of my conversation

with Jaron as he sat across from me with the receiver up to his ear.

"That's when the crazy bitch stabbed me, nigga! And when I woke up, a nigga was fuckin' cuffed to a hospital bed. I don't know what they got when they raided my shit or what they know," he confessed.

"Do you know who's on the case?"

"I don't know shit. Once the doctor cleared me, they transported me from the hospital straight here, and I've just been keepin' my head down ever since. I haven't met with anybody yet. No lawyer, no nothin'."

"And you not gon' say shit when the time comes?" I quizzed.

His neck swiftly turned from side to side. "Nah, never, but listen," he said, leaning in closer to the screen. "I need to get out of here. You talked to Devil? Is he gon' help get me a good lawyer?"

Already knowing the answer, I shook my head. "I don't know. How you doin' in here? Anybody fuckin' with you?"

"Nah. I'm good. I can handle myself if it comes down to it," he assured me.

The bitch in his voice and the hand tremors he was trying to hide, said different. He wasn't cut out for the life he was living. Raking in the money was all fun and games until a nigga had to sit down and do his time. There was no telling what he would say if the cops dangled immunity in his face.

"Aight, bet."

"Talk to him for me, Dash."

I gave him the okay as I stood to my feet. "Yeah, I will."

When I got back to the car, Devil was about to light a fresh blunt, which hopefully would calm him down. "What that nigga say?" he asked before flicking his lighter.

"He said he's not gon' talk."

"Bullshit. How'd he look?"

"Scared," I admitted.

"Exactly, nigga. I don't trust that mothafucka."

"He wanted me to talk to you about helping him get a lawyer."

Devil clenched his jaw. "You talkin' to me now and the answer is fuck that nigga. That nigga hates me more than he loves himself, and that's word to my dead nigga. He's gotta be handled before his musical ass starts singin' like a canary. If I go down, then we all go down. And you already said you ain't goin' back."

"I'm not."

"So, we need to do what we need to do to make sure we go home to the people we love. Fuck everybody else."

"You don't trust your own blood that much?"

He puffed his blunt a few more times before passing it to me as we hit the highway. "I already told you, if he takes me down, everything we've worked for over the years will be for nothin'. The nigga ain't cut out for this street shit. The moment the fuckin' cops start talkin' greasy to him, it's over and you know it. I don't trust shit a mothafucka say, ever, especially when it comes to my money. Business is business, family or not."

I shook my head, knowing not to go against Devil's decision. The feds had a hand around his throat and if it came down to him going home to his kids or giving his brother the benefit of the doubt, he wasn't going to bet his last on Jaron. A little sibling rivalry never hurt nobody, unless you were the Mitchell boys. Devil and Jaron may have grown up under the same roof, but they lived two totally different lives. Justin and I had been boys since we were twelve years old, and it didn't take long for me to figure out that he had a better chance of surviving on the streets than he did living under the same roof as his father. Out of the two of them, Jaron was always favored, while Justin was always called a demon and abused daily. So, instead of rebelling against it and trying to prove his parents wrong, he hit the streets at fifteen and submerged himself in the game. He took on the name *Devil* to remind niggas of just how bad he really was and never looked back. Devil had made it clear that his mind was made up and that Jaron's fate had been sealed. People would do anything out of desperation if they thought they didn't have nothin' else to lose. Silencing Jaron was Devil's way of making sure his brother didn't fuck him over first.

"So, what you wanna do about him?" I questioned.

He passed me the blunt. "I know you just got home from school, nigga. I wouldn't ask you to get your hands dirty like this. I just want you to know what my decision is. I'ma have him handled on the inside. We get him out the way and you have my word we'll deal with Cecil Warren's bitch ass next."

Just hearing the name Cecil Warren made my blood run hot. There was a special place in hell reserved for his ass.

"I told you I didn't trust that mothafucka years ago, and now I'ma handle his ass. I want that nigga to bleed," I professed.

I was too focused on my own get back to figure out when Gotti would decide just how she'd get her revenge by blowing up Cecil's career. There was a part of me that wondered if she would hate me for the rest of my life when she found out I was going to kill her biological father, but my hatred for him ran just as deep as hers. She and the world were better off without him. I was going to take that nigga out execution style. No mercy, no fucks given.

Jaron

It had been a few days since I'd seen Dash and had a conversation with him, and I still hadn't heard anything about a lawyer. From the moment I was brought into the jail, I was on high alert. Watching my back became a full-time job, and I *needed* Devil to come through for me and get me a good lawyer to beat whatever the cops were trying to throw at me. If all I had to rely on was a public defender who didn't give a fuck whether I walked free or not, then I was fucked.

"Lunchtime, inmate. Let's go!" the overweight

correctional officer yelled into my cell.

I dragged my feet, heading into the cafeteria only to see a stack of blue lunch trays piled high and a long line ahead of me. I grabbed a plastic spork just before slop was plopped onto each of the sections on my tray. At the end of the line, I had a choice of a choice of unsweetened tea or two percent milk. As much as I didn't want to eat or drink anything, I had to keep my strength up. I cast my eyes out onto the sea of inmates, searching for an open seat at one of the octagon-shaped tables. The moment I started walking in the direction of a seat, one of the inmates brushed past me, bumping my shoulder so hard that it knocked my tray out of my hand. My jumpsuit was instantly covered in different hues of brown and red slop trying to pass itself off as chili.

"C'mon, man, what the fuck?" I griped while swiping my tray off the floor.

He snickered. "Better hold on a lil' tighter next time, snitch."

All the muscles in my body seemed to tense up at once as I snarled at him. His sleeves were rolled up to his elbows, and he was clenching his jaw as tightly as I was.

"What the fuck did you just call me!" I roared. My fist balled up in rage. The tighter I held it, the more it began to tingle with numbness.

"You heard what the fuck I said, snitch. Ain't that what your lil' light-skinned ass is, a snitch?"

"Fuck you, nigga, I ain't no snitch! Everywhere I go, my face good!"

"Not in here, pretty boy. I'll have a snitch like you cleaning the soles of my shoes with your tongue by the end of the week if I want you to."

"I already told you, I ain't no fuckin' snitch. Who the fuck told you that shit?"

"That's the word on the street," he told me.

"Well, the streets are always talkin', you just gotta be smart enough to know who to listen to."

His forehead caved with wrinkles. "You callin' me stupid, mothafucka?"

"I'm just sayin' you can't believe everything you hear in the streets," I replied, trying to diffuse the situation before it went any further. In that moment, I could hear my father's voice in the back of my head saying, *'You always want to offer your enemy peace first. Give them a chance to surrender on your terms. Violence is always secondary.'*

"Do you know who the fuck I am?" he growled.

"I don't give a fuck who you are. You need to step the fuck outta my way before I wash you in front of all these mothafuckas in here!" I barked back.

I looked around at all the angry faces staring back at me. There were correctional officers at each exit, but there were far less of them than there were of us. There was nowhere for me to run and nobody to come to my rescue, so I had to stand my ground and fight. I tracked his gaze as he charged towards me. I gripped the side of the lunch tray as tight as I could and swung fast and hard across his face, snapping his nose in two.

"Ahhhh, fuck!" he yelled, while holding his nose to stop himself from leaking blood all over the floor.

"Yeah, mothafucka. What's good?"

When it came to an ass whooping, there were no rules, no code, and no referee. All that mattered was the win and changing the narrative of my name throughout the jail walls. If niggas were gon' talk about me, I couldn't have them thinking I was a snitch, especially when I never said anything to anyone.

He quickly retaliated, landing a blow to my chest. I brought a fist to his face, staining it with his blood. His neck flayed backwards like tree limbs caught in the wind. He staggered backwards before lunging forward and jabbing me in the ribs. His fists opened and closed rhythmically, but every time he swung at my face, he missed. I gained enough strength to charge forward and wrestle him down into a headlock before a swarm of guards pulled us apart.

"Don't you ever fuckin' disrespect me, nigga!" I yelled as

the guards wrestled me down so that my face lay flush against the sticky cafeteria floor. "Hold up—what the f—what the fuck are you doin, nigga?"

"Devil says hi," one said before jabbing me in the side three times with a knife.

*****

MY EYES CRACKED open, and I blinked rapidly, trying to clear the blur from my vision. After noticing the beeping heart monitor to my right, the cold steel bedrails, and scratchy, bleached bedspread laying over me, I knew I was back in the hospital. I'd been on the verge of death on two different occasions and survived both times. I had no idea why God kept showing me favor, but I was not about to waste my life anymore. I was going to go after exactly what I wanted and fuck anybody who was in my way.

I reached out and found the call button for the nurse. The second I shifted my body to the right, I winced in pain. I couldn't believe my own brother had gotten a fuckin' guard to stab me after I'd asked for his help to get me out in the first place. If this was his plan to get me out of the way, then he was no brother of mine. Impatient, I pressed the call button once more, needing some pain medication so that I could rest and try to figure out my next move. The door creaked open and instead of the nurse I expected to see, there was an older black man standing there with a white button-up shirt, slacks, and a shiny badge clipped to his hip with a holstered gun on the other.

"Hello, Jaron."

I grimaced. "You don't look like no nurse to me."

"I'm Detective Cecil Warren. How are you feeling?"

"I feel like I got hit in the side by a fuckin' Mack truck, other than that I'm good."

I glanced up at him, and immediately felt like I'd seen him before, but I couldn't place him. To be in his late-forties or early fifties, he was still in good shape, and had a full head of hair. I could tell by the way he walked that he'd had his fair share of bitches back in the day.

"Lucky for you, the doctors say the knife didn't pierce any vital organs. Do you remember anything about the attack?"

I shrugged my bruised left shoulder, careful not to move the right side of my body too much. "Niggas is gon' be niggas. Some words were exchanged and boom," I said nonchalantly.

"Seems like you have more enemies than friends these days, Mr. Mitchell. Do you know who may have ordered the hit on your life?"

I shrugged my bruised shoulder. "What makes you think it was a hit? Maybe it was just some shit that happens in jail. You treat niggas like animals long enough and sooner or later, they'll start actin' like 'em."

He shot a sly grin my way before walking over to place his attention on whatever was goin' on outside of my window. He kept his hands in his pockets as if he was cold or had something to hide. What I wasn't about to tell him was that it was my own flesh and blood who'd ordered the attack. I wasn't going to make shit easy for him.

"We raided your apartment and your vehicle, Jaron, and found your stash of drugs and money. And then not so long after, you end up in here? Do you know what that tells me?"

"What?"

"That somebody wants you quiet. Somebody like your supplier, perhaps. Give me a name."

"I don't have a name, and even if I did, I ain't no snitch," I reminded him.

"You have options. There's witness protection, there's—"

"You think witness protection is gonna save me? You're askin' me to testify against my— I ain't no snitch, aight? If he ever found out, he'd kill me."

"Looks like he may have already tried."

"Yeah, well next time, I'm sure he won't miss."

"He won't unless you help me help you. Don't you wanna be around to see that baby of yours grow up? You know, I tried to get your baby mama to flip on you, but she wouldn't help me. I'm hoping you're smarter than she was."

"How does me helpin' you help me at all? I'm dead either way."

"Tell me who your supplier is, and I'll get you immunity, witness protection, anything you need."

Just the mere mention of Tati made the reality sunk in that I had a baby on the way with a crazy ass bitch. I was stuck between a rock and a hard place. I wanted to be there for my seed, and I didn't want to go back to jail, but a snitch was a snitch for life. I would have to skip town if I opened my mouth. "I need money," I declared.

"That may be able to be arranged."

"I don't need maybe's, I need a definite yes. You're asking me to commit suicide, and if I gotta do that, then you and your whole department gon' pay up."

He snorted. "I don't think you're in the position to be making any demands, Mr. Mitchell."

Something hadn't been sitting right with me from the moment he stepped into my room. It wasn't until I turned and caught his reflection in the bathroom mirror that I was able to study his face for a few seconds and realize where I'd seen him before.

"Actually, I think I am. You see, when you first walked in here, I knew I'd seen you somewhere before," I mumbled, pointing my index finger in his direction.

"Excuse me?"

"You were on the surveillance footage handing over money to the niggas that robbed me for everything I had! You were behind that shit the entire time, weren't you? But why?" I confronted him, playing the only card I had left in my hand.

His face was unreadable. There was no fear in his eyes and no invitational smirk across his lips. Something told me he was banking on me making a mistake so that he could take me down and wipe my chance at immunity right off the table.

"Listen, Jaron. It's your brother, Justin, that I want, not

you. He's the big fish in this scenario. Help me bring him to his knees."

"My brother? What do you want with my brother?"

"Cut the shit, alright? I know he's your supplier. I know everything about his operation, I just need someone not chicken shit to testify! For some reason, all my potential witnesses keep going missing. Do you know anything about that?"

"I ain't sayin' shit until I get my money," I repeated.

"I can get you $10,000."

"$10,000? I can't get out of town with that shit. I want $100,000 cash, or I ain't sayin' shit."

He flexed his jaw muscle. "Give me your word that you'll testify against your brother and his entire organization, and you'll walk out of here a free man. That's more than enough."

"I'll walk out of here a free man and you'll pay me what I want, or I'll take that surveillance footage and turn it in right to all your fuckin' fellow cops. Then, we'll see how much you're respected when you're behind bars with all the mothafuckas you put there," I warned, "those are my conditions."

"$50,000," he bartered.

"Fine. You give me the money, and you can have the USB with the footage on it and my testimony against my brother. How soon can I get discharged and get the money?"

"I'll draw up the informant paperwork and get everything in motion and work with the doctors to see if you're good enough to get discharged. The moment they give you the greenlight and you give me the footage, we can make sure you're on your way to your new life by tonight as long as we have a deal."

"It's that simple?" I questioned, frowning at him.

"Yes, it's *that* simple. Do we have a deal, Mr. Mitchell?"

I looked his non-trustworthy ass up and down before willingly extending my hand to make an alliance with a snake. "We have a deal."

He left, and my mind immediately started running overtime. The truth was, since my spot had been raided, I didn't know what was still there or what wasn't. All I could do was hope and pray that the only leverage I had wasn't gone. I slowly reached over to pull the phone to me to try and call Bellamy. To my surprise, since I was still technically in police custody, I couldn't make any outbound calls from my room. As soon as I got out and was able to get cleaned up, I was going to go straight to Bellamy to ask her to leave the city with me and also find that USB so I could get paid.

Bellamy

I swung open my front door to see Jaron standing there. My nose immediately recognized the Gucci Guilty cologne radiating off his skin.

He smiled with bright eyes. "Hey, you."

"Hey yourself. What are you doing here, Jaron?"

"What I tell you was gon' happen when I got out? I told you I was comin' to see you, right? Well, here I am."

"Are you serious right now?" I asked, rolling my eyes.

"You actin' like you hate a nigga, Bells. You hate me?"

I sucked my teeth. "Jaron."

"Aight, listen, yes I'm serious about doing what I told you I'd do."

"And what's that?"

"It's over between me and Tati. She tried to kill me, and yeah, she's the mother of my unborn child, but that's not a good enough excuse. I'm done with her."

"Good for you, Jaron, but what does any of that have to do with me? All that drama that you're tied to, that's not my thing. Never has been, never will be."

"And I respect that, and that's why I'm here to ask you to

leave the city with me, tonight."

My eyes widened with surprise. "Leave the city? Jaron, you just got out of jail. Can you even leave the state?

"Trust me, I'm good. I can come and go as I please."

"Jaron, this is a lot all at once. I—"

"Leave with me, Bells. We can start a new life on the West Coast. We can do music. We can launch your career. We can finally be free to be together the way we always wanted to. Please, just come with me. You're the only good thing I have in my life."

"What about your unborn baby?" I asked. Sure, he could leave my sister, but could he turn his back on his own flesh and blood? And if he chose to do that, he wasn't the type of man I needed to be with.

Jaron sighed. "I'ma be honest, aight? I—I haven't thought all the kinks out, but I promise I'll make it work. I swear on that. I just want it to be me and you alone, even if it's for a few days. Ain't nobody ever held me down like you have, and I need you by my side," he said, before stepping forward to kiss me.

I was unable to open my eyes even seconds after his lips left mine. I could still feel the softness of his lips on mine as each of his words tugged at my heartstrings. He always knew exactly what to say. The two of us met by chance, and the chemistry between us was undeniable from the second we locked eyes with each other. I would've been a complete fool to let the smooth-skinned, gray-eyed tall, athletic man pass me by. It was clear that I had his heart, and he had every piece of me, and that was all that mattered.

"I hate you so much," I said, pulling him back into another kiss.

"Mmm, I love you, too."

"What did you say?"

"You heard me, Bells. I ain't been doin' shit but thinkin'

when I was locked away, and you were the only one I thought about each and every day. Remember when I told you that you were the one I wanted to be with and you asked me if you were the only one? The answer is yes. You're the only one I want to be with. And to prove that to you, I got you something."

I smacked my cherry red lips. "And what's that? Another song or something?" I asked.

"Nah," he said, pulling a ring box out of his pocket.

My eyes widened. "Jaron, that better not be what I think it is."

"I guess that depends on what you think it is."

He opened the box and there was nothing inside. I frowned. "What the hell, Jaron?"

"I wanna buy a ring, but I don't know your size, so this is me promising you that when we touch down wherever we're going, we gon' go to the jewelry store and we gon' fill this box, Bells. I promise you that."

I looked into his sensual gray eyes, knowing it would never really be a goodbye between us. If I accepted his impromptu proposal, I knew was going to miss Gotti and my family, some more than others. But I would've been completely fine skipping out on more of Mama's Sunday dinners if it meant I got to live out the fairytale I'd created in my head. Ring on my finger or not, I was ready to trade in my last name to become Mrs. Jaron Mitchell.

"When are we leaving?" I asked.

A wide smile spread across his face. "Tonight. Just give me a few hours to get my shit from my spot, get the money together and we out, just you and me."

"Are you going to come back here?"

"No, meet me at the Delta terminal at LaGuardia in three hours."

"What if Tati is home? I don't want you going over there. What if she tries to attack you again? Are you going to tell her that you're pressing charges?" I asked, bombarding him with question after question.

"I'm not tellin' her crazy ass shit. I'm just going to get my clothes and shit."

"Shit? What shit?"

"Remember when I had you stash some of my shit for a little while?" he asked.

"Yeah."

"There was a USB flash drive mixed in with my stuff, and it's real important that I find it."

"What's so important about it? What was on it?" I asked, already knowing the answer.

"It's the only leverage I have to make sure we get our new life."

"Leverage against who?"

"This dirty ass fuckin' detective. I got proof on that drive that ties him to some shady shit, so in exchange for the footage, he's gon' pay up."

"You're extorting a fuckin' cop, Jaron?!" I asked as an army of butterflies swarmed my stomach.

He reached out to grab my hands. "I gotta do what I gotta do to make sure we good on money and get the fuck outta here. I want you by my side, Bells."

"Okay." I nodded. "I'll be there."

He flashed a warm smile. "Good. Make sure you put a smile on that face, aight? You know a nigga love to see you smilin', Bells."

Just his words alone had me cheesing like a kid in a candy store. "Okay, okay. I'll see you later. Be careful, Jaron. I love you."

"Love you, too," he said before turning to leave.

I let out a loud huff as I let my back crash against the door. My phone dinged from the couch. I walked over and swiped it up, opening an email from Jerome Massey from Complex Records. It had been months since I'd sent him my song and it had been crickets ever since. I figured he was all talk and nothing more, but the email he'd sent proved different.

Bellamy,

My apologies for taking so long to reach out to you. I just got around to listening to your song, and I love it. Your voice sounds amazing in person and on a record. I really feel like we can do something big together. Respond back if you're interested, and I'll connect you with my assistant to set up a time for us to meet and discuss next steps with your music career.

Talk soon,

Rome

I could barely believe my eyes. As excited as I was about the opportunity that had been presented, I had more pressing shit to handle. Not only did I have to pack up half my life in a limited amount of time, but I also had to call Gotti and get that flash drive back before I met up with Jaron at the airport. That flash drive was the key to my happily ever after with Jaron. I closed the email and made a mental note to myself to respond when I got to the airport or once Jaron and I landed at our next destination.

Chapter Seventeen

Gotti

I was on my way home from dropping off a package at the post office that was addressed to the police precinct where Cecil worked, when Bellamy called.

"Hello?" I answered.

"Gotti, what are you doing?!"

"Sitting in traffic. What about you?" I asked.

"Packing!"

"Packing? Where you going?"

"I don't know, and I don't care, but Jaron and I are—"

"Hold up," I said, cutting her off, "Jaron?"

"He proposed, Gotti."

My eyes widened. "He what!? With an actual ring or was it one of those hypothetical proposals? Like, do is there a picture of the ring on your finger you can send me?"

"I don't have one yet," she admitted.

"What? Then, how the hell are you engaged?" I asked, quickly realizing my tone was coming off more judgmental than I'd originally planned, but she needed to hear the stupidity in her words.

"We are starting fresh, leaving tonight and grabbing a ring once we touch down."

"Touch down where though, Bells? You really don't have any idea as to where you're running off to with him?"

"Who knows and who gives a fuck? All I know is we're meeting at LaGuardia and that I can finally kiss the bullshit job at Sephora and bartending goodbye, ride off into the sunset with my man, and finally put my everything into this music. I think it's romantic. Like, it's perfect. For the first time in forever, shit is literally perfect for me, Gotti. Or it at least it can be…I need you to meet me somewhere and bring the flash drive I gave you."

My eyes widened. "The drive? What do you need that for?"

"It's not me that needs it, it's Jaron."

"What does he need it for, Bells? Tell me the truth."

She let out a long sigh. "He says he needs it to get money from your godfather, Bells. He's not a good man."

"I know," I told her.

"So, do you have it? Where can we meet up?"

"I'm sorry, Bells, but I don't have it anymore."

"What do you mean you don't have it anymore? Where is it? What the hell did you do with it, Gotti? You told me you'd hold onto it!"

"I did, and then I found out how much of a monster my godfather really is, Bells. It's—trust me, it's deeper than you know, and I don't want to even talk about it, but just know, the drive is in a good place and justice will be served," I promised her.

"What the fuck am I going to say to Jaron? He already brought it up, and I had to act like I'd never heard or seen it before. I don't want to start off our new relationship with a foundation of lies, Gotti!"

I sighed. "I know, and I'm sorry. Just—I don't know, just know that I did what I thought was right, okay? And if it all works out, none of us are going to have to worry about Cecil Warren ever again."

"Fuck, Gotti! You better pray you're right. If not, I'm fucked!"

Instead of trying to continue to convince her that I knew what I was doing or trying to talk her out of running off into the sunset with Jaron, I just stopped talking. Bellamy's life sounded the furthest thing from a fairytale, but I had no room to judge. My shit was just as funky as hers was, whether she could smell the shit from the roses or not. It was clear that everything Jaron had put her through up to that point was water under the bridge. There were so many questions I wanted to ask her, but she'd made it clear there was no chance in hell that I would be able to change her mind.

"Do you two have to leave tonight? Can you just sleep on it before you make any final decisions?"

"Mmm, no can do. I'm packing because we're literally meeting back up in a few hours. Besides, I'm too excited to sleep!"

"And you feel like you're ready to trust him again with your heart?" I asked.

"I've always just wanted somebody for myself, and I really believe he's the one. Jaron is my person, Gotti. I tried to wean off of him and it's like we're magnets. I—I can't explain it."

I shook my head, hearing the pure elation ring through her voice. "No, trust me. I get it...all too well. Congratulations, Bells."

"Do you really mean it, or you just sayin' shit?"

"I mean it. If you're happy, then I'm happy for you, girl."

"Thanks, because I really do love him, Gotti. I do."

I sighed. Before I could muster up a response, a call beeped in with a 2-0-2 area code. "Hold up, Bells. I'm getting another call. Let me call you back." I clicked over and answered. "Hello?"

"Hi, is this Ms. Golani Evans?" a woman asked on the other line.

"This is she."

"Hi, my name is Jennifer Pewter, and I work with the human resources division for the Department of Justice. I'm calling to congratulate you on the job offer at the Department of Justice's Bureau of Justice Assistance."

"Oh my God, are you serious?" I squealed.

"Yes, ma'am. This job is located at the Department of Justice's headquarters here in Washington D.C."

"Wait, Washington D.C.? I interviewed at the office here in New York."

"Yes, that position has been filled, but there was another one just like it available in D.C. Are you still interested in accepting the job offer?"

"How long do I have to consider your offer?"

"One week."

"Um, okay. Thank you. Is this the best number to reach you to let you know of my decision?" I asked.

"Yes. I will also follow up with an email, so you can send your decision there as well."

"I will, thank you so much for calling."

"You're welcome, Ms. Evans. Have a great day!"

"Thanks, you too!"

I hung up and sighed. I'd been waiting for a phone call like that for months, yet I'd never felt so torn. My heart was in New York with Dash, yet the next stage of my life was knocking at the door, and I didn't know what to do.

Tatiyana

My heart nearly exploded in my chest when I heard keys jingling in the lock followed by a banging on the front door. The landlord had come and replaced the locks from the raid, and Jaron's key no longer worked. I hadn't seen him since the incident, and I was more nervous than ever. I slowly walked over and opened the door for him. His jaw was clenched and his stance was widened.

"Jaron, I—I'm surprised you came back."

"Look, I only came to grab a few things, Tati. I'm not doin' no back and forth shit with you."

I quickly shook my head. "That's the last thing I want to do, Jaron. I'm just glad you're okay. I—I'm sorry for what I did."

He frowned. The coldness in his eyes was chilling. "Just let me come and get my shit, Tati," he said, walking past me and heading toward the bedroom.

I followed him down the hall and stood in the doorway of our bedroom, watching him throw shit in a bag while looking for something. "Jaron, what's going on? What are you looking for?"

"Nothing. I told you I'm gettin' my shit and I'm out. I don't wanna talk. I don't wanna hear no apologies. I don't want nothin' from you."

"Why are you still lying to me? The police told me that you're involved with drugs, Jaron. They want to take you down."

He stopped packing to look up at me. "What else did they tell you?"

"They want me to flip on you…"

"And did you?" he asked.

"No! Of course not! You're the father of our unborn son, Jaron. I would never do that to you. Tell me what's going on. Let me prove I can hold you down."

"Son?"

I nodded slowly. "After the incident, I went to the doctor just to make sure the baby wasn't in distress and everything was still okay. They did an ultrasound and that's when I found out that it's a boy."

His face softened. "Damn, I'm gonna have a son?"

I bobbed my head before stepping closer to him. "Yes, baby. I'm carrying *your* son."

He backed up, and I reached out to grab his hand to put it on my stomach. He let his hand soften against my stomach as he rubbed it. I flashed my eyes up at him before placing my other hand on top of him.

"I know you said you don't want to hear apologies, but I am sorry, Jaron. I—I've only ever wanted to love you, and I don't know, love just makes me so fuckin' crazy, and I know that these hormones aren't helping, but I just—I just want us to be together and be a real family."

He sighed. "Look, I know I ain't been the best nigga to you, Tati. And I'm sorry for that. I never should've let shit go on this long if I knew I wasn't ready to fully commit to you the way you wanted me to."

"Jaron, all of that can be put in the past. Just put the bag down, baby. Let's figure this out together."

He shook his head. "Shit ain't that simple no more, Tati. I wanna be a good parent with you to my son, but as far as you and me, I'm done, Tatiyana."

"Then let's make it simple, Jaron. Whatever you want me to do, I'll do it."

"The best thing you can do for me is leave me the hell alone, and I'll do the same for you."

My stomach dropped to the soles of my feet. All of the oxygen began to deplete from my lungs and it became harder to breathe. "No, you—you don't mean that. Please, Jaron—please don't leave me. I can't have another fuckin' person leave me!" I screamed.

He tossed his bag over his shoulder and walked past me. I chased behind him, stopping in the kitchen. He stood in silence, looking down at the floor that he had previously bled out on. I'd taken things to the point of no return, and I was losing the man I loved because of it.

I stepped up behind him, wrapping my arms around his waist. He turned around, and I buried my nose into his chest. "Let me show you I can make you feel good. I can fix this. Let me fix this, baby," I said, ignoring the faint scent of another woman on him.

"Tati, stop," he said.

I stood on the tips of my toes and gently kissed his neck and collarbone. "I can show you what real love is, baby. I know I've hurt you and you've hurt me, too, but I'm willing to look past all of that for you...for us."

I let my hands travel down his chest to the slight bulge in his pants. I continued to kiss and nibble at his neck, feeling the bulge rise as the seconds fleeted past us.

"Tati—"

"Shh," I said, gently pressing my lips against his, "let me show you how sorry I am, baby..." The moment his bag dropped to the floor, I knew I had him.

*****

I WOKE UP hours later wrapped in the arms of my bedsheets with no Jaron in sight. I sat up and looked around before no longer dawdling in bed.

"Baby?" I called out, poking my head inside the bathroom. "Jaron?"

I made my way out to the main area and saw all of his belongings were gone, including the bag he'd dropped on the kitchen floor. It suddenly became clear that he'd dicked me down and dipped out soon after. I felt like the ultimate fool. There I was thinking I'd seduced him and he'd been the one playing me. I debated whether or not to call the detective and tell him I changed my mind and that I would work with him to take Jaron down, but I couldn't. Jail wasn't good enough for him. If he thought he was going to get away with continuously taking my heart and stepping on it, he was wrong. I was a good woman, and he was not going to rob me of my chance to be a real family with our son.

With the iPad in hand, I navigated through the cracked screen and opened the Find my iPhone app to track him. My heart palpitations increased as I watched the screen. I could see he was on the road and headed toward LaGuardia Airport. Without a second thought, I darted back down to my room and dove in the back of my closet and pulled out a gun. After the raid and getting out of jail, I decided to get the gun as protection. As much as I knew I had to stay clean or they'd arrest me and probably take my son, I couldn't fight the urge to hunt Jaron down and demand his love. It was either our family or the streets, and if he didn't make the right choice, I wouldn't allow that gray-eyed devil to play me again.

Chapter Eighteen

Jaron

I was running late and rushing to get to the airport after meeting up with Cecil to get my payout. As soon as he handed me the money, I'd handed him an empty flash drive and signed some papers that said I'd testify against my brother in the case he was building against him before jumping on the interstate. Little did he know, I'd planned to be long gone before the ink fully dried on the bullshit I'd just scribbled on. I didn't have the best relationship with my brother, but I would never flip on him. With one hand on the wheel, I tossed a few pain pills to the back of my throat and washed them down with some water. I was still sore, but nothing was going to stop me from getting the fuck out of New York while I still had the chance.

I glanced at my phone and saw *Justin*, Devil's government name written across the screen. With everything that had gone down, I couldn't believe he had the nerve to call me after trying to have me killed. I wanted to cuss him out, but if I answered that meant he'd have confirmation that I'd gotten out. Shit was about to blow up right in Devil's face, and he didn't even know it. That crooked ass cop had it out for him, but that was far from my concern at the moment. I rested my hand on the volume knob, contemplating whether or not to turn my music down and answer or let it rock and reach out to Devil when Bellamy and I landed. The ringing ceased, making my decision for me. Seconds later, the phone rang again with a picture of Tati and I on the screen.

"Fuck," I mumbled before sending her ass straight to voicemail.

I still didn't know how I'd gone from knowing I was going to leave Tati to dickin' her crazy ass down one last time before I left, but I had to do what I had to do to get her off my back. Sneaking out like a thief in the night wasn't how I planned for shit to go down, but I figured by the time she woke up, I'd be long gone. As I followed the signs to the Delta terminal, I turned my phone off completely and made a mental note to delete her and formally move forward with pressing charges against her for trying to kill me.

BELLAMY TURNED TO face me with a ghost of a smile stretched across her face. I returned the gesture, instantly feeling a wave of relief wash over me.

"I made it! I'm here!" I panted, jogging over to her.

"I was beginning to get nervous that you stood me up or somethin'," she said.

I laced her fingers with mine as we stepped up to the first available kiosk, ready to book the next flight to the West Coast. "Never that, Bells. I meant everything I said to you earlier."

"Good, because I did not try to squeeze my whole life into two checked bags for nothing."

"Damn, girl. Why'd you pack so much shit?" I chuckled.

"Um, you neglected to tell me exactly where we're going or how long we'll be there, remember? A bitch didn't wanna be unprepared, baby."

I chuckled again. "You just threw some shit in a bag and said fuck it, I'm goin' with my nigga, huh?"

"That's exactly what I did. I haven't told either of my jobs shit, I'm just packed and ready to roll with my bae, straight YOLO shit."

I laughed while pulling her into my arms. "Straight YOLO shit," I repeated before pulling her lips onto mine.

A few innocent pecks and a long lip-lock later, we both

turned our attention back to the kiosk screen to look up flights. "Looks like there's one to San Francisco leaving in two hours," she said, staring at the screen.

"Fuck it, let's book it. We'll rent a car and take our time making our way to L.A."

Bellamy started entering our information and then turned to me. "How are we paying?"

"Straight cash," I said.

"Okay, well we're going to need to go up to the desk and actually talk to someone. You got your I.D.?"

"Oh shit..." I mumbled, turning away from her as she stepped up to the desk.

"What's wrong? Don't tell me you're having second thoughts."

"It's not that, I...don't think I have my I.D."

Bellamy turned back to the airline worker as I continued to feel around in my pockets. There was nothing but my phone in there. My entire wallet was missing. "Fuck!" I grumbled.

"Is there anything he can do?" Bellamy asked the worker.

"You can purchase your tickets now for a later flight and try to run back and get his I.D., but there's nothing I can do if you miss the last call for boarding."

Bellamy sighed and turned to face me. "Let's just go back out to the car and figure out something else. Maybe it's in there."

I let out a frustrated breath before nodding. "Aight."

"Can I be honest?" she asked, her suitcase wheels gliding across the slick floor with ease.

"Always."

"I had a bad feeling about this from the moment I got here. Something just wasn't sitting right with me and now with us not getting the flights, reality is starting to settle in a bit. Like, do we really know what we're doing, baby?"

"I thought you were down for me, Bells. I thought you were my day one."

She frowned and stopped walking so she could grab both of my hands. "I am. I didn't mean it to come out like that. I'm right here with you, ten toes down."

"Good," I said, pulling her into a kiss.

As soon as I pulled my lips away from Bellamy's, my ears were met with the sound of Tati's voice. "What the fuck is going on here?"

My heart sank to my feet. Tatiyana was standing less than six-feet away from us with tears smeared across her cheeks.

"Tati!" Bellamy shrieked, fixing her glare on her sister.

"Tati, what the fuck are you doing here? How did you even know I was here?" I asked, fuming with rage. Once again, she'd taken shit way too far.

Her nose twitched as she crossed her arms over her pregnant belly. "I was tracking your phone and it led me all the way to the Delta terminal, so I figured you had to be in here somewhere. This whole time I'm rushing here wondering what the fuck you could be doing at the airport. Imagine my surprise to find you two here together, bags all packed and shit. So, what the fuck is going on?"

The pain in her eyes pierced mine. As much as I knew I needed to say something, my mouth instantly went dry, and my brain couldn't function enough to form a sentence. I was sure my non-responsiveness was telling enough. Bellamy stepped up and grabbed my hand. "Tati, I'm sorry you had to find out like this, but we—"

"What? Don't tell me he's fucking you too!" she asked in a raised voice as one eyebrow arched higher than the other.

"We're in love," Bellamy corrected her, "and we're leaving the city. What you two had is over."

Tati's eyes narrowed as she shot her sister a chilling green-eyed stare. Goosebumps covered my arms as I studied her demeanor. From her curled upper lip to her jerky movements and rapid blinking; she was clearly off, and Bellamy and I both needed to tread lightly. She'd already tried to kill me once, so I didn't put it past her to try again.

She steepled her fingers together. "You wanna know something funny? I saw the two of you kissing from afar, and I said wow, you can just see the passion dripping off them. I wish I had that. And as I got closer and realized just who you were, I said wow, she's the little slut I always knew she was."

Fuming with zero chill, Bellamy delivered her sister a stony stare. "Fuck you, Tati. You need to leave. You're making a scene and nobody wants you here!"

"How long?" Tati asked with a pained grimace written across her face.

I sighed. I knew what Bellamy and I had, was a violation of the bond she'd shared with her sister, but we couldn't help ourselves. It was finally time we came clean.

"None of that even matters because I said what I said. It's over. You need to move on, Tati, and find happiness with somebody else," Bellamy suggested.

Tati scoffed as she picked a piece of lint off her clothes. "Why? So, you can fuck around and find yourself underneath him just like you did this one?"

My skin tingled with fury. "Listen, let's take this shit outside, and I'll tell you everything. You really about to get everybody hemmed up in this mothafucka!" I said, taking note of the small group of people who'd actually stopped to shamelessly watch the drama unfold.

Tati's face clouded up with rage. "Fuck a scene! You think I give a fuck about these people in here? I'm not leaving until I get all the answers I fuckin' came for! So, tell me how long you been fuckin' my man?!" she yelled, blasting her voice over ours.

"You're gonna fuck around and get us all arrested, *again*," Bellamy warned her, staring icily.

She was right. The crazed look in Tati's eyes and the way her hand clutched her purse was enough to let me know she wasn't thinking straight. She was going to fuck around and take us all down because she couldn't handle her emotions. The last thing we needed to do was get thrown out of the airport and banned from flying the friendly skies. If I couldn't get out of the city, I knew it would only be a matter of time before either Cecil or Devil caught up to me. I glanced around us and could see eyes on us at all angles. My pulse raced as I waved her away. "Tati, just go the fuck home. It's over, aight? I'm sorry, but it is what it is."

"I told you I'm not going anywhere until ALL my questions are answered!"

"It's been months! Months, Tati! Is that what you want to hear? Does that make you feel better?" Bellamy blurted out. "God, I'm so fucking sick of you!"

"What did I ever do to you to make you hate me so much?" Tati asked her.

"It wasn't personal, Tati. I tried to fight it. We both did! But what's done is done, and we can't undo it. We fucked around and fell in love and the quicker you accept that, the quicker we can all move on from this," Bellamy explained to her.

Tati belted out a devious chuckle. "You think you got it all fuckin' figured out in that stupid ass head of yours, don't you? Hate to break it to you, sweetheart, but he's not the knight in shining fuckin' armor that you think he is because not even three hours ago, he was dicking me down in our apartment! Go ahead and ask him, and nigga, you better not lie!"

Bellamy snapped her neck back toward me. "Is what she's sayin' true? Did you fuck her, Jaron? After everything you was sayin' to me earlier, givin' me empty promises in that fuckin' empty ring box!" she asked in a wavering voice.

"Hold up. Y—you proposed to m—my fuckin' sister?"

I swallowed hard as my unfocused gaze bounced back and forth between Tati's elevated eyebrows and Bellamy's jutting jaw. My worst nightmare had come true. They were both bombarding me with questions that I knew I'd have to answer to one day. They were going to force me to choose between the woman carrying my seed and the woman who held my heart. Before I could say anything, I felt Bellamy's fist crash into my chest, invading my personal space.

"Fuck you, Jaron! I'm done for good this time!" Bellamy said through a face full of tears. "I can't believe I trusted you again! After all your bullshit and your lies! You ain't shit!"

I grabbed Bellamy's arm, refusing to let her walk away from me. It was time I finally set the record straight. "Hold up. Listen, Tati, I told you the truth when I came to get my shit. The only reason what went down went down is because I was tryna get the fuck outta there with no issues. I'm done! I'm pressing charges on your ass, and I mean that shit," I snarled.

Tati's eyes widened as they glistened with tears. "Y—you'd send me to jail, Jaron? Even after everything I told you? I—I told you we could put everything in the past and you—I thought you couldn't beat me down any lower, and I still tried to work shit out with you! I still tried to be there for you! And what did I get out of it in the end, huh? I knew you wasn't shit but a liar! All you do is lie and break my heart and cheat and lie and lie and cheat! Guess I gotta find somebody else to help raise my son!"

My brow crinkled. "Don't fuck with me, Tati! I don't fuck around when it comes to my fuckin' seed and trust, I'll have full custody as soon as you give birth!"

"And ride off into the fuckin' sunset with my fuckin' sister and have my son growin' up thinkin' his aunt is really his mother? I'll eat fucking nails before I let that shit happen! YOU CANNOT HAVE MY LIFE!" she screamed while drilling her index finger in Bellamy's direction.

"Bitch, I'll beat the fuck outta you!" Bellamy warned, charging forward.

I quickly spun her around, gripping her clammy hands and restraining her arms. "Yo, Bellamy, you gotta chill! Airport security is fuckin' coming. Shut your mouth and calm the fuck down!" I barked.

"Fuck you, Jaron! My sister though? Any bitch in the world and it had to be her!" Tati yelled at my back. "If a bitch like Bellamy can have you, I never did. And as for you, don't you ever fuckin' say my name again. You're no family of mine!"

A security guard approached her, wrapping his hand around her arm as two more shuffled behind him. "Ma'am, you're going to have to come with us."

"Don't fuckin' touch me!" she griped, snatching her arm

away.

That's when the other guards proceeded to grab her to try and restrain her. She yanked away and finally dove her hand into the bag I'd been watching her clutch since she rolled up on me. My eyes bulged when I saw the gun she was inching out of her purse.

"Tati, No!" I yelled before four shots rang, out and everything faded to black.

*****

I WOKE UP to bright fluorescent lights shining over me. I squinted as my ears took in the sound of the blood pressure monitor whirring just before the cuff squeezed my arm numb. *Fuck,* I thought to myself. I was *back* in the hospital. I'd been there three times in a short time span and started to think it had become my second home. My eyes closed again as my mind raced back to what had landed me there. The last thing I remembered was the crazed look in Tati's eyes just before she pulled the trigger. I reached out for Bellamy, trying to push her out of the way and felt a bullet pierce my back before hitting the ground. I shot the top half of my body up, heart racing. For a split second, I thought I'd dreamt it all up. It wasn't until I looked down at my legs and realized I couldn't feel them that I realized my new reality. The bullet I'd taken to the back had left me paralyzed from the waist down.

My stomach quaked as the door to my room opened. I didn't know who was going to be on the other side. So many people wanted to see me dead, and I wasn't surprised if someone had come to finish the job.

"Hi, Jaron, I'm Kathy, your evening nurse. Since you're awake now, is there someone we can call for you?"

"There's no one already here for me?" I asked, hoping Bellamy hadn't been harmed.

She lowered her head. "No, not yet. You got out of surgery

almost two hours ago, so I'm sure once your family gets word, they'll be on the way," she assured me.

"Thank you."

She turned to leave. "I'll let the doctor know you're awake so he can come in and answer any questions you may have."

"No—wait," I said, slowly lifting my arm to stop her, "tell me what happened."

The somber look on her face told me everything I needed to know, but I still needed to hear the words. Instead of responding, she walked over and turned on the TV for me and put it on the local news. There were dozens of police cars lighting up the Delta terminal like the Fourth of July over our incident. Tati had caused them to ground all outgoing and incoming flights until the situation had been cleared up.

"This is Jeanine Dandridge with WTSD News 7 reporting live from the LaGuardia Airport where we're told a woman charged into the Delta terminal with a loaded gun and fired the weapon four times. Authorities are saying there were two people wounded and one fatally shot. That is all the information we have for now. Back to you at the station, Jessica."

With my eyes glued to the TV, I didn't know what to think. *Two injured.* I knew I was one, but who was the other? Most importantly, which situation would be easier to live with?
If Bellamy was dead that meant the woman I loved was gone. If Tati was gone, that meant my unborn son was gone too.

"You were there, right?" Kathy asked me as she filled my water bottle with ice cold water and put two pain pills on the table she'd slid in front of me.

I nodded. "Yeah."

"You're now a walking testimony."

I scoffed. "I can't walk anymore."

She tucked her bottom lip underneath the top. "I'm sorry, I—I didn't mean to offend you or make you feel less than. You've gone through a big ordeal."

"Do you know if they brought the other injured person in here? Who was it? Do you know? Can you find out for me?"

"I'm sorry, but I can't disclose that information. I could lose my job."

"Please," I begged, "I need to know who the other survivor was."

She pressed her lips together before leaning in close to me. "I don't have names, but all I can say is the other person was a female, and she was pregnant. I hope that helps you in some way."

Tears swelled in the back of my eyes as flashbacks of the day rolled through my memory like waves during high tide. I quickly bobbed my head, and she left. The second the door closed, the tears began to fall. I'd finally gotten the answer to my question, and I was sick over it. Out of the three of us, Bellamy was the only one that didn't survive. Without Bellamy, my heart was going to be devoid of emotion. She and I both knew that love was the next of kin to hate. In the end, we were just two fools in love that thought getting a happily ever after would be simple.

Never in a million years did I ever expect for my life to turn out how it did. I'd paid the ultimate price for running through lovers, and I wasn't sure if I'd ever fully recover from that. I had to live out the rest of my days knowing that my secrets and deception cost me the love of my life. Knowing Bells, she'd probably haunt my ass just to make sure I never forgot it. The only reason I had to fight to stay alive was the anticipation of my son being born. I slammed my eyes shut and prayed that my son hadn't been harmed in the midst of Tati's crazy antics. Whether I pressed charges against her or not, I knew there was no way she wouldn't face jail time for what she'd done.

I pressed my palms against my face, swiping the tears away. Just before I was about to turn the TV off, a breaking news bulletin shot across the screen. "Oh shit..."

Gotti

I shot up in a cold sweat in the middle of the night. There was a chilling, unsettling feeling that washed over my body as I let my hand explore Dash's side of the bed. His side was cold, which told me he'd been gone for some time. Unable to return to a deep sleep, I turned on the TV. After swiping my phone off the nightstand to find out where Dash was, I saw a flashing news bulletin pop up on the screen.

"This is Karen Washington reporting live at the scene where Detective Cecil Warren's body was just recovered from the Hudson River. This news comes hours after an anonymous package was delivered to the precinct with video footage showing the detective allegedly participating in corrupt work with known criminals across the tri-state area."

"Oh, my God!" I said, slapping my hand across my mouth.

My hand trembled as I went back to my original task, calling Dash. I needed to know if he had anything to do with Cecil's death. The decision to either thank him or reprimand him for doing things his way depended on what his answer was. When he didn't answer, I called Bellamy to tell her the news. I knew it was late as hell, so it didn't faze me that she didn't answer. Plus, she could've still been 20,000 feet in the air flying to her final destination with Jaron. I sighed and flopped back down against the pillow until I eventually found sleep again.

I woke up six hours later to the sunlight peeking through my blinds and my phone creviced in between my fingers. I called Bells back-to-back after seeing that she hadn't returned my phone calls, and I still hadn't received an answer or a text, which was unlike her. As soon as I hung up, Dash shot me a text, asking me to meet him on the walking path to the Brooklyn Bridge at sunset. Knowing I needed to talk to him about my job offer, I agreed and decided to get up and start getting myself together for the day.

*****

LATER THAT NIGHT, Dash and I walked across the Brooklyn Bridge, taking in the magical view of lower Manhattan and the Statue of Liberty. With all that had been going on, I'd basically put the job offer on the backburner and neglected to bring it up to Dash. Knowing I had less than seventy-two hours to respond, it was now or never.

"It's beautiful up here," I told him.

"I used to come up here just to walk and clear my mind. Plus, the air is a little fresher," he said, taking my hand in his.

"Dash, there's something important I have to talk to you about," I confessed as I stopped and turned to face him.

"What is it?"

I let my eyes fall to the ground. "I got offered a job with the Department of Justice."

"Word? Congratulations, G!"

I shot him a brief smile. "Thanks, but…it's in Washington D.C. and I have to give them an answer tomorrow, and I don't know what to say. I'm honestly torn. I wanna be here because you're here, but then again, every piece of this city just brings so much pain, from losing my father to all the shit with my mom, it's just too much. This city is too much."

"Fuck the city then," he told me.

"What?"

"I think you should take the job, G."

"Taking the job means I'll be moving away."

"I said, take the job. You need to get the fuck out of this city now more than ever."

"But what about us?"

"What about us?"

"So, you don't care that I'll be states away?"

"You won't be."

"What do you mean?"

"I'm coming with you. Shit, we both need a fresh start."

My eyes lit up with excitement. "Are you serious?"

"Yeah. I told you, you gonna be my wife. Whenever you move, I move," he stated it as if it was a proven fact.

"Wife? Oh, you using serious commitment words, baby. Do you know something I don't?" I giggled.

"All you gotta do is say yes, G," he said, pulling a diamond ring out of his pocket.

My eyes widened as a joyous smile split my lips in two. "Yes to what? You haven't asked me anything."

"You're not going to make this easy for me, are you?"

I cheesed. "Nope, not one bit."

I could barely believe my eyes as I watched Dash's tall ass get down on one knee. The man I never knew I needed was about to propose. "Golani Evans, you are as beautiful as your name. I knew from the first day I saw you that I wanted you to be mine, and that I wanted to protect you. I never knew that would lead to falling in love with you or being here asking you to be my wife. Will you marry me?"

I sucked in a faint gasp as tears of happiness sprang from my eyes. "Yes, Dashiell Graham. I will be your wife."

He smiled before sliding the custom princess-cut diamond on my finger. "Is that why you brought me up here?"

He shrugged. "I figured you needed to be reminded how fuckin' special you are."

"God, I love you," I leaned down and whispered against his lips.

"I love you, too."

Dash stood to his feet, and my body crashed against his. I was the happiest I'd been in what seemed like forever. I'd fallen for Dashiell Graham harder than I'd ever fallen for any man in my life. A large chunk of me was scared shitless. My biggest fear was losing myself in the savage, beautiful man I'd fallen in love with seemingly overnight. The love we shared was no ordinary shit. It was us. Our hearts had been tested, strained, bent and broken, only for us to find solace in one another. I'd found my peace in a thug, and he'd found his in me.

I unwrapped my arms from around him when my phone rang. I looked at the screen to see *Bellamy's Mom* written across my phone. Surprised, I hit accept and put the phone up to my ear.

"Hello?"

"Golani, hi—it's Bellamy's mom," she sniffled.

"Hi—Mrs. Daniels. What's going on? I've been trying to reach Bells all day, and she hasn't been returning my calls."

"You don't know, do you?"

I frowned. "Know what?"

"I'm so sorry, Golani, but Bellamy's dead. Tati killed her."

Feeling faint, I let the phone slip out of my grasp and hit the ground. My heart quaked with sorrow. What had started out as one of the happiest moments of my life had been tainted with the tragic news of my best friend's death. I let out an ear-splitting scream as an abundance of tears poured out of my eyes until I could no longer see through them.

"G? G! What is going on? Who was on the phone?" Dash asked, concern racing through his voice.

"Her sister...she—she killed her," I said, barely able to form a complete sentence.

I was screaming and crying like a hungry infant as feelings of guilt and blame chained themselves to my heart. "I should've fought harder. I should've stopped her from going to the airport! I can't believe that! What am I going to do without her, Dash? What am I going to do?" I screamed.

Dash scooped me into his arms and carried me all the way back to the car. My heart was in a trillion pieces, and I didn't know how long it would take for me to pick them all up and put them back together.

"Damn. Why would she do her own sister in like that?" he mumbled, while glancing over at me as he drove.

I kept my focus on whatever whizzed by through the window and didn't initially respond. It hurt too bad to even think about talking about Bellamy in past tense, let alone speak her indiscretions out loud. I didn't know the full story, and I knew I couldn't stomach finding out all the details leading up to Bellamy's death. I knew what she'd been doing behind her sister's back and it was no surprise to me that Tati had probably found out and went off the deep end.

Dash reached out and rested his hand on my thigh. As much as I appreciated the gesture, I didn't even flinch. He spoke up again. "G?"

"She um—she was with this guy named Jaron that she's been on and off with for a little while now. He was dating her sister, having a baby with her and yet, him and Bells just couldn't leave each other alone," I confessed.

"Jaron? You know his last name?"

"No. I just know he's into music and he's got g—"

"Gray eyes?" he asked, finishing my sentence.

I finally turned my eyes to him. "Y—yeah. How'd you know that?"

"Damn, I didn't know he was mixed up with all that. I didn't even know the nigga had a baby on the way."

My forehead puckered as I wiped my nose. "How do you know him?"

"He's my best friend's brother. They don't get along either."

I huffed, feeling numb. Sibling rivalry was just one more

thing Bellamy could've put on her list of all the things she loved about Jaron. As much as she and Tati hated each other, they had more in common than they thought. They both fell for the same man for the exact same reasons. They were both serial lovers and lovers of love, and they despised each other for it.

Chapter Nineteen

Dash

Three months later.

A lot had changed in a little over three months. Since Cecil had been dealt with, and it had been proven that he'd been a dirty cop for years. All of the open cases he was tied to were dropped. We were all finally free. G had been grieving the loss of her father, best friend, and the relationships between her and her godfather and mother all at once. Everything she thought she knew about her life was a lie, and some shit like that would be hard for anybody to deal with. It wasn't until after the funeral that Gotti felt the full realization that somebody else she cared for was gone and there was nothing she could do about it. It had been ninety-three days, and Gotti had a drawer full of anxiety and mood stabilizer pills to prove it. I knew death all too well, whether permanently or figuratively. The feeling of emptiness she had would never fully go away. So, I'd been helping her fight through her depression by cooking, cleaning, feeding, and bathing her. I was her alarm clock, her butler, her chauffer, and personal assistant. Anything she needed, I provided without question. I would've scratched her scalp while watching every season available of *Grey's Anatomy* on Netflix if she asked me to.

Her mother called every day for the first month and eventually, stopped calling altogether. I knew first hand that if you wore your guilt like a chain around your heart, it would drive you crazy, and Gotti didn't need her bullshit when she was trying to work through her own. Her mother didn't agree with Gotti's decision to be with me, let alone marry me, but neither of us gave a fuck. I was the only one who she could really depend on at the end of the day. If anything, her depression made us grow closer together and learn each other. No matter how many different shades there were of Golani Evans, soon-to-be Graham, I was happy to have her in my corner.

With me leaving the city with Gotti, Devil needed to have someone in his corner he could trust, so I had a sit down with both Devil and Jaron in an attempt to help them make amends. Once Devil learned he was going to be an uncle and all the craziness behind the story of Jaron's baby mama killing her sister and attempting to kill him, he agreed to try to be there for his brother since he would be raising his son on his own while also trying to adjust to life in a wheelchair. With Jaron becoming a father and his baby mama being locked away in a mental institution, Devil needed to be there for his brother more than ever. I'd planned to travel up and down the East Coast from D.C. to New York every couple of weeks to check in with Devil once Gotti and I were settled and she started working, but it made me feel better to know that this may have been their chance to have a good relationship. Thy were family at the end of the day.

I looked around at the wall filled with stacked boxes and totes ready to be packed and shipped to our new beginning in Washington D.C. She'd managed to work it out with the human resources division to push her start date back, allowing her to grieve the loss of Bellamy and close out her lease. It was our last weekend in the city, and we wanted to make it special by getting married. Planning our private ceremony was the only thing that brought a smile to her face.

She walked down the hall from the bedroom and flashed me a quick smile. "Hey."

I stopped, letting my eyes fully soak all of her in. "Hey."

"What?"

My eyes traveled from the high, bushy ponytail on the top of her head, down to the sports bra, oversized sweatpants and mismatched socks she was wearing. She looked absolutely beautiful.

"Why are you staring at me, Dash? What are you thinking about?" she asked, tilting her head to the side.

"How I'ma have to start calling you Double G or GG or somethin' once you officially become mine," I told her.

She smiled. "I've always been yours."

I walked over and kissed her forehead while pulling her into a tight hug. "I know."

"You're the only man I've ever truly loved."

"Oh yeah? How'd I manage to get that title?"

"Because you give the best hugs," she said, nestling her head against my chest before letting out a quick chuckle.

I flashed her a gentle smile. "I'll take that."

She lifted her head to look around the room at all the boxes. "I still can't believe we're really about to leave New York."

"How you feelin', G? You ready?"

She huffed. "As ready as I'm gonna be. I'm nervous, you know?"

"You're the smartest and hardest working woman I know. You got this, baby," I encouraged her.

"Do you have everything you need for tomorrow?"

I bobbed my head. "Yeah, I'm good."

"So, you're ready to become a married man?" She teased.

"As ready as I'll ever be, G. I told you that you were gon' be my wife, didn't I? This is just me making good on my promise."

If anyone ever told me that one day I'd meet a woman who made every nerve ending on my body stand on end and make me want to give her the world, I wouldn't have believed them. G made me a better nigga. I could honestly say I was happily in love with a woman who loved me for me, and I couldn't wait for her to become my wife.

Gotti

I woke up the morning of my wedding day, feeling a welter of emotions over everything I'd endured for the past few months. I was in the dark for a long time but was happy to finally be at a point where I felt like I was persevering. I spent a lot of dark days rooted in my depression, wondering when the pain would all end and if there was a way I could just fast forward through the heartbreak. Between the crying in the shower to waking up from my sleep in the middle of the night with a face wet with tears, I'd been fighting my depression like I was fighting for my life. I knew better than anyone that you couldn't have rainbows without rain, and I was finally ready to embrace the light at the end of the tunnel and embark a new chapter with Dash.

I arrived at the Bethesda Terrace and Fountain in Central Park. There was no one there but the two us, our officiant, and photographer. Dash had arranged for the entire park to be shut down for the duration of our ceremony. My eyes took in the scenery around me. There were large trees in grassy areas that carpeted the ground, birds splashing in the large fountain, and decorative rock formations.

My hand glided against the sandstone of the large staircase as *U Move, I Move* by John Legend and Jhenè Aiko played in the background. I slowly cascaded up each step to the top of the bridge where my husband-to-be stood. As soon as my eyes met his, tears started pouring out. Dashiell Graham was the one and only thug I ever loved. He saw my imperfections as perfection and fed my soul in ways I never knew I needed. He was too good to me, even when I didn't have the strength or desire to be good to myself. When I got to the top of the stairs, I saw Dash standing there wearing a heather gray suit with a red tie and a red rosebud boutonniere in the buttonhole of his left lapel. As soon as I was in arm's length of him, he pulled me into his arms and kissed me.

"Dashiell and Golani, we've come together to celebrate the unbreakable bond that the two of you share. We come together to continue to nourish and water it so that it remains strong in love, truth, and all understanding."

"In talking with you both, I've learned that when the two of you first decided to be together, you didn't know where the path of life would take you. And yet, your love has remained through some of the hardest times in both of your lives. So as you stand here in front of each other today, I want you to reflect over your time together. Remember the good and the bad, the smiles and the tears. I want you to ask yourself, was it all worth it? If so, we may now go into the vows. Golani, you can go first," the officiant told me.

I laid my eyes on Dash as they began to mist with fresh tears. "Dash, things between us has moved as fast as your name since day one. We've laughed. We've cried. We've fought. We've made up. Nothing about our love story is perfect. We've seen the best and the worst of each other, and yet we're both still standing here today; still choosing each other as we always have. Today, I promise to continue to love you in the good and bad times to come because I know nothing will be too big for us to overcome. I may not know everything there is to know about love, but I know that it's impossible for me to live without you. You have been my rock and my shield, and I fall more in love with you every day. I stand her today with an honest heart saying that I love you more now than I did yesterday and will love you even more tomorrow."

Dash reached out to wipe away my tears with his thumb, and then enveloped my hands in his. "G, when we were apart, I would have these vivid dreams about you. Every night it was different. Sometimes you'd be pregnant, others it would just be visions of us kicking it, but there's one dream in particular that I remember, and it was just like this. That shows me that my heart knew I was going to marry you before I did."

"Words will never be able to express my gratitude for you. The forgiveness you've shown and the love you've given me, even when I didn't deserve it. You are the anchor in the storm of my life and the only woman who has my heart. You are my queen, and today, I commit myself to you for the rest of my life."

"Let us bow our heads," the officiant stated. "Dear heavenly Father, we come to you today to say thank you for the bond that you've created between Dashiell and Golani. We ask that you continue to bless them as they embark on this new chapter in their love story. May they continue to learn from one another, lean on each other in their times of need, and be there for each other when things are going well. In Jesus's name, we pray, Amen."

"Amen." Dashiell nodded.

"Amen," I added.

"Now we will have a Bible verse read. I'll be reading from First Corinthians, chapter thirteen... Love is patient and kind; love is not jealous or boastful. It is not arrogant or rude. Love does not insist on its own way; it is not irritable or, um, re-resentful; it does not rejoice at wrong, but rejoices in the right. Love bears all things, believes all things, hopes all things, endures all things. Love never ends. Now, to symbolize your new life together in Washington D.C., I understand that you two want to do something special," the officiant announced.

"Yes." I nodded as Dash pulled out a small card out of his pocket and handed it to me. We walked to the edge of the bridge as I held a card in my hand.

"Here's to the future because we're done with the past," I read.

He pulled out his lighter and set the small card on fire. We both watched it burn for a few seconds, and then he stomped it out. We walked back over to the officiant, who then proceeded with the rest of the ceremony.

"Dashiell, please place the band on Golani's finger, and repeat after me. This ring is a token of my everlasting love for you. As I place it on your finger, I am committing myself to you."

I held out my finger as he slid the diamond band on it and repeated the words. Next, I slid the band on his finger. Dash and I took turns kissing each other's wedding bands as we stared deep into each other's eyes.

"By the power vested in me and the state of New York, I

now pronounce you husband and wife. Dashiell, you may kiss your bride."

I held Dash's face in the palms of my hands as he put his hands on top of mine and kissed me deeply. We were finally turning the page and getting our happily ever after.

The End

a note from k.l. hall.

Reader,

Thank you for reading *To the Only Thug I'll Ever Love*. Please, if you've made it this far, I hope you'll consider taking a minute to tell me what you thought about the book in the form of a **book review and/or rating**. Don't hesitate to let me know what you'd like to see from me next! I thoroughly enjoy reading your reviews and hearing from you as well! I'm always striving to attract new readers and retain current ones, and reviews are one of the easiest ways to attract readers. If you loved the book, tell a friend, and most importantly let me know!

All my love,

K.L. Hall

P.S. I created a special playlist just for this book. Check it out by clicking here. (E-Book Only)

about the author.

As a serial storyteller, K.L. Hall's fictional stories straddle the intersection of classic Urban and spell-binding Romance. Her writing style is a fusion of eminently relatable female characters, and the flawed, yet desirable male leads who love them.

Reader Faves:
In the Arms of a Savage: *(Peaked at #1 in Women's Fiction)*
As Long as You Stay Down: *(Peaked at #2 in African American Erotica)*
Awakened: A Paranormal Romance: *(Peaked at #1 in Erotic Science Fiction)*

Sign up for my mailing list to stay up to date with new releases, giveaways, sneak peeks, and more! Click this link: https://bit.ly/38RMpV5

Connect with me on social media:

Facebook: https://www.facebook.com/authorklhall
Twitter: https://twitter.com/authorklhall
Instagram: https://www.instagram.com/officialklhall/
Website: https://www.authorklhall.com

Other novels by K.L. Hall:

Diary of a Hood Princess 1-3
Rise of a Street King: The Justice Silva Story *(Spin-Off to the Diary of a Hood Princess series)*
Where He Belongs: A Disrespectful Love Story

Love Me Harder: A Sin City Love Story
Broken Condoms and Promises 1-3
In the Arms of a Savage 1-3
Built for a Savage: Blaze and Camille's Love Story *(Spin-Off to the In the Arms of a Savage Series)*
A Ruthle$$ Love Story 1-3
Fallin' for the Alpha of the Streets 1-2
The Most Savage of Them All: The Wolfe Calloway Story *(Prequel to the In the Arms of a Savage Series)*
When a Gangsta Loves a Good Girl
Caught Between my Husband and a Hustler
The Illest Taboo 1-2
To the Only Thug I'll Ever Love

Novellas:
Bi-Curious: An Erotic Tale
Bi-Curious 2: Tastes Like Candy
House of Cards 1-2
A Savage Calloway Christmas *(Christmas novella to the In the Arms of a Savage Series)*
Lovin' the Alpha of the Streets: A Valentine's Day Novella *(Valentine's Day novella to the Fallin' for the Alpha of the Streets Series)*
Awakened: A Paranormal Romance
As Long as You Stay Down

Children's Books:
Princess for Hire
Princess Twinkle Toes & the Missing Magic Sneakers
Little One, Change the World
Adjust Your Crown: A Self-Love Coloring Book for Children of Color

Non-Fiction:
Authors are a Business: The Booked & Busy Course Mini Book

TO THE ONLY THUG I'LL EVER LOVE
